THE DETECTIVE'S GARDEN

THE DETECTIVE'S GARDEN

A LOVE STORY AND MEDITATION ON MURDER

JANYCE STEFAN-COLE

UNBRIDLED BOOKS

This is a work of fiction. The names, characters, places and incidents are either the product of the author's imagination or are used fictitiously, and any resemblance to actual persons living or dead, business establishments, events, or locales is entirely coincidental.

Unbridled Books

© 2016 by Janyce Stefan-Cole
All Rights Reserved.
An excerpt from The Detective's Garden appeared in WG News+Arts as "Emil's Williamsburg".
Library of Congress Cataloging-in-Publication Data

Names: Stefan-Cole, Janyce, author.
Title: The detective's garden : a love story and meditation on murder : a novel / by Janyce Stefan-Cole.
Description: Lakewood, CO : Unbridled Books, [2016]
Identifiers: LCCN 2016011030 | ISBN 9781609531331 (alk. paper)
Subjects: LCSH: Widowers--Fiction. | BISAC: FICTION / Mystery & Detective / General. | GSAFD: Mystery fiction.
Classification: LCC PS3619.T4455 D48 2016 | DDC 813/.6--dc23
LC record available at https://lccn.loc.gov/2016011030

1 3 5 7 9 10 8 6 4 2

For Brandon. Definitely.

Teach me, and I will be silent;

make me understand how I have erred.

BOOK OF JOB

THE
DETECTIVE'S GARDEN

BROOKLYN, NY, 1995

Everyone likes to believe there once was a garden where all things were pure.

Life's a humbling lesson, Emil thought, facing his own gun. The intruder lit a cigarette with one hand, using a beat up old Zippo lighter sporting a Lucky Strike logo, but smoking a Gauloise, inhaled hard, exhaled slowly while demanding the deed to Emil's house. In the other hand was the Smith & Wesson .38 Special. Emil didn't care about losing the house; one was as good as another; a roof, running water, heat. But to take the garden—that was punishing.

He'd faced a gun before, on another summer night long ago, in Slovenia. With him then was a girl he hardly knew, Elena. They'd been lovers only a few days and would soon part—forever, he'd assumed. The man with the gun called her a thieving betrayer, and Emil, in the briefest of glances, saw his lover's fear. It ran across her face like the shadow of dark birds, a flock of evil black birds.

Guns make a lot of noise. Bang! The Big Bang theory; scientists say it happened very fast. There was a pinprick of something—matter, antimatter, dark matter?—and it popped, blew massively and the universe was born. Science would want to know what blew. The religious would say who made it blow. But Emil would ask why.

Thou shalt not kill, the Sixth Commandment, behind honoring mother and father. The first commandment is in regard to no other gods. Emil found it odd that murder was so low on the list, but he was an ex-homicide detective and would have put not taking life at the top. The question was whether he was facing a killer now, or an amateur bent on getting even. Either way, at such close range, Emil would be dead if a bullet left the chamber.

He was told to sit. The one with the firepower gives the orders; Emil walked slowly to the other side of the marble table and sat. The garden was quiet all around them, only the crickets with their obsessive rubbing, on and on, and the suffocating heat. It was going to be a long night.

PART ONE

SHOOTING PEPPERS

ONE

And the Lord God planted a garden in Eden, in the East; and there he put the man whom he had formed. And out of the ground the Lord God made to grow every tree that is pleasant to the sight and good for food, the tree of life also in the midst of the garden, and the tree of the knowledge of good and evil.

BOOK OF GENESIS

Sunday night, June 18th, Emil Milosec sat alone in the dark. He felt secure in the leafy haven of his garden, an oasis he and Elena had created: a twenty by eighty foot hedge against the cheerless urban surround.

He hadn't yet fired his revolver. Hadn't yet, his former partner Detective Mike Dunn might say, gotten pissed off at God. Sitting with a glass of a full-bodied pinot noir, he innocently thought about original sin: Adam and Eve, the first fornication; a garden, Eden, no zip code. It was a topic Emil rolled over like worry beads repeatedly massaged. He had his own ideas of Eve's shape and Adam's manhood. He had his own ideas about everything, his wife said; everything but himself.

Even his mother had warned against his arrogant questioning. "Only God can know," she'd say, wagging a finger in his face. "Too many ideas fill that head of yours, my Emiloshka." She'd threatened to drill a hole on top so all the questions would pass out of him. Young Emil imagined steam, like from a kettle, whistling out of the hole in his head, forming words in the air. He began to think anyone could read his mind and for a time tried to think in code.

Was that first coupling transcendent? He would like to know. Did Adam perform—not too fast, not too slow? Did Eve respond with all she had? First times are usually a disappointment, he reflected. His was, with a whore he paid twenty-five hard-earned dollars to break him in. The Bible is prudish on details; how the first sin went off that we're supposed to regret for all time. No, he didn't buy it, not one single word of the Genesis story. As for regrets, he figured each and every one of us did a good job creating our own.

Emil leaned forward, hearing a rustling sound toward the rear of the garden. He thought he'd seen a possum the other day by the back wall and wondered if they were nocturnal and what they ate. Or it could be Mrs. Noily's cat Sam nosing around. He took another sip of wine.

Why not make Eve the same way as Adam, out of dirt mixed with God's spit? Or like the giraffes or strawberries or ice, the way they came about? Why take Eve out of Adam's rib? That all but guaranteed a form of incest, didn't it? Was that the snag in the story that led to the first calculated criminal, Cain? Was murder written into the DNA all that long time ago? Or was the chaos of humankind the result of a blurry law laid down in secret behind closed doors: No touching! Just to keep the demon semen in check? Then why not make the first couple neutered?

He remembered it was Father's Day. Earlier he'd heard giggling children on the street out front. Elena hadn't wanted kids; she'd said not every woman did. She'd joked, said breeding was too Darwinian. Emil had wanted her: her body, her sex, *her*. The other cops on the force had families, but his life was not the same as theirs. He inhabited two separate worlds, one colored by violent death, the other by Elena, and he thought he'd kept the two carefully apart. Elena once said, "You can be a perfectly good mother without having children."

Emil's meandering thoughts were cut short by the noise of drunken rummaging from next door. The clash of cheap aluminum chairs, a swear word in Spanish, a belch. Emil tensed. Some nights his neighbor Franco called out, saying what the liquor made him say.

Tonight, very drunk, he jeered, "Amigo! You there? Sí, I can smell you! Digame, how do the peppers grow, hah?" He stopped to laugh. "Still barren like your wife?" He took a breath, changed his tone: "May she rest in peace."

"What's with you and the peppers, Franco?" Emil called over the fence between them. Since spring, every time he saw him, Franco brought them up.

"You don't know, hombre?"

The way Emil saw it, if his neighbor didn't own his dump next door he'd be out on the street. He growled, "Go sleep it off, man."

"What? You want to shoot me?" Franco called. "Pale-blooded blanco; go ahead, shoot me with your shiny pistola! If you have los cojones, amigo." He broke out in a raucous laugh, repeating, "Los cojones." In the morning he would have little recollection of his beer-soaked words.

Emil lingered after Franco finally retreated to his cave of a house. His mind wandered back to Adam and Eve and their short-lived joy. So what was it, one blissful go next to the silvery stream, the peaceable animals hearing Eve cry out in earthly delight? The thought of them prior to the hissing, whispering snake, a sexless, childlike pair wandering through a flawless setting for all eternity—whose idea of perfection was that?

His garden had a flaw: the bald patch Franco alluded to that once flourished with peppers and nasturtium. He hated peppers. He'd told Elena and asked her not to grow them. She laughed, said, "Peppers speak to passion." Then the seeds stopped growing, lay barren, to use Franco's word.

The other day Franco called to Emil. He was walking home with a bag of groceries. Franco was seated, aimless as usual, on his front steps in the afternoon warmth. Emil stopped on the sidewalk, shifted the load of groceries. "What's it this time, Franco? Someone took your parking space again?"

"But you told me the streets are free, any car can park where it wants!"

Franco would place traffic cones, stolen from construction sites, in front of his house to reserve his space on alternate parking days. Emil told him it was illegal and Franco finally gave up the practice, but only after receiving twenty summonses.

"Good to know you're obeying the law," Emil said. He turned to go.

"Amigo, wait," Franco yelled so anyone within five miles could hear. "Come see what I have." He leaned out, looked up the street. Lowering his voice, he said, "Now *that* is hot chili."

Emil turned to see where Franco pointed. Mrs. Noily's tenant—Lorraine, no, Lori, or was it Lorene?—slowly descended her front steps. The men watched as she walked, heading in the direction of the subway, her hips swaying to a private rhythm. She was tall with long hair falling below her neck, in jeans, a size too small white T-shirt, and a red patent-leather purse slung over her shoulder. She carried a large portfolio under her left arm. The air held still until she turned the corner.

"Phew! Poca flaca but mine if she wants me," Franco said, nodding approval. "That could be the devil with the red dress, like the song, no?"

"What is it you want, Franco?"

"No, that dress is blue; devil with the *blue* dress." He looked toward a cloudless sky, nodded. "Blue, sí, mi amigo—"

"All right, I'm gone—"

"Amigo, no, come see my peppers. Venga."

Emil went with him because he thought he'd bring up the topic of painting Franco's scarred south wall and was surprised to see a thriving pepper patch tucked along the fence outside the kitchen door. Yellow, red, and orange nasturtium trailed alongside three robust pepper plants. The buds hung like ornaments, the leaves polished green. Emil stared dumbly at the plants, an exact replica of Elena's.

Franco laughed, slapped him heavily on the back, and challenged, "My very own, hah? Su esposa linda, mi amigo—a very generous lady." Grinning, he handed Emil a few seeds from his pocket and told him to try again. Back in his kitchen, Emil tossed the pepper seeds into the trash.

The garden was abundant everywhere else, a profusion of color, mingling scents and buzzing bees; dizzying on hot summer afternoons. Mornings, he'd be out early with fresh anticipation: what flowers had opened in the first pale light as he slept; the great mystery of how a flower chooses the exact moment to open. Time slipped gently by as he deadheaded roses, pulled stray weeds, and hand-squashed fat green aphids that would suck the life out of the blooms. Only the pepper patch was a sore that wouldn't heal. He blamed himself. Elena had pickled them each autumn for condiments over the winter, relishes and spreads and spicy yellow chutney. There were still rows of neglected jars in the cellar. He'd managed to avoid the patch, to slink past it because Elena was dead and seeing the empty dirt made him know her death all over again, and the paralyzing ache of loss.

Franco's backyard was something else he tried to ignore. Once a garden had grown but now junk littered the place. Dolls' heads, forgotten kitchen utensils, a rotting toilet seat, a pile of bricks from some abandoned project; Franco's sloth. The south side abutted a black cinder-block wall that was splattered with illegible graffiti. The only readable word, sprayed an angry sulfurous yellow, was "heel." Through his bedroom window the heel greeted Emil each morning, rain or shine, winter through autumn, the shrill, indecipherable message. Whose heel? A dog? A person? He wanted to paint the blocks white, plant a vine to soften the surface. He'd tell Franco his idea and offer to pay for the paint, but would his neighbor ever sober up long enough?

Emil the cop knew Franco had every right to live as he liked; there was nothing criminal about a generally disorganized lazy man. Elena hadn't shared Emil's resistance, and much as he might object to it in himself, he'd been bothered that she wasn't bothered by Franco, that she overlooked his bouts of loutish drunkenness. There had been that slip of her that eluded him, that part of her that answered to no one. She was so contained he sometimes felt he was only a complication at the edge of her world. And there was too the inevitable cop's distrust—reasonable or not—that all was on the up-and-up between his neighbor and his wife.

TWO

Now the serpent was more subtle than any other wild creature that the Lord had made. He said to the woman, "Did God say, 'You shall not eat of any tree of the garden'?"

Book of Genesis

Monday morning, June 19th, Emil's eyes, menaced from the night, appeared darkly circled. The early light made him seem older than he was. He'd seemed older in some ways since childhood. There had been a sunless room under the roof rafters in the house in the old country. As a boy Emil hid up there and listened to the sounds of his family below, and to the coo of mourning doves under the eaves. From his mother too much talking, from his father too little, his sister recalibrating the balance between them, as if that were the purpose of her life. His memory of the old country was of darkness. Not the place itself—so full of mountain light—but something else, vague and under lit.

He'd sat in the garden too late, Franco's taunting words circling like angry flies. He told himself, "I *should* shoot him with my pistola." He finally went to bed and had a vivid dream.

In the dream he lay trapped on the bed as malignant black crows flew through the open window. They had blood-red eyes and carried Elena's jewelry out in their beaks. Beside him a very young Elena lifted herself off the bed. She moved toward the window, her silhouette obvious through a sheer nightgown, nipples two sharp points pushing through the fabric. At her bureau she pulled out lingerie, tossed shimmering panties and dark satin bras into the opened crow beaks. Able to move again, Emil ran to the window. The garden shifted to his mother's from the old country. Elena leaned against a wall. The crows were now clumps of black grapes hanging low above her head. Franco sat on a stone bench looking at her, his gritty laughter carrying up to Emil in the window, looking down.

Dreams disturbed him with their irrationality. Elena said they were only the unconscious puffing smoke. "Or maybe something's hidden in there. Why not analyze the dreams?" she'd say, tapping his forehead.

But he scoffed at that idea: "What should we do, slit open an eagle's entrails and read the blood drippings, the feathers?"

"That would be omens, I think."

"Either way."

Emil said that to his wife, but he did try to replay his dreams, to grasp hold of them before they dispersed like morning mists, tantalizingly, as if they wanted to be chased. But it was impossible, like holding water in a cupped hand. And if a dream troubled his sleep and he emitted soft wounded-animal sounds, Elena would tap his head, saying, "Knock, knock!" He'd mumble, half awake, "Who's there?" "Dream a little." "Dream a little who?" And she'd sing, "'But in your dreams, whatever they be, dream a little dream of me.'" And he'd feel easier because of her singing.

Monday, the start of the work week, but not for an ex-cop. He'd have stayed in bed, but a morning garden was chaste; its breath sweetest, the light a gentler wash. He was no good at lounging anyway. Not like Elena who could sleep for hours on end, lie in bed like a cat. He sometimes lingered with her on weekend or holiday mornings, but a sense of expectation—or suspicion—kept him alert.

He'd forced himself up and was in the garden earlier than usual, kneeling before the tomato plants. He concentrated on tying the last of the tall stems to a notched bamboo pole. Then, as he stood, his eyes fell on the empty dirt where the peppers had grown. He hadn't meant to look, but the dead patch was impossible to avoid now that Franco was drumming it into him. Not even weeds grew there, as if a child's grave had planted itself on that spot. Emil shifted his weight. A cloud skittered across the sun, dimming the light. Something is wrong, he told himself. "No," he said aloud, sloughing off a gnawing uneasiness. He no longer had to pay attention to every passing cue. But how does a guy stop being a cop?

He returned to the tomatoes, two neat rows, four tidy plants in each. Insignificant yellow flowers already hinted at the little green balls, the ripe red tomatoes to come. He touched one lightly with his long fingers; there would be a plentiful crop this year. Tomatoes were a favorite, but he preferred flowers.

Elena wanted an apple tree. It started around the time of the pepper patch, he thought. Or, no, was it before the peppers? "An apple tree," she said, "endures."

"You want to tempt me, is that it?" he joked. "You could hold a strip of rotten herring in my face and I'd be tempted." She wanted the apple tree smack in the middle of the garden. It made no sense. He remembered reading somewhere that flowers captured the smile of God. He'd told Elena this, hoping to amuse her, to deflect her from the wished-for tree.

But she'd said, "Atheists are the most religious people in the world!"

Would Adam and Eve have quarreled over a tree? Wouldn't God have made all horticultural decisions? But then what were they supposed to do all day before they fell?

There had been an orchard at Elena's father's summer estate in Trieste. Emil thought she was reminiscing. He treated her wish as a friendly disagreement between them. Some mythical remnant from her girlhood, he told himself. But was he wrong? Had he dismissed her unfairly? Was he a man who could figure out a killer but not his own wife?

The snake tempted Eve first; *she* got to Adam, who, according to Emil, ended up looking pretty much like a sap. Couldn't the snake just as easily have lured Adam first, in a very different narrative? Looking out, he saw there was barely room for an additional tulip bulb, never mind a tree. The garden was ripe and beautiful and almost perfect, and he was aware that he alone stood between this state of grace—a garden—and the chaos of Franco.

He walked the path over to Elena's two robust lavender bushes. Their scent called up pleasurable memories, like sniffing postcards of forgotten places. Emil reached down to rub a branch between his palms. He felt in a lighter frame of mind. The morning gloom had lifted. It hadn't been gloomy, only a few passing clouds and his mood, but the day was now wide open and deeply blue, and he responded to it. He was about to go back inside for another stab at the newspaper, empty the dishwasher, get some sort of day going, but he stopped again by the pepper patch. The dirt sifted through his fingers like sand. Could someone have tampered with the soil? Could there be an underground influence at work, some chemical poisoning?

He laughed at himself: Detective Emil Milosec—retired first class, cited with the department's highest honors, and here he was thinking like an old maid. "Underground influences! Come on," he said. If anything was wrong, that patch had been deliberately sabotaged, and the logical suspect would have to be Franco. Some plot between him and

Elena to drive Emil mad. "I'm letting that bastard get to me," he said, touching his head. "The man isn't capable of plotting more than a can of beer."

He brought his hands close to his face again to breathe in the soothing scent of lavender. He stood for several minutes. The bitter peppers used to grow up against the fence between his and Franco's property. Why had he so despised their very presence? Was it Franco? He was Latino; didn't they all like spicy food?

Back in the kitchen, he made himself a second cup of espresso and forced a look at the newspaper, but it was no good. Two years since Elena's death, and then the peppers died. Swigging down the coffee and rinsing his cup under the tap, he dried his hands and headed for the garden door.

He marched straight to the narrow tool shed in back. Bands of gray-and-brown sparrows left off their incessant pickings, swept out of his path. The door to the shed stuck before pulling open. From within came the cold breath of the dark. Reaching in, his hand brushed against strings of spider webs. As a boy spiders had horrified him. In a recurring nightmare he'd be trapped by thousands of silver webs spun across his bedroom door. Today he ignored the sticky, sickening feel of the spider webs, pulled out a shovel, and slammed the door shut.

By the time Franco called to him from the other side of the high fence, Emil had already broken a sweat shoveling nearly two feet deep. "Amigo, that is some racket so early."

Emil kept digging.

"Listen, man, you want a break? I'll get us coffee, Bustelo. What do you say?" Emil shoved deeper into the earth. "Hombre, maybe you need a beer to relax yourself, huh?"

Emil kept digging, shook his head. "A beer?" he said. "At seven thirty in the morning?"

"I am being *poh-lite*."

Emil stopped shoveling. "Polite? Last night you wanted me to shoot you."

"So now you dig my grave?"

Emil went back to digging.

"It is the pepper patch, sí, amigo? That you dig? Unless you plan to visit China the slow way?" Franco laughed at his own joke. "Ayee, I have my headache this morning." He waited. "The sound of that shovel is no help."

"So take an aspirin, amigo."

"You know, why do you trouble the place that won't grow? Maybe the ground is still crying for La Señora Elena, you ever think of that?"

Emil leaned on the shovel. "Franco, don't take this the wrong way: Screw yourself."

"No, see, hombre, earth can cry. We don't think so because we put buildings on top and roads; still, the earth feels; under all that shit she lives."

Emil listened and all he could think of was Franco's dump of a building and his trashed backyard. Elena saying he never gave Franco a chance. Sure. They used to talk through the fence, she and Franco, and sometimes out front. Once, home early, he'd seen her step out of Franco's car.

Elena Morandi worked as a diplomatic translator for the Italian and Austrian Embassies. Her clothing had flair, suited to luncheons, cocktail parties, and dinners, political events where appearances mattered; fluid dresses and smart suits; a fine figure, pure class. That day he saw her was warm, her bare arms slipped through a sleeveless yellow dress with narrow brown stripes. She laughed before thanking Franco, leaning into the car. Thanked him for what? Emil was out in the garden before her key was in the downstairs lock. He pretended he'd been outside for some while, though he still wore his suit. He too dressed well and was noted for it at the precinct, for the cut of his dark suits, his tall frame filling them just so. "Emil! You're home early," Elena said, seeing him come in through the garden door. He stood along the frame. "You look lovely," he said. She smiled. "A lunch?" he asked, all nonchalance, the noncommittal smile he sometimes used on suspects. "Mmm, Italian," she answered before going upstairs to change. Emil watched her leave, loosened his tie, came inside to pour a glass of rosé from the refrigerator, and returned with it to the garden. From the other side of the fence he heard Franco whistling softly to himself. Disgusted, he threw the wine on the pepper patch. One time he urinated on it.

Franco sang songs to her, she said, and once in a while recited. "Recited *what*?" an incredulous Emil asked. "They're in Spanish, poems. Very sweet," she answered coolly.

He said through the fence, "Recite me some poetry, Franco."

"*Poetry*?"

"If you can. Or sing me a song."

"No," he muttered. "Am I Falstaff?"

"What did you say?"

"I am no monkey act. You have the wrong man. I am going for beer, una cerveza; you want one?"

"No, wait, don't go just yet." Emil leaned the shovel against the fence. Franco stood silent on the other side. "Why did she grow the peppers?"

"Su esposa?" Franco shrugged. "How do I know?"

"She grew them for you, didn't she?"

"Listen, why don't you … try something else? Try an apple tree. Manzanas are good fruit. They keep away bad things."

Emil's head was beginning to tighten. When they first came to America he suffered severe headaches. His mother would place him in a shaded room and lay warm washcloths on his forehead and massage his neck with her strong fingers. He was beginning one now. The tree quarrel each spring … then the peppers; they were a recent addition, no more than two or three seasons before Elena's death. A nerve at the base of his neck began to throb.

"Did she want an apple tree?" he asked.

"Why would I know that too?"

"Maybe you did something here, huh? For her, like poison … "

Franco laughed. "Keep talking like that, amigo, you will be drinking beer with me soon."

Emil shook his head, almost angry. "I don't—"

"Sí, sí, you told me many times: no beer."

"Did my wife drink beer with you?"

"Once or twice, to be polite."

Adam and Eve never had a chance. If God created the snake, he also created the sin, its potential. The snake was a plant—Eve set up, Adam born to take the fall. He said, "I am going to ask you a second time, Franco, did you poison my ground?"

"A little weed killer. Not a big deal."

"Not a big deal, huh?" Emil turned and walked into the kitchen, not fast, not slow; deliberate. He was calm, but underneath was something bitter, like chewing off his own hand, grinding the small bones and cartilage to a pulp, the crunch of tissue between molars. Only later would he understand that what he had chewed was his pride.

Inside, he pulled his backup revolver from a kitchen cabinet, lifted the gun out of its holster, and unlocked the safety. The weapon was instantly familiar in his hand, as much second nature as holding a garden trowel. He walked back outside, and the kitchen door closed hard behind him.

Franco, from his side of the fence: "Amigo?"

A helicopter passed somewhere off to the left. Emil raised his arm. His icy fury concerned more than a poisoned patch of ground, more than a drunken neighbor who may or may not have been too friendly with his wife. Focus hammer-locked, exterior steely cool, he took aim.

He'd discharged his service revolver exactly once in the line of duty and missed on purpose. The perp was a skinny fourteen-year-old running from the scene—a narrow alley—armed with a gun that was too big for him. Emil and his partner, Mike Dunn, stood safely behind a doorway. Emil stepped out and in a split second guessed the kid's aim would be off if he fired. It was a fifty-fifty wager. He called out to drop the gun; the kid didn't; he raised the weapon, but before the boy could get off a single round Emil fired just to his right. Feeling the breath of the bullet that nearly grazed him, the boy dropped the gun and froze.

There was only Franco on the other side of the fence when Emil squeezed the trigger and fired two rounds deep into the pepper patch: Bam! Bam! The noise cracked the air. Every tree branch emptied; birds flew off in a mad flapping of wings. The silence that followed was nearly as deafening as the shots. It was broken by a bouncy Latino song from a passing car radio that penetrated the backyards before moving on and retuning the morning to its near-dead quiet. Two craters splayed into the earth where the peppers once grew.

"Hombre? What did you do?"

Emil, calm as still waters: "You know, amigo, you should paint that scrawled-over warehouse wall of yours white. I think it's filled with tears."

Franco pealed out his rasping laugh. He seemed to eventually find everything funny. "She said so too, La Señora."

"And you refused?"

Franco sighed. "I did not truly refuse, I more neglected. Then maybe I forgot."

Emil looked up at Franco's ugly wall. The sulfurous HEEL was there, defiant as ever.

Franco spoke in a low voice: "I will tell you a secret, amigo."

Emil clenched his jaw. "What's that?"

"I never told her. I don't like peppers." Emil didn't react. "Also, she did not like peppers too."

Emil looked up at the sky, then down at the ground. "Did she ask you to poison the peppers?"

"No, that part was my idea. But to help her."

Emil let out his breath. "And planting peppers in your yard?"

"For her, that she asked me. It is probably a good thing you just now shot where they grew, because now the apples can grow there."

"What else did my wife ask you to do?"

"Why do you say this?" Emil was quiet, the pistol limp in his hand. Franco said, "Tell me, amigo, where is that weapon pointed now?"

Emil studied the gun, held it sideways in the palm of his hand. He pressed the thumb piece, pushed open the cylinder and dislodged the empty casings, letting them fall into the pepper-patch hole. He relocked the safety.

"I'm going to make you a deal," he said. He kicked at the dirt with his right foot. "I plant an apple tree; you paint that black wall white. For her, see?"

Franco laughed but quickly suppressed it. "A big job painting that wall, señor. But okay, okay. Maybe." He yawned.

"No maybes."

"No?"

"No."

"Okay, but no more bullets."

Emil was quiet again on his side of the fence. Some minutes passed. He said, "That's that."

"That is what, amigo?"

"The pepper patch is dead."

Franco couldn't help his laughter. "Sí, muerte." He laughed again. Then, almost reverently, repeated, "La muerte. Maybe now we can have some little quiet peace around here?"

Emil walked away, closed and locked his kitchen door, shutting the garden out. He placed the revolver back in the cabinet and went upstairs, where he dropped onto the bed in his clothes and fell into a deep, dreamless sleep. He awoke three hours later; ate lunch, then emptied the cylinder and cleaned the gun with Hoppe's solution. He returned the four rounds, adding two more, and replaced the revolver in the cabinet. Then he walked down the basement stairs.

In the basement he methodically dumped all the jars of pickled peppers into a heavy-duty plastic garbage bag. The cellar was immaculate but he poked around for whatever else needed throwing out. In a corner he found a few things that had belonged to his sister and his mother. He found the army citation for his father, who died in the war. He threw it into the bag. His mother's old teapot went in with a loud cracking of pottery against broken pickle jar. Terra-cotta pots, stacked neatly on a shelf, went in, smashing on top of the other breakables.

He stopped when he came to a postcard of Slovenia he'd sent to his sister, postmarked 1956. He lifted the card to his face half expecting to smell the fresh mountain air of Lake Bled pictured on the other side. He turned the card over and studied the photo of that long-ago lake with the storybook castle nestled on an island in the middle. Upstairs in a drawer he kept a tiny plastic replica of the castle. He stared at the postcard for a long time, finally throwing it in with the other fragments.

He tied the bag closed—tight—and dragged it upstairs. Out front he shoved the bag into the garbage can, to be collected in the morning.

The rest of the day drifted into what Elena called the unavoidable debris of life. He cleaned the not-very-dirty stove then went up to his office on the third floor to look into bills and other paperwork; things she normally saw to that he'd still not gotten the hang of handling himself. He'd rather clean the stove. But he'd noted some depletion in a mutual fund Elena had set up. Those accounts went up and down, she'd explained. But, looking more closely, he decided market fluctuations didn't explain it, that a little too much money was missing. He wasn't certain and had no idea how to find out whether he was right or not. He spent some time looking over the forms but gave up. He'd study the case more closely another time.

Anybody else would have grown furious suspecting a loss of funds. Emil grew restless having to think about the question at all. If it were up to him they'd have placed the money she'd invested under the mattress, where, Elena would have pointed out, it would earn nothing. He didn't care. Having known great poverty did not translate into his having a love of money. They had a good life together he'd say whenever Elena spoke of improvements, of things they needed.

Late afternoon dissolved into evening spent in Elena's day room across the hall from his office. The garden door remained locked.

Tuesday morning, June 20th, the graffiti HEEL on Franco's wall was there to greet Emil when he opened the bedroom shade. Ahead of sky or tree or another person's face, each morning his eyes fell on that misdemeanor mischief scrawled on a wall. As he stood in front of the window, his left hand on the frame, a dream from the night came back to him.

In this dream he was a cop again and he was trying to tell the other detectives something important. He began to shout until his voice grew hoarse, but the other detectives only stared blankly as he ran from one to the other until he was bellowing into their faces about a crime he could not name. He woke up breathing hard and lay awake, sweating, eyes locked on the ceiling until sleep again overtook him and the dream left him, until just now. In real life Emil had never raised his voice with the other cops. The dream made no sense; only the feature of him yelling came back, whatever crime he had been so anxious to report vanished like an overheard whisper.

As he washed up he thought about the apple tree he'd agreed to plant. He'd already decided on a miniature crabapple, imagined the branches draping over Franco's side of the fence once the tree grew tall enough, and the spray of tiny white flowers in spring. A crab was a *Malus* same as any other apple tree. But he knew way down in the rigidly scrupulous part of his brain that he was cheating, that Elena wanted a real apple tree, the kind that yields pies and tarts and sauce.

First he'd have to dig out and bag the dirt, toxic from whatever the hell it was Franco did to the ground, cart it out to the curb, and then haul in new dirt. A tree couldn't safely be planted until October, so the question was what to do with the hole in the meantime? He skipped over the question of how he had come to agree to plant the tree Elena had so long desired. Elena ... she knew how to lie beneath the green trees. The thought that Franco's wall might actually be painted and planted filled him with a kind of dumb elation.

His face in the bathroom mirror looked tired, but at fifty-eight, Emil Milosec was not without appeal; he'd be lying if he tried to say otherwise. The black hair, lightly peppered with gray, was not thin or receding; he'd have a full head to the end. As he lathered his cheeks, a bit of cream stopped up his left nostril. He blew it out with a sharp exhalation. Elena sometimes waited until he said something disagreeable at the breakfast table before informing him that a dab of shaving foam clung to the hairs inside his ear. He in turn would wait a minute or two before wiping it off. A silly game; she would stick out her tongue then resume reading the newspaper. Her smart small face and pointed tongue, the full lips. As he leaned up against the sink, razor in hand, he felt his penis erecting itself and he looked down at his shorts. She would spread herself on the green, green ground. Corridors of green.

He usually ate breakfast in the kitchen, but today Emil went outside with his coffee and newspaper, as he and Elena had done on summer weekends. Sometimes they fucked after a breakfast of crêpes Suzettes, their fingers sticky with apricot jam.

The morning that greeted him was dull; the afternoon promised to be brutal. The late-night news had warned of a heat wave. A hazy bowl of foul air was already coagulating over the city, a thick, gauzy film. Rain would be a godsend, heavy clouds to feed a thirsty earth, but no rain would fall this day. The past few summers had been dry; by August nearly all the Eastern seaboard was toughing out some degree of drought. This year looked to be more of the same.

Emil sat down at the round marble table and took a bite of toast. The *New York Times* lay in front of him. He opened the Metro section first; the dummy blotter he called it, filled with snapshots of local foul play. He'd read the section regularly when he'd been with the force. "A cop could learn a lot from what goes on in here," he'd told Elena on so many mornings, though it was Elena who'd gotten him hooked on reading the papers in the first place. His toast sat hardening on the plate as he read about a man who walked into his father's hospital room, slashed the old man's throat, then whacked the eighty-year-old in the next bed with a hammer and, while he was at it, sliced his sister's throat. And why did he do that? This is what the police would want to know; what sort of motive lay behind such savage behavior? There was always a reason. Knock, knock: Emil, why did you fire your revolver?

"We do this," he once told Elena. "We take this wonder of tissue and bone and blood and brain, this fragile body, and we beat and violate and torture and destroy it in our unending hatreds; we find ways to justify murder. . . ."

She stared at him. "Of course we do."

"Why do you look at me that way?"

She lowered her eyes. "It's as you say; we find a way so we can go on."

"I didn't mean us—you and I."

"No . . . but something . . ."

"What?"

"No, it isn't important right now."

That was all she would say, nothing else. Her private mysteries were like restless phantoms.

His father had cancer, the son told the cops, and he took it upon himself to end the misery. It was obvious. The roommate had been abusive, he added. Oh, an eighty-year-old? They can be cranky, but to end up in some deranged man's idea of justice, snuffed because he maybe said something disagreeable about the hospital food?

Looking up through breaks in the grapevine growing along the pergola, Emil glimpsed an unnatural greenish-white sky. He was already warm in his shirt. And the murderer's sister? The brother disapproved of her lifestyle; unmarried and living at home with her kid while he was out driving a cab. Cabby, tough job, thought Emil, underappreciated. He disliked taking cabs himself. And the sister's child, now orphaned; had the killer—the child's uncle—thought of that?

The guy snapping wasn't much of a surprise, but it bewildered Emil even though to a lawman those sorts of goings-on were as common as skin. What about all the other frayed citizens who didn't snap? The parents, say, of a four-year-old with leukemia whose health insurance had dried up. You couldn't tell them the insurance guys were anything other than legitimized crooks. Or the woman hurrying home from work to fix her kids' supper when a guy slips out of the stairwell, forcing her to her knees at knifepoint for a quick sodomy before taking her cash. Why didn't they snap? Why only pockets of snappers and not the other way round? For all the years Emil had been a criminal investigator the question never left him: why the citizenry was mostly docile.

His shirt, which was loose, felt close. The heat nagged, forced its way up to his verbal brain so he had to fight from stating the obvious, from declaring out loud, "Jesus, it's hot!" He'd have to get the sprinkler going. He preferred to hand-water; it took forever but what kind of hurry was he in? Besides, hand-watering showed up problems: eaters, wilts, a million fungi looking to have their way. A heat wave, like a plague, requires vigilance. Emil was calm as he thought of watering and droughts, heat and smog.

For now his thoughts steered nicely clear of the day before, of having fired the two rounds into the pepper patch. He'd thought in the night that the shots could have attracted attention—locking the stable door after the horse is out—but nothing had come of it so far, and twenty-four hours had now gone by. His cleaning the revolver was good training; a cop's automatic response to having fired his weapon. That he had no business discharging the weapon in the first place was not yet a sore he was ready to rub. Worse, he did not know why he fired. Had he intended, for even a flicker of a second, to shoot his neighbor?

Emil sometimes imagined what his former partner, Detective John Michael Dunn, might have to say. They'd spent enough time sharing crime scenes and car-seat lunches, had talked over plenty. Mike might say Emil was shooting at God.

God was in the dirt, was he, Mike?

Not precisely. But the God who made your wife sick deserved a bullet, right?

So I was mad at God, shot the dirt instead? That's the idea?

Grief's not a tidy package, Milosec, much as you might like it to be.

"Neither is your God," Emil said aloud to the empty garden.

But a temporary calm disallowed any real analysis. Instead, Emil behaved like a dazed man who has just walked away from a car crash, ignorant for the time being and numb as to what has befallen him, of his reasons for having fired two bullets into his garden on a Brooklyn morning in June 1995—two years after the death of his lovely wife.

He crossed his legs, picked up what was left of the now rock-hard toast, smeared jam on it, and moved on to the Science pages. The impossible certainty of the scientists amused him. Let them explain the criminal mind. What, genetics, upbringing? Given time, would science get to the bottom of the whole loving show? Birth to death, and all the issues in between?

Lately he'd been wading into articles on the universe. There was the idea of nothingness and possibility: the cosmological constant energy and its opposite twin, dark matter, in an expanding universe—if that made any sense. Some of it knotted his brain. Like the theory of the shrinking universe. But where did that leave the expanding one? He figured it couldn't do both. He didn't mind the idea of nothingness as much as he minded searching for false comfort. Nothingness, according to Emil, was preferable to a fabricated faith filling in the void, a distraction papered with promises of heaven and hell. Chaos made more sense; laws of physics and this and that randomly coming to be. When he read about things like string theory, he pictured the cat's cradle game his sister used to play on his outstretched fingers.

The headline of today's Science section read, "Beginning a Bargain Basement Invasion of Mars." Emil raised his head, looked out onto his glorious garden, and smiled.

PART TWO

CRIME SCENE

ONE

If you do well, will you not be accepted? And if you do not do well, sin is crouching at the door; its desire is for you, but you must master it.

Book of Genesis

Emil folded the paper closed and stood up. He felt jumpy, getting on his own nerves. He'd take a stroll through the garden, that's what he'd do. But only visitors strolled. The gardener is constantly taking measure, on the lookout for surprises—good and bad. Something always needs adjusting or plucking, to be taken note of; a garden, like a person, is rarely at rest. At least, that was the way Emil Milosec saw it. Tucking the paper under his arm, hands behind his back like a gentleman surveying his estate, he walked the path to the *Dicentra*—the bleeding heart. Only two blooms were left, its moment of glory over with the waning spring. He bent to pull off a stem gone yellow. It snapped hollowly in his hand. He thought he heard the phone ring and turned back toward the house. Who would be calling?

He stopped at the pepper hole while thinking what annuals would work there until he planted the tree: A couple of lacy euphorbia might work well, and white verbena, and some blue and white lobelia? First the two shell casings would have to be fished out.

The phone rang again.

Emil looked up at a sparrow bustling among the thick English ivy that crept along the stuccoed facade of the house. He heard the irritating bleat of a car alarm in the distance and thought he saw something lying in the pepper hole. He stood perfectly still, the bleeding heart stem still in his hand. He didn't want there to be something irregular lying in the hole. He turned to watch the sparrow duck into the leaf-covered wall. That ought to be removed, he told himself about the ivy. Each summer Elena had remarked the same, and he had agreed, but they'd let the ivy continue to grow up and up, like Jack's beanstalk. They'd let it nearly cover their bathroom window so they never needed a curtain and inside was lit a pale green as the afternoon sunlight filtered in. They liked the rustling sound of leaves when a breeze whiffled through. It's probably a dried leaf in the hole, he told himself, prematurely fallen off Mrs. Noily's old maple. He bent down for a closer look.

"What?" he asked himself with the softness of a child who hopes, by speaking in a hushed voice, some lurking darkness will go away. He went down on his hands and knees and thrust his head over the pepper hole. A second later Emil jerked up and was on his feet. "What the hell?" he said, but not loudly; softly, softly, very controlled. He looked down again to be sure of what he'd seen: There, resting on the earth where Elena's peppers had once grown, beside the fence between his and Franco's yard, lay a cleanly severed, neatly positioned finger.

"A woman's," he said in a whisper. "A woman's pinkie," he added, just as softly.

His mind involuntarily snapped into cop mode: timeline, evidence, motive . . . story. Yesterday's movements replayed—no getting around it now—an interior film of him digging the hole, unlocking the safety in the kitchen, firing his Smith & Wesson snubby, two bullets. Bam! Bam! Franco. . . .

Was it true Elena disliked peppers?

He stood still, so still, as if he were not breathing. He tried to see time move, to catch every fleeting detail in composite. It was a game he'd played at crime scenes, where he tried to actually see time: Now was now, but what happened then, when the victim was harmed; how did the bad guy or girl behave during the crime? Could he replay that tape, bridge time like a video rewind of the critical moments?

But the game wasn't working and that left him back at the day before: the shots fired in a moment of fury. Was it fury, or angry longing for what was missing? That would be Mike Dunn's take: striking out in anger over Elena. Yes, he'd discharged his weapon, but he could not say why, didn't want to say why, or did not know how to say why. . . . But that finger had a separate life from the pepper hole and his fired bullets. Why was it in his garden? Where was the pinkie's owner? Who placed her finger in the pepper hole, just where he happened to have released the two rounds?

Emil rubbed the back of his neck. His head throbbed. He needed a cup of coffee. This was a multi coffee discovery—all-day coffee. This was what-the-crap-is-going-on serious; this was ruining-your-day real. *This*, Emil told himself, as he left the garden for the comfort of his kitchen, is a crime scene.

As a cop, Emil drank scads of coffee. Gallons. By the end of the workday his stomach felt as if it could etch steel. He drank espresso at a time when it was considered foreign, except in Italian or Turkish restaurants, something un-American from the other side of the Atlantic. He'd had to bring in his own stove-top espresso maker and hot plate. There were no latte joints around the corner when Emil started out in blue. He suffered plenty of ribbing over his miniature cups of dark caffè. The faint accent he worked so hard to conceal didn't help either, only added to the general sense that Emil was never going to be one of the boys.

Things would have been plenty worse if he hadn't been so good at catching killers. Detective Emil Milosec had pretty much seen it all before his copping days were done, witnessed all manner of dead body from the bizarre and grisly to the almost comic and the nearly unrecognizable as human. He'd seen his share of dismembered body parts, bits that would never add up to tell the whole sordid tale. He wasn't the nauseous sort but the chore of viewing violent death up close remained an ugly one. He'd been fast at reading a corpse. If a stiff had an arm up and a twisted left leg facing the toilet bowl, Emil drew his conclusions and then waited to see what forensics and the medical examiner had to say. He'd stick around a scene listening on the side while the other cops talked. He figured they were full of it if they claimed they understood a corpse. Emil understood that a dead body had once been a living, breathing person with a story to tell and that that person's narrative was related one-on-one to the perpetrator's story. He would say, "Everybody has motive at one point or another to get rid of someone. The trick is finding out who is willing to act on it." In time that approach made him the better cop.

It was seated at his desk, his mind abstracting, that brought a crime into focus, deductive reasoning, he'd say, tapping his head. At the stationhouse they called him "the Thinker" or Rodin because of the way he sat at his desk to figure things out alone, to theorize, as they put it. The other cops liked gut for solving crime. With the tougher cases, as the medical examiner's final report, the witness statements, scene notes, and so forth shuffled through, they'd dump the lot on Emil. "Give it to Rodin," they'd say, pronouncing it, *Row-dan*. "Milosec'll get to the bottom of the bad guy's id; call on his pal Siggie Freud. Right, Milosec: Where's your mama?"

Emil's success rate in solving crimes allowed things to relax to a degree where procedure was concerned. Once he saw what he felt he absolutely needed to, he tried to steer clear of any further physical contact with a crime other than the suspect interviews, where he'd get looks from his partners for the "oddball" kinds of questions he'd ask. At a crime scene, once he took things in, he spent his time looking out a window, if there was a window, or at the surrounding landscape, if the corpse was located outside. Prospect Park was one location he enjoyed, albeit a murder in the park or nearby was what usually brought him there. Often he was the butt of coarse crime-scene humor, like the Canopy Case, as it came to be known. That day it was raining lightly over Prospect Park, the leaves like softly veiled gowns over seminude tree branches, the air drunk on the earthy smell of early spring. It was an address he could only ever visit, never own, the sort of place he'd have wanted for Elena, a locale not frequented by homicide detectives. The spacious, well-appointed co-op apartment overlooking the park contained the bloodied body of a murdered woman.

Within twenty minutes, his back to the victim, Emil declared, "A woman did it." Even Mike Dunn ignored the remark. A .22 revolver had done the work, a small, low-caliber weapon that would have been fired at close range. "A lady's gun," Emil said to the day outside since no one was listening to him. The victim, Connie Bortense, was flung to the side of the bed with a bullet to her left ventricle, the aorta shattered. Mike Dunn commented on the sheer white muslin canopy over the bed, said his wife would go for that sort of decorative touch. Connie's blood had splattered up to the canopy, leaving a pattern of deep red dots, dashes and curlicues.

"It's obvious the victim didn't put up a fight, so how come her dress is all torn?" Mike asked.

"The jerk tried to make it look sexual," offered the uniform cop who'd been the first to arrive. Connie's black panties were pulled down to just below her knees.

That's when Emil said, with not one thing else to go on, "A woman, definitely. Bank on it." There followed some muffled laughter regarding maybe a lesbian did the job, so that would explain there being no semen and how faked the torn garment looked. Plus, what self-respecting guy would leave the panties up that far? Emil didn't mind the gallows humor, even if it was at his own expense; there had to be a way to live with constant murder, a cop on the job day in, day out.

Mike tugged at his pea-green sports coat—which seemed to be growing smaller—hearing Emil repeat that a woman did it. Mike had lasted longer with Emil than any of the other detectives he'd been partnered with, and he'd actually grown to like him. He'd grown protective too of what he knew the others regarded as Emil's eccentricities, gathered some understanding of how his partner's mind worked.

Previous partners had routinely asked to be placed with someone else. They couldn't work with the Slovenian, they'd say. He could be a filthy commie for all anyone knew, never mind he was now a US citizen; he was *different*. A desk sergeant, overhearing one of these complaints, said, "Milosec's no communist. I don't know what he is, but have you seen his wife? Pinkos don't marry that kind'a broad." He flapped his wrist and sucked in his breath for emphasis.

"Yeah, I know what he is," said one of the detectives. "He's something up his sleeve."

"Like what?" the desk sergeant wanted to know.

"Like a dead rabbit."

The others laughed, but uneasily. Like it or not, Milosec was still one of their own.

Maintaining a balance between the other cops and Emil, Mike winked. "So, you saying we got a girl-on-girl thing going here?" he asked, though they all knew the victim was married.

"I don't know about that," Emil answered. "Let's see what the husband has to say."

"You're thinking a threesome now, huh?" the uniform cop called out.

"Keep it down, Kelly," Mike warned.

"How much is really ever clear?" Emil said, but low and more to himself.

The forensics officer joked, "Husbands are always the last to know."

Emil smiled.

"People know their sexual styles; even you can't argue with that, Milosec," Mike put in.

"Anyhow," Emil remarked, "it's too clean." He meant the crime scene, the killing.

"Guys can be clean," Mike answered. Emil looked at him. "Okay, all right, then what's the motive?"

"Jealousy, but I think it was the wrong woman."

Mike knew Emil was already edging toward fingering someone in the building, but he didn't see how. "I can't imagine for the life of me what in hell you have *jealousy* on?" When Emil failed to comment, Mike added, "You ought to write books, you know that? You're way out on a limb this time, Milosec."

Emil did not think it necessary to point out that motives in murder were few; anger, jealousy, greed, fear. His job, as he saw it, did not include convincing others. In the end he was right about Connie's killer.

He was just too quiet for the other cops, too contained, his silences confused with disdain, suggesting a sneaky European quality that made the other cops uneasy. Emil just didn't try to fit in. He never thought to try and that was viewed as an offense. Not intended, maybe, but just who the hell did Milosec think he was? Invitations rarely came to him for the after-work drink. He'd agree once in a while, a scotch and soda, Mike dragging him along. Or after a particularly tough case everyone had invested in, even the captain coming along; a grim case, not much to really celebrate, but the job was done, a hazardous person removed from circulation, impossible for even the most hardened cop not to feel some satisfaction. He'd obligingly buy a round, but Emil never instigated a beer out with the boys, except maybe with Mike. Even that was rare.

Sometimes it seemed Emil only went along for the ride. There was the case that took them out to Connecticut, tracing a murder weapon. Mike drove while Emil took in the scenery. The gun had come from an antiques fair in Greenwich, a German piece manufactured in 1937. Mike asked Emil on the way back to the city, "Did you know they could do that? Sell a gun at a roadside flea market, call it an antique: no permits, no paperwork, no nothing?"

Emil was looking out at the Merritt Parkway, at the many trees lining the roadside, the dark areas suggesting a vast forest full of unknowns, but he knew suburban houses were bundled along the other side of the deceptively narrow corridor. He had come along because he enjoyed that route, called it a treasure. He sometimes took his wife over the

Merritt for day trips in summer. "Flea markets are notoriously beyond the fringe," he said. "I'm just surprised the piece worked."

Mike continued, "If the rich mother hadn't lent sonny the cash and kept the receipt, how would we have found the source of that weapon? And, I mean, the guy goes to his mom to borrow money to kill his wife? What kind of man is that?"

"Takes all kinds," Emil said. "Maybe mom was soft on sonny and, you know, daughters and mothers-in-law, a murderous mix."

"Not so fast, Einstein. You're saying the *mother* is involved—"

"No!" Emil cut in. "It was ... I was joking."

Mike scratched his head. "You were making a joke? Give a guy a heads-up next time, will yah? Poke me when it's time to laugh." He looked over at Emil, the car speeding toward Brooklyn. He was eager to get back to the precinct; the day was nearly over and he had a long commute home to Long Island. He popped the red lamp onto the roof, leaving it flashing without the siren. Suddenly slamming on the brakes, Mike swerved right to avoid hitting a dog standing in the road. Emil's head banged into the side window as the car stopped hard on the narrow, grassy shoulder.

"Jesus! Did you see that! Right in the middle of the frigging road. Shit, I could've killed him, stupid, dumb dog."

Emil reached up to touch his head.

"You okay?" Mike asked. Emil nodded. "I hate it in movies when they kill the dog; people is one thing, but to kill a dog in a movie, that's criminal, it shouldn't be allowed. Yah know?"

Emil said, "I don't really go to the movies much, Mike."

Mike looked at him again before pulling back onto the highway. "Sorry, Milosec. I must've looked away."

"I'm fine."

Mike asked him, "So no movies, huh? I mean, never? Elena either? You watch TV, though, right? I mean, TV's not banned?" He looked over at Emil again, seated tall in his impressive dark suit, the smart tie. Emil suggested he keep his eyes on the road. Mike hadn't really expected an answer, and he wouldn't want the ribbing to go over his partner's limit.

There was the case of the book editor who took her best friend's life. Emil was nearing retirement when a new captain insisted he no longer be permitted to sit at his desk while his partner worked the field. Emil returned to the scene but let Mike do the talking. Mrs. Friedlander was an editor with a small publishing house that handled mystery writers. She worked with three or four clients from out of town, doing most of her work at home, going to the office only for staff meetings. She killed her friend one day and tried to use an interoffice fax as an alibi. Emil named her as the prime suspect in well under twenty-four hours.

Mrs. Friedlander found lipstick stains on Mr. Friedlander's underclothing and it was the same shade she had given her best friend for her birthday. The lipstick was Estée Lauder, the expensive, long-lasting kind, and it was still on the murdered girl's lips at the time of discovery. Emil noticed right away how fresh the color looked.

Mike got the details. The nuts and bolts came via Mrs. Ryder, from the apartment below the Friedlanders'. Mike learned a lot from Mrs. Ryder, who was often at home with little Scotty Junior. There was plenty of trouble in that household, Mrs. Ryder said of her upstairs neighbors. "She was thinking of having a baby," she added, meaning the murder suspect, Mrs. Friedlander.

"Yeah ... and how do you know that?" Mike asked.

Mrs. Ryder nodded several times. She continued, "I've heard plenty." She said she didn't like to pry but the bathroom vents acted like a PA system between the upstairs bath and hers. "Mrs. Friedlander—Doris—was crying to her friend on Linda's birthday. A few of us went up to eat cake and sing happy birthday, and that was when Doris gave her the lipstick. Doris is a suspicious person by nature," Mrs. Ryder volunteered, but in the case of Mr. Friedlander, Mrs. Ryder felt she had grounds to be. "I don't care to malign, but there is something oily about that man."

"Mr. Friedlander?" Mike asked.

Emil, playing a game of staring with Scotty Jr., shifted in the child-sized chair he'd taken while Mike did the interviewing.

Mrs. Ryder looked down at Emil. "Well, yes, that's who we're talking about, isn't it?"

"And you're familiar with the deceased, Linda?" Mike asked.

She turned back to Mike. "It's a small building. Doris is a neighbor. We got to know each other. Linda was over all the time; it was natural."

"I see. And you say the victim, Linda, comforted Doris Friedlander?"

"Right after the party I heard Doris crying. She must have gone into the bathroom. She told Linda her husband was seeing someone, that she wanted to get pregnant, but how could she now? Like that. What a stinker … I'm sorry, but it was Linda all along. Some best friend."

"How do you know this, though, Mrs. Ryder?"

"What? Wait!" Little Scotty had let out a bloodcurdling cry. His mother ran to retrieve him. Emil stood up, brushing off his trousers.

"About the victim, Mrs. Ryder, and Mr. Friedlander?" Mike pressed. "You were saying?"

Mrs. Ryder held her whimpering son and shot a disapproving look at Emil. "The lipstick, Detective. Doris confronted him. The underwear had that shade on it. That's what I said a minute ago."

"Right, but can you be certain, Mrs. Ryder? Certain enough for, say, life in prison or lethal injection?"

"Well, I'm not *absolutely* certain about Richard Friedlander and Linda. I never saw them in bed together, if that's what you mean, but I heard Doris yell at him, *'How could you? I gave her that color.'* ... Do we have the death penalty in New York State?"

"I'm asking is there a chance you're wrong, Mrs. Ryder?"

Forensics had already matched the lipstick. "It's circumstantial," Emil said in the car after the interview, "but it'll probably stick." He told Mike to go ahead and bet on it.

Mike pulled a handkerchief out of his pocket. "As a rule, I don't bet," he said, blowing his nose. They were headed back to the precinct to get a warrant for Mrs. Friedlander's arrest. "What'd you do to that kid back there, Milosec?" Mike asked as he parked the car.

"Nothing. He blinked first."

"The kid's four years old, for pity's sake; you couldn't'a let him win?"

According to Emil, the human factor would weigh in against Mrs. Friedlander no matter the outcome of a trial: Taking a life was bad enough, but to kill a betraying friend had to wreck whatever peace of mind might be left. "In the Bible," he told Mike, "Mr. Friedlander and the best friend would have been stoned to death, quite likely with Doris Friedlander tossing the first rock."

Mike said, "The Bible, right. What I don't get is, why off the supposed other woman? Maybe she's a miserable so-and-so for lying and so on, but it's the bum husband deserved to die."

Emil shook his head. "Nobody deserved to die, Mike, not for one or for ten thousand rides on the sheets."

"Well, which is it? Biblical stoning or no penalty for fornication? You can't have it both ways."

"I don't want death for fornication."

"But you want the biblical justice?"

"I don't think I meant that either, Mike," Emil answered. Was Mike saying Emil was an Old Testament scold? Was that the kind of man he was or that Mike thought he was? He didn't think so, but even he could see that his preoccupation with the Bible was odd, especially in an atheist. He was bothered plenty by that conversation.

Mike Dunn had been Emil's final partner, the only one to get close. Emil had strong ideas that came with him to the job, for which he was overqualified anyway. He'd taken classes in criminal psychology at City College, and while a student it occurred to him that his boyhood dream of becoming a police officer might not be the best, but he'd thought for so long about being a cop that he couldn't see another way. He was not a man to shift his heading without a struggle, and there hadn't been time for that. His mother and sister were counting on him; police work meant a decent job with benefits and respectability, and they needed the money. There was no cushion in the Milosec household; if something broke it stayed broken. At the time Emil's pretty sister was washing dishes at a five-and-dime-store soda fountain, with her perfect legs displayed for all the men to see.

The top brass didn't get why a talented mind like his stayed on the force. They didn't much care for Detective Emil Milosec. They said he had an ego the size of Kansas, and that was only the front part. He was averse to casual conversation, and they didn't think he showed sufficient respect. But he was too good at copping to dump. Everyone said *his* was the uncrackable case; who knew what went on inside the Thinker's head? And it wasn't just at work; people often felt when they talked with Emil Milosec that he would rather be somewhere else.

Mike Dunn was a clean cop. They had never discussed the question, but Emil guessed he and Mike had been paired once and for all by a process of elimination. Detective Dunn had his own sense of justice, balancing cause and effect. A woman killing a brutal husband was legally wrong, for example, but why should she be a beat-up victim her whole life? He thought the law ought to allow for that; there was murder and there was murder—compassion should have a part to play. If Emil answered that the law could not accommodate each crime, Mike would ask, "Why not? All life ever is is accommodating for this, accommodating for that; why not the law?"

Some of the other officers Emil had been paired with had a sense of right and wrong that seemed ad hoc: one day one method, something else the next. They could punch a perp or treat him easy, depending. To Emil this behavior was one step away from the jungle, and such an approach to enforcing the law frightened him. If the others thought Milosec was too stiff, he thought they were a little too creative. He could barely remember the names of those early partners before he started outpacing them all.

Emil respected that Mike was not a hard man. Mike didn't agree with him about the other police officers. He said the job had the potential to do that to a man, wear him down until he started to blur bad guys and good guys. "They can't all be as starchy as you, Milosec," Mike said.

"What about you?"

"I don't like a complicated life so I go by the book; doesn't mean I have to like it." He shrugged.

Emil and Elena had twice gone to barbecues out on Long Island, to Baldwin, where Mike and his wife, Danielle, lived with Mikey Junior and little Dannie. There would be a mountain of food: chicken, burgers, hot dogs, potato salad, ices, cake. The house had a wide, flat backyard with swings, a plastic pool, hundreds of toys, but not much of a garden. Elena liked Danielle, partly because she too was foreign born, and attractive, but she couldn't understand why there was no garden. Emil saw how the kids were drawn to Elena. The five-year-old had a little girl's crush on her, "The pretty 'Lena.'" He was surprised to see how naturally she horsed around with them. With him the kids were polite but kept their distance.

He commented on this in the car on the way home after the first visit. "Did I ever say I did not like kids?" Elena said. "Children are free of motives. But the mothers must socialize them and then … they are no longer free."

Emil looked at her. "You've thought about this," he said.

She looked at him. "I think once in a while, yes."

Emil feared she might be having second thoughts about not having children. But he didn't want to ask and maybe open up a topic that had no bottom.

Mike and Danielle occasionally met up in the city for dinner with Emil and Elena, for steaks; a night out, a babysitter with the kids. The ladies drank white wine, the men whiskey. Emil enjoyed himself on those nights; the women's presence softened his edges. He and Mike avoided talking shop, poisoning the meal with tales of murder and mayhem. Even

Elena was briefly carefree, laughing easily when Mike would tell one of his jokes, even harder when Emil would ask for an explanation. The couples were an unexpected pairing, a friendly blink in time.

Mike Dunn was killed during an arrest six months after Emil retired. His new partner failed to detect a concealed weapon, a pistol hidden in a cowboy boot.

After leaving the force, Emil assumed he would never again see another violent crime up close. The only murder for him these days was the occasional noir detective program on public television. They'd invested some, realized income from the top-floor rental, and were comfortable. Elena continued to work, though less at the embassies, taking freelance translation assignments she could work on at home. They'd gone back to Europe twice, mostly to view gardens in the cities they chose to visit, steering clear of their countries of origin.

Emil had gotten the hang of life without victims and suspects, crime and punishment. He took a French class—awkwardly—because he'd always wanted to speak French to Elena in bed. But she was gone these two years, a body part had turned up in the garden, and whatever life Emil had managed to make for himself since Elena's death appeared to be in jeopardy. Once again he was staring into the jaundiced eye of a crime.

TWO

When the Lord saw how great was the wickedness of human beings on earth, and how their every thought and inclination were always wicked, he bitterly regretted that he had made mankind on the earth.

Book of Genesis

Emil's popularity was not boosted by his having made detective in under a year on the force. At the time he was sleeping in the dining room of the rundown house they'd bought in Brooklyn, purchased with grief pay and GI insurance from his father's death. Insurance was what made Emil think something was shifty about a mom-and-pop double murder that had been set up to look like a mob hit. "They were after the insurance money," he told the detective in charge of the case. "It's a ploy; they're Italian so the idea is maybe a bad loan, but this is not the mob in this; it's family," he repeated.

The older detective, who'd heard him the first time, looked him over. "Says who?" he said, in front of everyone, to the upstart in uniform. The detective looked willing to let it ride on the mob, or at least not be instructed by some foreign kid fresh out of the academy. Emil's beat partner suggested he put a lid on it before they both landed in hot water.

Emil decided to investigate on his own. He had plenty of time to follow up on hunches; his mother was dead, his sister, Lisle, had married and moved out, and he was alone. Moving the mattress into the dining room meant saving on the heating bill, leaving the three other vacant floors like an icebox. He'd managed to replace the roof and gotten the mechanicals updated, but the interior of the house was badly wanting. Eating and solving crimes were all Emil had money for; he thought, back then, he should probably sell the place but he liked the idea of owning his house—the American dream no matter how dilapidated. He bought a brand-new suit and pressed his shirts on an ironing board in the kitchen for the promotion to detective. The other detectives called the new man "Milo" when he first came up, a moniker tweaked out of "Emil" and "Milosec," not intended to endear. They said he'd gotten lucky but that his luck would run out.

As it turned out, "Milo's" luck stuck, and the business of being an officer of the law soon began to seem pointless. If making a garden was ultimately futile, solving crimes was a bottomless pit. His method involved emptying himself, like an actor for a part, in order to fill up with a crime's unique narrative. Ninety-eight percent of all murders are committed by somebody the victim knows; the psychological autopsy of a crime is nearly always based on that given. Emil Milosec was a homicide profiler without knowing it. Once he had his storytelling method down the work became routine. It was a job; instead of fixing plumbing leaks or heart valves, he fit together puzzle pieces, the behavior behind a murder. He found nothing noble in the endeavor and began to develop headaches whenever he had to serve an arrest. Once the culprit was out of his hands the headache would disappear, unless he had to testify. Testifying in court brought him nearly to the point of migraine.

Elena reacted curiously toward the headaches, as if she expected them. By then she was living with Emil and she helped him as his mother once had, darkening the room, bringing him aspirin, encouraging him to sleep it off. But there was an expression on her face. She'd look at him knowingly and say, "Another killer caught?"

The coffee began to bubble. Emil poured milk into a small pot to boil. He found it a reassuring ritual: the bubbling coffee and steaming milk, the rich smell of fresh-ground beans, something primitive and reassuring. There was a brand-new espresso maker on a shelf in the pantry. Elena bought it for him, but Emil preferred the old stovetop method. Her American coffee maker still stood on the counter, unused these two years. Seated at the kitchen table, facing the window that looked out on the garden, he opened a tin of almond biscotti and placed one on a flowered plate next to his cup. He was aware of going through the motions, moving slowly to give his mind a chance to catch up with events outside.

He dipped the biscotto into the hot espresso and waited until it was drenched without falling apart in the cup. Holding the biscuit upright before taking a bite, Emil saw the image of the finger in the pepper hole. He put the biscuit down. There was pink polish on the dead fingernail, and the shade seemed familiar. He remembered an ecru gown of Elena's—a filmy number with a wide skirt that swished when she walked; very feminine, with a satin bustier—that she'd worn to a police racket, some benefit ball or other. To go with the dress her nails had been painted a pale pink, much like the color on the severed finger now haunting his garden. He ate the biscuit, chewing thoughtfully, took a sip of coffee. He rarely hurried.

Elena painted her nails infrequently, partly because the practice struck her as silly—applying varnish to the body—but also because the enamel chipped so easily, especially working in the garden. Clothing was a different story. She'd been acutely feline—possessive, sharp, but never fussy in her dress because she was confident and knew what suited her. Emil compared her, when shopping, to a hungry jaguar on a hill. While he groomed to distance himself from a job that regularly brushed up against the brutal, to Elena a garment was a statement of personality. "Who are you?" he asked her once, in Saks Fifth Avenue—a store he thought should be abandoned by humanity and eliminated from the face of the earth. "I don't know who you are when you shop for dresses."

Though he enjoyed her elegance, and even insisted upon it, that night of the ball, as he watched her dress, he worried she would outshine the other wives. Like their husbands, they tended toward the lumpy. The police commissioner and the mayor would be there. Emil had recently been decorated for solving a grisly triple murder of underaged girls. He would be singled out, but so would Elena, and she'd be envied by the other wives. The extra attention would be agonizing for him. He gently mocked her that night, but he was also proud and maybe even a little afraid of her. At times Elena's physique aroused a quiver of violence in him.

He carried on, especially in summer, when the neighborhood girls went around in skimpy outfits. Elena would laugh at him and ask, "What is wrong with you?"

"They go around half naked; do they know what they're doing?"

"It's hot out!"

"I know it's hot, but I'm not half naked; you're not."

"We are no longer twenty."

"Seriously, Elena? Breasts falling out, legs bared to the pubic hairs—no wonder men get only one idea."

"Men are born with only one idea, Emil. If this troubles you so, go to someplace like Iran. There the women are shrouded in veils, the hijab, and buried alive in chadors head to toe. Listen, even as a small girl I was told always be with your girlfriends, arm in arm. They all said this, mothers, aunts, grandmothers. If you are seen alone people will talk. I did not understand. It's good for people to talk, I thought. But later I understood. Men cannot behave so women must behave for them. Who made this up? I have to hide *myself*, or they'll say I am inviting men? Never mind about a woman's pleasure."

Emil watched her as she spoke. "Mmm, a woman's pleasure . . ."

"Should we stay off the streets? Wear black sheets to look like insects? Maybe the men should hide under a veil instead? Imagine sucking veil fabric into your mouth all day? In the heat."

"I could suck some fabric off you right now, if you feel constrained in any way."

Elena smiled. "Go to Tehran!"

"Seriously, this doesn't bother you?"

"Women are beautiful, Emil, and there is nothing to be done about it except for you to suffer."

He had to agree, women are beautiful and they are everywhere, but the cop in him knew, right or wrong, they spelled trouble. "Women—glamour and sex, it's like rye whiskey and gasoline," he told Mike Dunn. But Mike never had a problem with it: "Without sex and gasoline we'd be out of business, ever think of it like that? Jeez, Milosec, whadda'ya want the world to look like, anyhow? You worrying that apple-in-Eden thing again? We wouldn't be here without that famous apple, huh?"

Emil finished his coffee and resisted eating a second biscotto. Outside in the garden was a clue to a crime, and it was probably sex and gasoline all over again. He asked himself, What about this finger? Why? How? It occurred to him that the rest of the body might still be alive. The amputation of a finger wouldn't kill anybody. But he'd seen no blood, and that was not a good sign. It was the sort of conclusion Elena would come to: that the rest of the woman was alive, in big trouble perhaps, but alive. She might say to him, "Why assume the worst just because you are police?" Emil answered to himself, Probably dead, one way or another.

Nothing came to him as he sat. He was as blank as an empty house. Why a finger in *his* garden, like some Sicilian vendetta? Standing in the kitchen doorway, he went over the night before: His bedroom window above the garden had been open, but he'd heard nothing unusual. He'd locked up before going to bed around eleven thirty. Other than the yelling dream he'd slept well. Had he slept through an intruder? He must have. . . .

He put the dishes into the sink and opened the garden door. Stepping outside, he heard Franco whistling to himself next door. He pulled back inside. "Dammit!" he cursed under his breath. "Why's he up so early?" It was way too early for Franco, and this was the second morning in a row. He knew Franco couldn't possibly see the finger, but he did not want him nosing around. Franco Montoya was a good way to get an item like this broadcast throughout the borough; with a few drinks under his belt, he'd start to boom everything out. For now Emil wanted to keep this little problem to himself. He stepped all the way out, coughing loudly so Franco would be sure to hear.

"Hey, amigo? You over there playing with your peas?"

The air was still, not a shred of breeze. "You over there, Franco?"

"You mean me? Sí, I am here; where would I be?" Emil moved with purpose, as if he were going about some important chore. Franco called out again, "Amigo, how about those tomatoes; they going to be big this year? Like in a woman's blouse? You know what I am saying, hombre?"

"Uh-huh, sure to be a D-cup, every round one."

Franco laughed loudly from behind the fence. "That's a good one, mi amigo. A D-cup! Ha ha, que grande. Very funny."

Emil thought Franco might already be drinking. He was too loud, rowdy, like he'd been at it for hours. Franco once told Emil that during the holidays, from Thanksgiving through Christmas, he ate his Cheerios in beer every other morning. He did this to try to celebrate. By drinking only every other day, he explained, on Christmas morning he would be confused as to which day was on and which was off the beer. It was a good system to fight off the sorrow of the season. Christmas was sad, he said, because nothing had turned out the way it was supposed to, and poor old Jesus (he said "Hay-seus," in the Latino way) had probably died on that miserable cross for nothing.

"So the world wasn't saved after all?" Emil asked.

"Not yet, I don't think so, amigo. Do you?"

Emil disliked beer; the brew guts on the other cops, especially the uniform guys sitting in squad cars all day. Beer- and doughnut-choked bellies; it was everything that was wrong with the NYPD. Those cops couldn't run two blocks if their lives depended on it. Emil had kept trim and strong, had allowed no fat to ripple along his flesh, still a size sixteen shirt and a thirty-four-inch waist with washboard abs. He regularly exercised, as Elena had, keeping her shape nearly to the end.

Without thinking, Emil gently massaged his stomach, watched

absently as a fly landed on the dismembered digit. That was when he noticed a small opal ring on the ground at the base of the finger, as if the ring had slipped off at the wrong end, where the palm should be. He'd missed that before? Had he missed a huge clue until just now? He thought the ring might be familiar but it was turned partially sideways on the ground, and from where he stood he couldn't be certain. A cold snake of fear slithered down his large intestine. What else had he missed? He swatted a gnat. Why didn't Franco go back inside his cave? Why was he snooping around? He needed to think, to examine the scene. Procedure required that he call the police, but Emil knew that no such thing was about to happen.

His canvas tool bag sat on a chair under the window behind him. Elena had ordered the bag for him from one of the pricier garden catalogs. It was smart-looking, beige with green piping along the edges and loops and pockets on the outside and compartments that were roomy enough for larger tools. At first Emil thought the bag too fancy, but he had come to see its merits and later complimented Elena on the gift.

He reached for the bag and walked the few feet to the pepper hole. Kneeling with his back close to the fence, he mentally thanked her again for the bag. He took his work gloves out of a side pocket and slipped them on. There was not much in the bag that morning: clippers, Elena's old goatskin gloves, some plastic ties and bits of green string, a trowel. His plan was to wrap the finger in one of Elena's gloves and slip it into the bag. He leaned over, bent down close until most of his arm was inside the two-foot-plus-deep hole.

"What are you doing, amigo?"

Emil shot to his feet. "*What?*"

"Did you have coffee, I am asking?"

"Coffee? Yes. Why?"

Franco imitated the way Emil talked. "Perhaps you would care for a dry martini instead, my friend."

"Have you been drinking, Franco?"

Franco peeled off his gritty laugh. "No. Sober as a mouse."

Emil smiled slightly. "A glass of orange juice might be more appropriate."

"Orange juice? Quieres jugo de naranja, mi amigo? I have it, juice, it will be my pleasure. Wait! I will get us a glass."

"No, no, Franco! Franco, I've had my breakfast. Read the paper, gardened. I'm out here gardening, as you can see."

"I don't see you gardening."

"No?"

"Uh-uh. I am behind my fence. I don't see nothing."

Before Emil came into his own method as a cop, he practiced all the usual techniques. He studied the scene with care, grilled witnesses until *they* felt guilty, faithfully followed every lead. He had once excelled in those notorious interviews where he'd get into the face and if necessary the soul of the accused. The clammy interview rooms would fill with nervous gas, the suspect's and the police officers'. Those nail-it-now, fart-filled sessions before a lawyer came on board to interfere with the purity of an arrest. He and his partner would try to trip the perp; convince him to take a plea, confess, comply, or simply turn rat. Sometimes a bit of rough stuff. Nothing that would show on the surface, no black eyes or swollen knuckles from a hand slammed inside a door; just a bit of shoving, mostly intimidation.

Then Emil learned to be more subtle. After all, he was originally from Eastern Europe, the virtual birthplace of Western torture. His secret weapon was silence. He'd be alone with the accused, a few conspicuous questions: "Why'd you do it? How'd it feel? Tell me anything you like. And by the way, where's your mother right now?" Then silence; a grade school-sized clock on the wall—ticktock, ticktock—long hands measuring time against huge numbers, five fateful black dots between each digit. "Try to see the big hand move," he'd suggest. "We have all the time in the world." A semi darkened room, no coffee, no smokes, no water, no toilet, no phone, no relief. "Let's talk. … " A smile. But he had detested the sport. Specifically, what it brought out in him, the involuntary hatred for the man—or woman—he meant to corner, trap, break, dehumanize. It was necessary to see the suspect as subhuman. No twisting of due process was too much to get at the suspect's knowledge of himself, melt him down to jelly and stick him to the crime.

But later, alone, Emil found a new clarity. His own imagination might be worse than a criminal's, but at least he no longer had to sit one-on-one in suspicious hatred of a man or woman who had become like a character in a dark tale. It was Elena who had shown him the possibilities of that approach. She gave him Dostoyevsky to read, *Crime and Punishment*. She said, "This will bring the mind of the murderer back to you. You will like it; there is even a bridge over a river, the Neva." He was skeptical of fiction, patronizing; carrying on about real life and a writer's version of it, having fun with imaginary crime scenes. She asked how he knew that if he didn't read books. In fact he was a slow reader and embarrassed, but he did end up reading *Crime and Punishment*. Three times. A dog-eared copy of it still sat on his bedside table. He saw it every day, a constant reminder of his missing wife.

He said to her after the first reading, "Raskolnikov didn't have to kill that old pawnbroker."

"No."

"He was in a state, not eating, overwrought."

"Why don't you read the book again?" Elena had suggested.

"Poor, trapped Raskolnikov tells Detective Porfiry to go ahead and find his murderer. Such arrogance."

Elena stopped folding the wash.

"Listen, Elena, this Porfiry is having a friendly chat with Raskolnikov about the murderer, all the while suspecting him. He asks him about the killer's conscience. Can you imagine me asking a suspect such a question? Raskolnikov basically tells the cop, 'What business is his conscience to you?'"

Elena picked up a sock, looking for its mate, not looking at Emil. "Interesting," she said.

"The detective, he's subtle, but Raskolnikov is so, so *complex.* Still, he gives himself away. You see? That's not what an innocent man would say. Do you see?"

"Read the book again."

Why was Franco hanging around? Why in hell was he up so early? He had to be up to something, and the something couldn't be good. This was the man who poisoned the ground that now held the pinkie. Was that likely to be coincidence? Emil felt the old stirrings of police-work ugliness reawakening.

Franco startled him again. "You have something in that tool bag, amigo?"

"*What?*"

"That white-and-green bag, the one she gave to you, huh, to her husband, a gift?"

"What about the bag?"

"Am I right? Su esposa, she gave you the tool bag and you did not like it at first."

"What are you getting at?"

"What would I be getting at, amigo?"

"How do you know about the bag, Franco?"

"I have ears, my friend, and besides, your wife would at times confide in me."

What in hell was Franco talking about? Elena confide in him? Emil had to pry things out of her. For years when they were first married she was often sad and silent. Emil would ask what was wrong, but she would only climb further inside herself, or she would say things he couldn't understand. "The wind," she might say, "the way it sways the trees, that can madden … can't you sometimes hear the way the wind torments the trees?" And she would sleep, escape into long hours of sleep.

"We are alike, you and I," Franco said. "Without our women. It is true, mine left me. The putana, la corazón negra putana, madre de vacas, la puerquita … You are lucky, cabrón, yours stayed with you until you were almost old together. That is a thing muy bonita, beautiful. Do you know what I am saying?"

"Yes, Franco, I know what you are saying. A thing muy bonita." Emil rubbed his neck. This was becoming impossible. There would be no escaping the reach of this day; Emil could already feel it closing in. He had to do something with the finger; he couldn't just leave it there to rot in the sun. On top of everything else, he was sweating rivulets from the heat. He raised his arm and wiped his face on his left shoulder.

His arm still raised midair, Emil looked up when the window on the top floor of his building pushed open with a hard whoosh. A woman's face appeared at the dark opening. Then her head of blonde hair poked through, followed by a pair of broad shoulders. A patch of floral nightgown was visible beneath the folds of two large breasts. Emil's tenant, Paulien Vandervell, leaned her head out, her nose extended to sniff the morning air, nostrils flared.

"Hijo. That woman is an animal, a horse," said Franco, not lowering his voice sufficiently for Emil, who pretended not to hear him. "Look at her, smelling the air like a pony. That putana has no man either, you know? If you ask me, she is a woman who likes the taste of little girls; that is no real woman at all. Look how huge she is!"

Emil's upstairs tenant wasn't *that* big. She was tall and large-boned with a round face that was too small for the nose and mouth it had to carry. Her features were hard to figure; they seemed to come apart, or were somehow mismatched, and when she applied her makeup too heavily, as she tended to, she resembled a blood clot.

She looked down toward Emil, standing by his tool bag at the pepper hole, and then at what Emil guessed she could see of Franco on his side of the fence. Emil couldn't tell if she'd heard Franco or not. She called out, "Good morning, Mr. Milosec. Phew! The heat is back."

"Sí," Franco yelled up to her, though she had not addressed him. "Like green salsa, muy picante, señora!"

Emil quickly called up, "Is that air conditioning working all right?" His tenant nodded, and maybe smiled at him, or maybe not; it was hard for Emil to see her clearly, looking up into the bright morning light.

Emil could go for days in his garden without seeing anyone; weeks would pass without a peep from his tenant or from Franco, and he'd spoken to Franco more in the last few days than he had in a year. Suddenly everyone was wide awake and staring at him on the morning a severed pinkie showed up in his garden. He couldn't believe it, but his tenant seemed to be staring straight into the pepper hole. She was leaning on her elbows, hands tucked in. He sneaked a look down, reaching as if to pull at a loose espadrille, but the pinkie couldn't possibly be visible from four flights up. Looking toward the top floor again, he thought he saw Paulien wink at him before withdrawing her head and disappearing into the darkness behind the window. A sheer white curtain swung closed behind her. His throat tightened. The window whooshed shut.

It occurred to Emil that Paulien might have heard the two gunshots the morning before, but he convinced himself that she would already have been on her way to work. In fact, she should be on her way to work now.

Franco let out a donkey snort of laughter. "Still, I would not mind finding out what lives underneath that nightgown, ha, amigo? We are not so old, you and me, for a bit of curiosity, no? I would accept if la rubia came down here from her tower to make us eggs. Huevos revueltos for me. After what went on last night, I can tell you, I am very hungry this morning."

Emil hardly heard what Franco was saying. "She must be calling in sick," he said quietly.

"I can't hear what you say?"

Emil was growing furious; why wouldn't the man let him be? "Nothing, Franco. I was just looking for a stick," he called back.

Time was wasting; he'd have to handle the finger, and soon. The possibility of working the case alone had already taken shape: Solve the mystery then present the whole story, open and shut, to the authorities.

He understood the penalty for failing to report a crime. Even if he successfully worked the case, there would be no way around that crucial omission. He looked over at his two neat rows of tomato plants, feeling caught—a fly on a sticky trap—but if he told the police, they would swarm, rip out his garden like locusts.

They'd be bulls in a china shop; nothing would be left untouched: his roses, the dogwood about to fully bloom, the lavender—all of it wrecked, and that included Elena because her ashes lay strewn among the flowers. The neighbors would see the bright yellow crime tape across his front door. There would be questions and stares, speculation. Worst of all, Emil would be in the spotlight; he would lose his treasured anonymity, become a topic in the neighborhood—a thought that filled him with dread. Yet the mystery had to be solved. The finger was young; the hand must have been lovely, the "death" of it cruel.

From the other side of the fence, Emil could hear Franco scratching his sandpaper stubble and yawning. It seemed to Emil that Franco had no idea what to do with himself, that his days lacked cohesion. He had retired from a civil service job with a pension and veteran's pay from serving in the marines. The few years since had melted into a meaningless muddle; Franco himself probably couldn't say where the days and years had gone.

Emil remembered when Franco's Tía Marta kept the garden next door. It was never lush like Elena's but it was pretty, arrayed with annuals in exotic colors, and made Marta proud. She was old now and nearly deaf, hanging on to life by a thread. Franco inherited the property from his mother, who had supposedly gained the building by questionable means. Elena probably knew the story but Emil had never asked her. He'd heard a gambling debt was involved. Franco's mother was said to have been a notorious cardsharp. The owner might have lost the deed in a game with her. That was one story. Other versions differed. One had it that the building had been bought for Maria Montoya by a mysterious lover. Another was that Franco's father owned it and had thrown the wayward Maria out but later regretted his action for the sake of their son and left the building to him. Who knew which was true?

Whichever the case, the place was now in pitiful disrepair. Leaks in the roof to be patched each spring, ancient electrical wiring, dangerously sloping staircases that all but hung off the wall. Franco fixed nothing. Besides old Tía Marta, there was a tenant who'd been in the building forever and was legally blind. He was called Oscar. He lived on disability insurance with his seeing-eye dog, Park. Franco called him "Oscar Park," and he called the dog "Oscar Park" too. Franco looked after Marta, buying her food and medicines, seeing to it that she stayed alive. He looked in on Oscar and the dog too. Recently he'd told Emil that he would soon fix things up, renovate. He'd secure a loan, he said; Emil would see, and some fancy tenants would move in, paying him top dollar. It was happening that way all over; why shouldn't it happen here? He was no fool. Emil would see what would become of Franco Montoya the landlord. Or maybe he would sell, go to Mexico or to a Caribbean island, drink piña coladas while floating in a cool blue swimming pool, a little paper umbrella open in the drink.

"Look at those two in la casa de Señora Noily. La blanca chica, amigo. You see? These people are coming, the artists." Didn't Emil know if he played his cards right he too could be a millionaire? When Emil laughed, Franco told him to stop working his peas once in a while and have a look around.

Emil tended to dismiss the idea that property values would rise in their sleepy, semi-industrial corner of Brooklyn. The neighborhood hadn't change much in a hundred years, other than demographics, the Latinos edging out the Polish, who'd edged out the Irish. The area was solidly working class with good factory jobs in light manufacturing. The blue collars weren't going anywhere, not the way Emil saw it.

Emil said, "Wait a minute, Franco; what did you just say?"

"Me? When? Now? I said I was hungry."

"No, the other part, about last night?"

"What about last night, amigo?"

"You said you were hungry after last night."

"I am always hungry after last night."

Emil tried to keep the exasperation out of his voice: "You said something *happened* last night, and you were hungry. What happened?"

"You are loco, amigo."

"No, amigo; you said something happened. What?" Emil's tone had become sharp.

"No, no. Too early in the morning for this game. Go back to your plants, amigo. Talk to your beans; beans are the natural friend of the police. To me you are making a big thirst." And with that Franco abruptly left his yard. Emil heard his retreating footsteps and then the back door banging shut. He stood, barely controlling his fury, like a horse ready to kick the inside of his stall. He now felt certain Franco knew something and was playing coy about whatever that information might be.

The garden walk meandered. Elena had designed a brick path to wind past the dogwood, the miniature star magnolia, the various flowering bushes, a multitude of blooms. A curve in the path made the garden seem deep and long, while moss greening the bricks made it seem old, as if the garden had grown forever just as it grew today. At the very back, almost hidden, they'd built a small raised pool. A few lily pads grew, and some goldfish swam in the shallow depth. The rear of the garden abutted an old brick wall that ran the length of the five houses on Emil's block and the warehouse wall that formed the miserable south wall of Franco's yard. Behind the brick wall was a narrow alley filled with weeds and debris that fenced-in the upper part of a parking lot that was no longer in use, taking up the block to the west. No one knew why the alley was there or who owned it. A locked gate at either end closed off the alley; Elena had argued for sealing the ends with brick against intruders entering the garden, though the wall had never been breached, not that anyone knew of. It was high, and the alley was very narrow. The factory across the avenue from the parking lot was closed, a behemoth manufacturing plant sitting idle that had once echoed with the hum of machinery and the sounds of working men and women. Twice a day Emil and Elena once would hear cars come or go from the parking lot, but that ended.

The plant closed down the year before Elena died. After a drawn-out labor dispute the owners sold the property to an investor who so far had done nothing with it. Everyone said the workers had overplayed their hand, killed their own jobs. It looked as if the new owner had no intention of restarting the factory that had once processed spices. Somewhere out of sight, local talk went, plans were being made; banks were talking to banks, and those locals would be the last ones to learn about what.

Emil walked to the pool and sat on the flagstone edge. The heat never fully penetrated this heavily shaded, peaceful spot. He closed his eyes, wondering vaguely what would become of the factory. Its silence felt like a hole in the fabric of the neighborhood, not hearing the workers calling out as their shifts ended, starting up their cars or walking home with lunch pails swinging at their sides, the scent of spices in the air, with cinnamon or white-sugar granules sometimes settling onto car windshields. How many jobs had been lost? Some said the plan all along had been to get rid of the workers, that the strike had been forced by management and that real estate developers were lurking. Franco wasn't the only one talking. Emil had heard the rumors.

He wiggled two fingers in the pond. A shimmering goldfish swam up, bumped against his flesh, and swam off. It was probably time to feed them. He idly pulled stray weeds from the base of the pond and tried again to piece together events close to home. He had not sat in the garden last night. He'd watched the news and before that a nature program about lions. He learned that a male lion will eat its own cubs if given the opportunity, to eliminate any potential rivalry. A pretty rotten method of population control, he concluded. He didn't know if Franco had sat outside drinking himself stupid or not. If he had, and *was* drunk, would he remember anything more than bits and pieces of any movement that might have taken place in the night?

Say Franco wasn't involved, though he was acting guilty as sin—which could just be the general guilt of the drunken personality—why was he snooping around? Did he hear or see something but couldn't remember what? Had someone entered the garden? Emil rubbed his temples. And had that someone seen Franco? He sometimes slept all night outside. And the finger? Again, why?

Emil's next thought was to preserve the evidence. He was avoiding the idea of his own refrigerator, but the flesh would soon decay in the relentlessly building heat. He looked up to what he could see of the ivy-covered back of his house. How beautiful the garden was from where he sat, secreted from the world. The air was filled with peaty earth-breath; multiple shades of green soothed the eye, while flowers in a bonanza of colors tempted an impossible optimism—all of it Elena's. He'd been possessive and even insistent as he'd worked alongside her to build the garden, but it was hers. The way her silk kimono swayed as she walked the brick path in the morning, holding her second cup of coffee, reaching out with a slender hand as she passed to pet a bud, caress a leaf or petal, the way she leaned to take in the odor of a rose or lavender stalk . . .

Did Eve eat most of the apple, leaving Adam with only a single bite? One lousy bite, his mouth filled with luscious apple and then instant transformation? Suddenly he saw Eve was female—voluptuous and vulnerable and desirable—and he pounced and took her? Emil knew the story was only a metaphor, but the cop in him kept taking it apart to unravel the motive, always without hope of success. However the original sin played out, his own garden was also now tainted. Beyond the manipulated imperfection of the failed peppers lay a terrible impurity. *Thou shalt not kill.*

Emil stood up; impossible to sit still with the appendage lying in the hole. He returned to the scene, lifted the tool bag and carried it to the shade under the lilac tree near the kitchen door. Above the door was a pergola he had built. Elena planted a Concord grape vine there that had grown up sturdy and wide, shading the space beneath. Why hadn't she planted an apple tree in the first place? And why hadn't that thought occurred to him before today? Because he'd wanted to dismiss the apple idea, make it go away. She could have started the whole garden with a single apple tree. Why didn't she?

He looked up to the fourth-floor window, wiping his brow with his forearm as if reacting against the heat. There was nothing visible from Paulien's windows. He had a sudden urge to whistle but stopped himself; he never whistled. Why would he whistle? At the pepper hole he removed his work gloves, dropping the left one as if by accident. He then swept down and in one swift gesture lightly, very lightly, grabbed the severed finger with the glove, careful to include the small opal ring. In four sprightly steps he was back at the tool bag; he gently deposited the glove with the finger and ring. He closed the bag tight and then reached up to make a fake adjustment to the grapevine. Fairly certain he had not been observed, Emil walked quickly into the kitchen.

He stood in the doorway and listened. There was no movement outside. The kitchen behind him was dark and cool. The sound of an oncoming plane grew louder overhead. Emil thought of all the people stuffed into that silver can sailing through the sky. Would any of them look down and see the garden way below and suspect something amiss in his green oasis? The plane passed and all was quiet once again. The finger was secured for now, and he could add evidence tampering to his other misbehavior.

THREE

The Lord said in his heart, "I will never again curse the ground because of man, for the imagination of man's heart is evil from his youth; neither will I ever again destroy every living creature as I have done."

Book of Genesis

Upstairs, Emil studied Franco's north-facing wall from the bedroom window. Was the surface newly scarred or damaged? He looked to the ground to see if there was any disturbance below. But how could he tell if anything was disturbed on that graffiti-scarred wall or rubble-strewn yard? Somebody could be hiding in Franco's junk piles right now for all he knew. He pictured a man or men rappelling down the warehouse wall behind the false mimosa someone had planted years ago, still bravely growing, half strangled. The razor wire along the roof did not look as if it had been cut, but that could be deceptive.

Okay, so one, possibly two men shimmying down the wall and from there entering his yard where a body part was deposited. Was that it? Or could someone have used the alley, scaled that wall directly into his garden? Less likely. Was the finger the only body part? Probably yes. And how did they get back out? Mrs. Noily's? With all her dogs and cats and that artist couple renting the top two floors? He didn't think so. The guy seemed odd. He'd once mentioned that he was an insomniac and worked out his constructions late at night; if Emil was bothered by any noise, he'd try to adjust. The woman, wife or girlfriend—Franco called her la chica linda—was all right, pretty and slim. What was her name? Lydia or Lynette? Always a hello, once said how much she liked the garden, what she could see of it from her windows, looking for an invitation, it seemed. Probably a flirt. With a night-owl artist and the dogs, the intruder would likely have left the way he came in.

Looking down now at his own yard, Emil saw Mrs. Noily's cat Sam saunter across the garden toward the kitchen door and—the tool bag! The cat quickly moved out of sight. Emil turned and dashed downstairs. Opening the kitchen door, he caught Sam sniffing at the bag.

Mrs. Noily had four cats skulking through her backyard, plus three dogs, each one large and dumb. Trouble threatened between the neighbors until Emil had a fence put up, high enough to discourage the cats from leaping over to his side. Only Sam, a bruiser of a calico, was unstoppable and regularly found his way into the garden. He'd park himself next to Elena's garden chair and purr furiously, taking loud and shameless delight in her reluctant touch if she agreed to pet him.

Emil quietly pushed the back screen door open. Sam looked up. Emil waved an arm. "Shoo!" he told the cat in a low voice.

Sam resumed his sniffing.

"Go on, Sam, get," Emil said more forcefully. The cat ignored him. With gusto this time, Emil hissed, "Scram!"

Sam sat perfectly still, glaring up at Emil, who stamped his foot. Sam swished his tail.

"Get the hell out of here. Damn cat."

Sam sneered.

"All right, have it your way." Emil walked to the spigot on the left side of the door, turned on the tap, picked up the hose, and sprayed the air near the cat. The water on his orange-and-white fur sent Sam flying into the lilac bush with a howl, up and over the fence, landing with a small thud on the other side. Emil put the hose down and turned the water off. He had been careful not to wet the tool bag.

Was the finger beginning to smell? He tiptoed over to the bag. The top was snapped shut, no flies circled, and he couldn't smell rotting flesh, the odor of death he knew too well. He froze when he heard Mrs. Noily's heavy back screen door screech open, then clang shut. Emil slipped back into the kitchen doorway. Normally things were quiet from her side, apart from the odd times her dogs would decide to bark in unison. She didn't garden much: two neglected rosebushes, some day lilies. Her yard had mostly shade from a rangy old maple. Her cats had the run of the place, and the dogs were let out early each morning to do their dumps in the yard, where the piles would then fossilize until Mrs. Noily's husband, Otto, saw fit to rake them together and pick them up. There was a grown daughter somewhere in another state, Michigan maybe, or Minnesota. Elena had figured the animals were her substitute.

Mrs. Noily called to Sam in her high-volume voice. She managed a restaurant, a cavernous seafood place out in Sheepshead Bay, and knew how to project. She was a tall woman with blonde streaks in her dark hair and was, as Elena had described her, a person with no sense of the internal.

"Saaammeee?" Emil heard her call to the cat. "Come here! What happened to our Sammy?" Emil heard a note of alarm in Mrs. Noily's voice. Her usual tone was of operatic self-assertion without a hint of reticence. "We don't want you ending up like poor Sissy." Emil heard Sam meow once as Mrs. Noily picked up all seven pounds of him. "Let's come inside now, Sammy," she baby-talked the cat. "Something evil is out there."

The door slammed shut.

Fifty seconds later the telephone rang behind Emil. He picked up on the fourth ring, his hello tentative.

"Detective Milosec?" Emil hesitated; he hadn't been called "detective" in a long while. Before he could decide how to respond, the voice on the line spoke again: "It's CeeCee Noily, from next door."

"I recognized your voice, Mrs. Noily." He couldn't bring himself to call her CeeCee.

"Yes, well, Detective, there's something wrong."

"Oh?" He was thinking, what kind of name was CeeCee anyway?

"I thought you should know someone broke my Sissy's neck."

"Sissy?"

"My ginger, killed her."

"Your cat?"

"I know your wife didn't like cats, may she rest, and I hold nothing against, but I thought you should know about violence like that."

He thought of correcting her. Elena liked cats; she just disliked Mrs. Noily's cats shitting all over her garden. "Are you sure the animal didn't just fall or was maybe hit by a car?"

"It was out back."

"Ah, I see. I'm sorry."

"Yes, and just now Sammy came running inside with a terrible fright."

"Could it be kids, teenagers, Mrs. Noily? They can be pretty cruel."

"How would they get in my backyard?"

"People find ways. But have you phoned the police?"

"I called you."

"I'm no longer—" Emil checked himself, changed course. "You did the right thing. I'll keep an eye out for anything … untoward. All right?"

"Untoward? Like gunshots?"

"What's that?"

"Yes, the other morning, Otto heard it too, coming from the Montoya place. There are types in that building, if you know what I mean."

"Types? In the Montoya house? A blind man and a deaf old aunt live there."

"And there's Montoya himself. …"

"He seems harmless enough, Mrs. Noily." He felt obliged to defend Franco, under the circumstances.

"You didn't hear anything?"

"What sounds like gunfire usually turns out to be a car backfiring. I wouldn't concern myself. …"

"But you'll keep an eye out for something—untoward?"

"I will."

"All right. Good-bye, then. But you'll let me know if you find out anything, Detective?" Her voice again communicated worry.

"Of course."

Emil had slipped so readily into the role of cop it was almost as if someone else had done the talking. He considered: There were now two events, an extracted pinkie and a murdered cat. Mrs. Noily was right about one thing: There was violence close to home. Emil sensed he was being drawn into someone's game, a crime in which it began to seem as if he might be one of the pawns. Of all the gardens in all of Brooklyn, he thought, why'd the severed finger wind up in mine?

A nervous flutter twitched through his bowels: He now knew at least two people had heard the gunshots, and of course there was Franco. Whatever the story line, the plot was thickening. What now? Follow the finger; see where it pointed. He smiled weakly at his lame joke.

He could call missing persons. He still had a few connections downtown. He could say he was working a private case. But to phone missing persons and ask, "Anyone report losing a finger?" Wouldn't that be funny?

He was pacing slowly between the refrigerator and the table, back and back again. He could start small, poke around the neighborhood, see if any other curious goings-on turned up. Visit the corner grocer, chat up the owner, Rudy: Anybody missing a ring, oh, and the finger that went with it? No. Rudy was a nasty presence and a meddling cheat. Buy some bologna from Rudy's Corner Market and the price of Rudy or his son Albert's thumb went into the total.

Emil was careful around Rudy, never more than a nod good-morning, nice weather. If no customers came in, Rudy would stand in the doorway of his shop, thick arms folded across a brown-stained butcher's apron, a rotund little czar in his grocery domain, a frayed toothpick inevitably wedged between his front teeth. His son Albert grunted and swore as he lifted heavy cartons into and out of the sidewalk cellar hatch. Rudy's prices were high and there was little local competition. Sometimes the meat in the case looked old, and the wilted vegetables might have been grown in a Dumpster. Emil had once worked for Rudy's father, Big Albert, delivering groceries on a rusty old bicycle with a wire-mesh basket attached to the handlebars. Big Albert had not been a cheat when Emil worked for him. Emil spoke only a few words of English at the time, and Big Albert was kind, teaching him the necessary words to do the delivery job.

If Rudy learned that Emil was on to something like a severed finger there would be no end of him sticking his nose into it. He'd make assumptions, worm his way into Emil's life. He already behaved with a trace of disdain because Emil had been an immigrant boy who'd worked for his pop. That his own pop was an immigrant's son didn't seem to factor in; Rudy was a true-blue, born-in-Brooklyn American. Emil imagined Rudy now: toothpick held aloft for emphasis, a fleck of whatever he'd eaten last balanced on top, fresh-picked from between his molars: *You found a girl's finger, you say? In the garden? That's something else, Milosec. You hear that, Albert? Milosec here found a corpse out back of his house.* Albert could pipe in, *No kidding, a body, and raped? You call the police—but, hey, you was a cop yahself, hah? That's right, ain't it, a cop yahself?* Revolting.

Emil picked up the wall-phone receiver and dialed his old precinct. A tired voice answered, "Tenth Precinct, Sergeant Maynham." Emil was quiet. "You have the precinct here; who's calling?" Emil hung up. He hadn't meant to dial the main desk. He put on his reading glasses, took another look in his black address book, and dialed again.

"Ten-oh, Detective Bracco."

"Hello, Bernie Bracco? Emil Milosec."

"Who?"

"Detective Milosec. Retired."

After a brief silence: "Name doesn't ring a bell."

Emil's mouth turned down. "Been off the force a couple'a years; you were just coming up from uniform?" Emil had helped Bernie when he made his shield to detective. Now Bracco didn't remember? He remembered.

There was another silence. Emil waited out the charade. "Milosec? Milosec. Yeah, yeah, 'the Thinker,' right? What can I do for you, Milosec?"

"Probably nothing, Bracco. Hear of any offbeat missing person reports lately, you know, something off—about the report, I mean?"

"We don't file missings up here, Milosec; you want the missing persons number?"

"No, no. It's not exactly missing yet. Just something I overheard at the local market. You know, the cop in me pricked up my ears, overhearing some guys talk."

"What exactly did you overhear?"

Detective Bracco's tone was disagreeable. Emil had brought this guy in, taught him what he could. At one time Bracco had been grateful, when he still needed help and looked up to Emil, who had avoided all the new-guy snubs and jokes when a blue came up, trading his uniform for plainclothes. Emil never minded a new face, tired of the stale ribbing and routine conflicts. Bracco had not behaved straight off like the others, was even somewhat polite, but now he sounded just like any other hard-nosed cop.

"Like I said, I only heard a snatch of conversation. Maybe a jewelry heist? Possible kidnap?"

"Well, ah, which is it: jewelry or kidnap? 'Cause if you got a kidnap, it's federal, FBI. We'd have to bring them in. You want the FBI; we could arrange a conference call?"

"No, I do not want the FBI. I can get the bureau myself if I want. I am asking, no reports came in on any odd robbery deals this morning or late last night, a general call?"

"Where's your address, Milosec? I'll send a car over."

Emil's stomach took a nervous flip-flop. He forced out a laugh. "No, no car, Bracco. That's not necessary. It was probably just some guys fooling around, I overheard, remembered this morning, thought I'd give a holler over there—just in case." He forced out another weak laugh. "But since all's well, how about we just forget it?"

Bracco was very quiet on his end of the line. He was cop enough to sniff out something irregular. Emil was cop enough to keep a hard silence. "Well, sure, you get a icky feeling in your gut you gotta act on it, right?" Bracco finally said. Emil laughed, sort of. "The missus okay and everything?"

Detective Bracco hadn't heard of Elena's death? "The missus is fine, Bracco; thank you for asking."

"Yeah, sure. So long, Milosec. Call us if anything solid turns up."

Emil hung up. "That was smart," he said aloud, standing by the phone. "Now add covering up and lying to tampering." The really ridiculous part was that the ten-oh wasn't even his neighborhood precinct. Wait until Bracco figured that out.

The phone call left a bad taste; Emil wanted to rinse out his brain. And the call had gotten him exactly nowhere. He hadn't been a dirty cop, had never been tempted, but he was beginning to feel like one now, or worse, like a criminal. Emil Milosec—quite possibly the most law-abiding citizen in Brooklyn—a criminal? He was a man who hated a misstep in himself more than he hated death. But he'd fired the gun, freely and without reason: a good start into lawlessness.

What was next on this boiling-hot morning? Emil stood in front of the kitchen window and said, "I should invite Franco over for a six-pack, spill the beans, buddy up with the amigo next door. Bring down Paulien, throw a party. What the hell? I'm knee-deep in shit soup; might as well break out the spoons and make it official."

FOUR

A garden shut up is my sister, my bride; a spring shut up, a fountain sealed.

Song of Songs

Emil tried to imagine what Elena would do with the thing out back. She might say, "It can't be left to decompose in the tool bag." And he might reply, "We could freeze it while I investigate."

"How?"

"How what, investigate?"

"No, how freeze it? In among the dinner items?"

"This is no time to be squeamish."

"Next to the frozen chicken?"

"No, you're right, that would be wrong—unsavory."

"What about dry ice? That old picnic chest in the cellar would hold it."

"Brilliant, Elena!" he said out loud. She always came up with just the right solution.

There was a place that sold dry ice just over the Newtown Creek into Queens. Emil had noticed it a while back when a floater turned up dead center in the middle of the creek, with neither Brooklyn nor Queens eager to claim jurisdiction. No one much cared to pull a waterlogged corpse with a bullet in its lung out of the toxic slime that passed for water in the creek. Emil and Mike were nearby and picked up the call. They were ferried out, meeting up with another small craft from the Queens side. A fair amount of time was wasted in crime-scene chatter on the boats until Mike took advantage of the situation by pushing the corpse's right arm. Using a ballpoint pen when no one was looking, he placed the stiff squarely in Queens by half an arm's length. "Hey," he said a minute later, dropping the pen into the creek, "I think our guy just chose sides." He was treated to a round of dirty looks from the Queens cops and a suspicious one from Emil.

Back in the car, Mike asked Emil, "What's the difference where the guy's processed? It got us out of it."

"No difference, I guess."

"Something the matter with you today?"

Emil had just finished his second reading of *Crime and Punishment*. He told Mike about Raskolnikov murdering the crone. He told how Raskolnikov has ideas: "That he can do whatever he has to, including murder, because he's different from everyone else."

"That's the guy in the book, right?" Mike asked, turning to look at Emil.

"Yes, in the book. Afterward, after killing her, he goes to sleep, has a fever, is delirious, but he's lucid too—"

"Yeah. Sounds like a novel," Mike interrupted, yawning. "High-strung. You ever read anything but the Bible and this Russian? I mean a juicy pulp now and again?"

"No."

"This isn't about me 'influencing' the crime scene just now, is it?"

"What? No, no. See, Raskolnikov has crossed the line and now he *really* can't be like other people *because* he crossed it. Even with his own mother he's exiled. He catches on too late, and he's going to pay, but in his head, see?"

"Pay in his head, huh? Right, but, you know, it's a *book* … not gonna stop crime. If that's your point, Milosec."

"Let's say a man thinks something especially vicious—"

"Like putting his dick inside his baby daughter?"

"Jesus. That's pretty foul, Mike. …"

"I tell you, a man does this, you cut his rocks off, and plus, he has given up the right to be out on the street again, ever. No Thanksgiving dinners for that particular pervert."

"Right. But say he only thought or dreamt this awful act."

"Either way, he's a sick prick."

"Just for thinking it? Or in a dream?"

"Are you trying to tell me something, get something off your chest?"

"No! I'm saying a thought is a thought. People imagine things. You can't stop that."

"So?"

"I don't know. Why does a guy imagine the hideous?"

"Milosec, if I had the answer to that I'd be called God, and taking home a way bigger paycheck. Right?"

Emil went very quiet for almost five full minutes.

"Milosec?"

"What do you think was the first thought, Mike? Good or bad?"

"I'm hungry."

"That?"

"No, I *am* hungry. So let's think about lunch, huh?"

Emil would take Elena's advice. He would drive out to the dry-ice place near Newtown Creek and preserve the finger. Now he was getting somewhere. Things were beginning to take shape, not very definite but better than the nothing he'd been doing since finding the finger.

But he didn't move from the kitchen table.

Emil had long relied on Elena to ferret out an answer, even if he didn't always let her know he was mining her. It was just the way her mind worked, her individual outlook, her elliptical way of processing facts. They'd had an unspoken bond between them: broken childhoods in common, dismantled by war. It was something they didn't discuss; their childhoods were taboo, a thicket of memories neither wished to enter but that infected their take on the world.

Elena had accepted her looks as a gift. She wasn't vain about being a beauty, though she had grounds to be. He'd seen the way other men looked at her, fixed their gaze. The features were not quite regular; her eyes a touch too small and deep-set, the mouth almost too full, tiny imperfections that worked to make the whole more intriguing. Her shape was youthful. She must have had a nervous metabolism, for nothing she ate, in particular the French breads and pastries she regularly devoured, left any evidence on her waistline. Her shape hardly changed from the day they met to the day she died. Even when the sickness came to own her she remained greedy to be herself. She was too thin at the end, a teenager's thin, yet she never dwelled on pain or wallowed in her bad luck. She mocked her illness and insisted she not be pitied. She wore lipstick on her last day.

He missed her most at meals, eating too fast without her company: good, bad, irritable, ironic—it didn't matter; Elena could make him laugh or forget. Even her silences, cloisters of nearly audible thoughts, were okay with him. Driving in the country, Emil had sometimes noticed solitary cows looking up at passing cars. In a herd, not so much, but a single cow would, wanting company, it seemed to him, as she chewed her cud. He felt he now understood those solitary beasts of the field. At breakfast he was all right, not a lonely cow out to pasture; he had his newspaper, the unknown of a new day. He was able to greet each morning without resentment. Dinners were harder.

She had an original sense of things. Insignificant things like the letters of the alphabet; *E*, for example, was favored. She felt it ought to have been placed before the letter *D* because *E* was receptive, feminine, while *D* protruded and puffed; an *E* could hold a *D* in check, as if letters had personalities. Some clusters, *TUVW*, say, were too militant, like they were wearing epaulets. She saw the alphabet in color with attributes beyond signifying words. Since she was fluent in four languages, Emil didn't think much about the extra significance she applied to letters. He told himself it was part of how she learned.

"What about *R*s?" he once asked.

"Soccer."

"Soccer?"

"Yes, always kicking."

"Not the lowercase."

"Lowercases are children."

He wasn't immune to little behavioral tics either. He preferred, for example, the white soup bowl with the blue edging—the last of an old set—almost superstitiously. And when Elena was up first for breakfast she always took the top half of the banana they shared each day. He felt she should rotate top and bottom, let her have the nasty nub of the umbilical bottom once in a while. Little things that could turn into big things but with them never did.

Elena had a particular way of reading the newspaper too. She looked for revealing stories, was after connectedness, human drama in meaningless muddles. Emil liked to listen when she found an odd bit to read out loud. There had been the morning she'd read him the article on the oldest living woman, Jeanne Louise Calment. He remembered it—there had nearly been a row over that story—how the one-hundred-fifteen-year-old had claimed she was not a worrier.

Elena's voice was low, her words spoken with a rounded accent that was not easy to identify, Trieste, her homeland, being multinational with many accents mingling. That morning was cool and sunny in mid-October. They were nearly finished with their first cups of coffee when she came across the oldest-living-woman story.

"What about this!" she began, turning to face Emil. "The oldest woman in the world says, 'If I cannot do anything about something I do not worry it.' Good for her! And she said, 'God must have forgotten her.'" She looked up briefly, smiled, read on: "She is French and lives in Arles. And—oh, Emil, Vincent van Gogh bought paints from her uncle's shop. My God, she is old!"

"Well, the south of France," he commented idly from behind his section of the paper, not yet giving her his full attention. "She would want to go on living."

Elena scanned the article. "She outlived her family by nearly forty years. And, let me see … she sold her apartment for an annuity years ago. The buyer assumed she would soon die and he would have had the place at a bargain. Ha! But he died first, in *his* seventies; the family still pays."

"Any foul play suspected?" The question was routine. Elena glanced away from the page to look at him. "A little shop humor," he added.

She continued after a pause, "What sort of price could she have gotten for an apartment then—in the sixties? Arles is not Avignon."

He put his paper down. "Didn't you just say she lived her whole life in Arles?"

"Did I say her whole life?"

"And that the fellow would have gotten her apartment at a steal?"

"Only if she died."

"How do you suppose she had an expensive apartment to sell if she and her family lived for generations as shopkeepers? What's Avignon to do with it?"

"There is nothing here about generations of shopkeepers. Or Avignon."

Emil eyed her; she was playing with him. "What about all those paints the uncle sold Van Gogh, *in Arles*? Do you suppose they were bought in a latrine? They were shopkeepers."

"Then how did she happen to have an expensive apartment to sell?"

"Did the paper say it was expensive? That's the question. Did it say twelve rooms with two fully functioning fireplaces? Of course not, because the French have passed on their apartments for centuries. There's none of this, this being driven out as people age because they can't afford to stay. It's a good system, the French."

"What on earth are you talking about?"

"About the south of France as a place where one might wish to live forever, *if* they had the rights to an apartment, to a house. And garlic in their garden for soups!"

"Garlic! That's not the point. Not worrying is the point. The oldest woman in the world is joyous; that is how she lives."

"No yogurt?" he asked. Elena ran her tongue across her teeth—not a good sign. "I must have missed the part where it said she was joyous."

"What are you suggesting?" she demanded. Emil pulled his paper up to his face without reply. Elena added, "Nor am I a worrier. . . ." Hearing this, Emil folded his newspaper. "You are staring at me with detective eyes," she said. "I fail to see why."

"And do you think you will see one hundred fifteen years?"

"Are you saying my time is nearly up? That someone else is due to take my place?" Her words hung in the air of their quiet kitchen. Emil frowned, his black eyebrows closing the crease above the bridge of his nose. "Well?"

"Elena, I . . ." He felt his blood begin to stir, somewhere between fear, fury, and lust.

Elena tossed her head back and laughed. She lifted her arms and stood, stretching like a cat, a suggestion of seduction in her posture. "Some of *my* coffee, Emil?"

"All right," he answered, relieved the moment had passed without offense. "I don't mind if I do."

He watched her. Admiring her behind as she stood at the counter, filling a mug, studying her movements, her slim form in a pale green silk kimono—the way the cloth followed the line of her hips. She turned and caught his eye.

That morning, the disease that killed Elena was nothing more than a seditious, microscopic sprout hidden in the inner soil of her body. And why should a renegade cell announce its presence any more than a seedling in the earth does, that has found a congenial spot, cracked its outer casing, and taken root? A pepper seed or a deviant cell, both grow knowing nothing more beyond an inborn function in a blind universe. It was a lottery, Elena told Emil when she first found out, a crapshoot that she had apparently lost. He understood: All is chance, and tough fucking luck.

She was especially lovely on that recollected morning as she passed

Emil the mug of coffee. He took in her scent as she leaned her hip lightly against his arm, the silk clinging, her slender wrist curved as she placed the cup in front of him.

He did that now, especially at meals, replayed conversations with his wife, like the one about the oldest living woman (living on at one hundred twenty, joyously or not—years longer than Elena). That pale green silk kimono still hung in the closet upstairs, untouched since her death. Time briefly paused as she came to him in the kitchen, almost real, her presence as alive as if she sat opposite him, just past the mustard-colored vase full of pom-pom dahlias. They'd bought the vase, which he now reached out to touch, centering it just so on the table, in Avignon not many years before.

Emil went upstairs to change into outside clothes for the trip to Queens. On his way out of the bedroom he turned back to fish his old badge out of the bottom drawer of his bureau. He was supposed to have turned in his shield upon retirement, and in fact he had. This badge was a fluke, an unintended spare. On one of their vacation trips he'd decided at the last minute not to take the badge along in order to be free of his cop identity for a couple of weeks, behavior that had been unlike him. Then the car acted up and they got a late start. Emil forgot where he'd hastily hidden the badge in case of robbers and never took the time to look for it. (Elena suggested he forgot on purpose.) When they returned home he reported the item missing. Two years later Elena found it underneath a stack of books and magazines on a bottom shelf in their bedroom. He decided there was no point in reporting it found. She was probably correct; he'd lost the shield on purpose. He turned it over in his hand now and tucked it into a flap in his wallet, thinking, Just in case. He didn't ask himself just in case what?

He was about to step out the parlor door when he heard the heavy clump, clump of his tenant's big feet on the stairs leading from her apartment down to the vestibule. He looked at his watch. She was very late if she was going to work. He waited until he heard the outer door open then went over to the window and peeked out from behind the curtain. He heard Paulien fiddle with the lock, then saw her moving down the front steps. His brain caught like a clutch between gears, seemed to screech and lock when he saw that Paulien's left hand was bandaged and tinged with a bloom of blood. "What's this?" he whispered to the empty room.

Paulien struggled with an overnight case in her right hand, her purse strap slipping off her shoulder. She moved slowly, the armpits of her sleeveless dress already wet in the heat. Emil briefly wondered where she was going with the valise, if not to work. Or if maybe later she would be meeting a man as big as she was, to spend the night. He involuntarily pictured her on her back, laughing, her large teeth exposed. But her hand? What did Paulien do to her hand?

She stopped when she reached the bottom step. Emil hurriedly locked his apartment door and opened the outer door to the street. Paulien looked up from the sidewalk and smiled. From the landing he could see into her dress. Her ballooning breasts were squeezed together into the vee of her neckline. She wore a pale yellow dress with a blue flower pattern. The colors of Provence, he noted.

Emil locked the door and turned again to face her. "Everything all right?" he asked, coming down the steps.

"Oh, yes, fine," she answered.

"What happened to your hand?"

"Nothing."

"Nothing? There's blood. Was it just now, upstairs?"

"No, I … really it is … someone will see to it at my work."

Emil knew Paulien worked in a hospital in some sort of laboratory. "Ah, yes, you're a nurse, isn't it?"

"I am a pathologist," she said. Her accent was thick. "A medical doctor."

"Right." He watched as she lifted her wrapped hand to push a few stray blonde hairs out of her eyes. The sun was pounding on both their heads. Paulien moved under the shade of the tree, a honey locust the city had planted at Elena's request because that particular type of tree can withstand harsh urban conditions. It was the only tree on the otherwise bare cement block. He stood above her on the first step. "Let me see that hand, please, Miss Vandervell." His tone had changed; he was not asking.

"What are you saying to me?"

"I'd like you to unwrap that bandage."

"Mr. Milosec, I do not see …"

"Now, please," he said, leaning forward.

"Look, I have just got the damn thing to stop its bleeding. I would not want to open it up again."

He came down the step, stood close to Paulien under the honey locust. "Are you concealing something, Miss Vandervell?"

She shook her head. "You are sounding ridiculous, Mr. Milosec. I am sorry to say that, but it is so."

Emil repeated himself: "Now, please. The hand."

Paulien placed her overnight case on the sidewalk and breathed hard as she began to unwrap the bandage. Emil felt his heart bounce in his chest, surprised that she'd agreed to do this, wondering why she would, though he'd used his most authoritative cop voice.

He watched Paulien closely. The pinkie in his garden was a lefty.

The bandage had been wound tightly several times around and took time to remove. Paulien worked the wrapping slowly, almost too slowly. Emil's head jerked back when her pinkie popped out. The last digit had been forced under her ring finger by the tight binding. The cut, which looked deep, was on the fleshy part of Paulien's hand between the base of her pinkie and her wrist.

She held up her hand for him to examine. "Satisfied?" she asked, exhibiting her hand the way a child would, almost bragging. The look on her face was one of apprehension mingled, he thought, with a suggestion of scorn; and did she seem excited by her cut? Emil said, noting her expression while feeling something like shame crawl under the skin of his face, which was hot, "That looks deep. Will you … they'll have stitches at work?" Paulien did not reply. Emil knew she was waiting for an apology. "I'm sorry," he said. "I thought—will you come inside and let me rebandage that for you?"

But she was already doing that. Emil stood by helplessly as she patiently rewound the hand. "Thank you, Mr. Milosec, for your concern, but I am late enough as it is."

"I hope you'll understand I was … glass in your apartment, some danger …"

"Obviously you are worrying; this was sweet of you."

That sounded all wrong to him, not the correct response at all. She should be furious; who did he think he was? He had just ordered her to remove the covering over a deep cut, and she was telling him he was sweet? There was something else in her voice that he noticed, something overly indulgent, almost cheerful, as if she were pleased with him.

"Good-bye, Mr. Milosec," Paulien said, moving down the sidewalk with her overnight case, holding her bandaged hand up so the blood wouldn't flow again.

Emil stood watching as she walked away. When she turned the corner he walked back up the steps to his house and unlocked the door. What in hell was the matter with him that he would approach his tenant that way? He felt utterly exposed and ashamed. He was also aware that something was off with what had just gone on, that something did not fully add up.

He entered the outer door, relocked it firmly, and then unlocked the parlor door, snapping that lock closed behind him with a hard click. There was no chance of going to Queens now; no, something was very wrong and he was making it very much worse. That was bad with Paulien. And the call to Bracco ... He felt dread, a prickly cold radiating through him, cold then hot at the same time. He'd been reacting blindly, swiping at thin air; it was time to think, to nail this beast hounding his garden. Sure, but where was he supposed to start?

PART THREE

THE OLD COUNTRY

ONE

She lulled Samson to sleep on her lap, and then summoned a man to shave the seven locks of his hair. She was now making him helpless.

JUDGES

Emil took his jacket off and retreated with it to the dining room. Here was the safety of silence and semidarkness, a good place to think—as long as he steered clear of the letters. Once he'd slept in this room, but now he only ever entered to rewind the old mantel clock. He stood by the window, one slat of the blinds peeled open so he could peer out beyond the gate, past the narrow growing area where Elena had planted *Ilex* that yielded perfect red holly berries in winter.

The only sounds were occasional footsteps, a car passing, him breathing, and the old clock on the mahogany mantelpiece, ticking like a second heartbeat. He'd bought the clock in the old country as a gift for his mother. Elena had faithfully rewound it each week, thinking it mattered to Emil. First his mother, then Elena; now it was Emil's turn, but he often forgot because he no longer used the dining room. It kept lousy time anyway; slow from the beginning, as if racing backward were the point.

Elena had accidentally broken the chime that marked the quarter, half, and hour; twisted the key too hard one day, snapped the spring so ferociously she'd felt it thrust against the wood. "I broke the chime," she told Emil that evening when he came home from work. "I killed the heart of that ugly old clock."

Emil tried to console her: "It's nothing, Elena, a useless clock. Consider it a happy accident, a break with the past."

She looked at him, alarmed. "Why do you say 'break with the past'?" He shook his head. "That clock is not innocent," she added.

"It's a *clock*!"

Again she looked at him with panic in her eyes. "But you know where it came from."

"It's not important," he said, watching her, "and not cheap to fix those old clocks either." He smiled to reassure her, but he meant one thing, she another. He moved toward her, but she turned away. "It doesn't mean anything, that old clock shop … ," he said. But she left the room, went upstairs to her day room and shut the door.

Though today was not the day to rewind, Friday was, he walked to the mantelpiece, glanced at his face in the mirror above it, took the key out of the small scalloped seashell it was kept in and placed it into the slot just beneath the numeral four. He carefully turned the key, felt the mechanism slip as it tugged on the key. Where were all the lost minutes? he wondered as he wound. Was there a collection, a dimension in outer space for all the lost hours and minutes from earth? He sometimes toyed with the idea of an invisible cosmic box containing all the world's missing time.

He thought similarly about the past: Where do experiences go? Do they just evaporate? Does only memory make the past real? Would scientists one day wake up and say there was no past, no future, no time; all was illusion? Or did the Buddhists already say that? Emil had a few vivid memories of his early childhood: glittering white snow, deep forest greens, and cloud pillows resting on azure skies. But he came up against a blank whenever he had to solve the problem of leaving Slovenia and coming to America. He couldn't remember the boat journey over but had strong impressions of his family walking alpine ranges, days and days marching on paths sometime only his papa could see. He was supposed to be afraid during that escape but he wasn't. There had been some trouble within the family involving his father's half-brother, Ivak. Emil knew that much, but there were foggy gaps, and it seemed to him that he'd arrived in America abstractly, separated out of time with only shapeless images of the long journey. All he knew for sure was what his sister, Lisle, told him, and that wasn't much.

He pulled out a chair and sat down at the table. It was Tuesday, a day like any other. A terrible event occurs, a plane crash, say, everyone killed, but it's still this particular day of the week all over the world; in Istanbul or Helsinki normal events and daily routines continue as usual. Children go to school, stores open, traffic snarls; nothing stops but goes on and on and on. The entire plane's passengers dead, and so what? With Elena's death he called out into the night, using his mother's phrase: "Dear God, dear God, what do I do?" He had only contempt for such helpless cries, but the pain was so acute that night that he cried out involuntarily. And there was, of course, no reply. Or comfort.

Though the event of a severed finger in his garden and his particular response to it meant very little in the overall scheme of things—made no ripple in the larger world—it began to matter very much to Emil why such a problem had visited him. And yet how long would it matter, and how intensely would he care? How long had he been with Elena and how long would she be missed the way he missed her today; missed like the severed finger removed from an unknown, hapless girl? It seemed to Emil that all gain in life was measured by loss.

Seated at the table, his face in his hands, he tried again to find the story of the dead finger but all that came were crowded thoughts, one bunching against the other. It was *her* garden. Elena hired those kids to help dig and drag out all the debris, fifty cents an hour she paid—good pay for a kid in those days. She could have put an apple tree smack in the middle in the very beginning. Didn't they have money for a tree? They had money. *She* had money. One tree. Why not? And why peppers? A message from the grave, was that what the peppers were? Not like peppers? But why grow them? Franco said … what does he know? "Oh, fuck! I have nothing to go on," he announced to the empty dining room.

His mind looping senselessly like a broken film reel, Emil's head fell forward and he dozed off and was instantly involved in a dream: Paulien stood before him, tall, large, wearing the yellow and blue dress, her left hand at her side, palm out. Emil stood close; in his right hand was a long hunting knife, and he began to slice the bodice of her dress. She threw her head back and laughed with those enormous teeth; he could see their yellowed backs. She lifted her palm and he saw the stigmata, the bloodied nail hole of the crucifixion. She shoved the bloody palm into his face—

He snapped awake, shutting off the dream. His mouth turned down in disgust. Dreams: a whole universe of them dispersed too—like the lost minutes. An atmosphere thick with time and evaporated hopes, jam-packed with billions of faded thoughts. What did any of it mean?

For a long minute he stared ahead at nothing. Stacks of papers, having to do with Elena, filled the table's surface, ghosts of her flesh and blood. There were passports, birth and marriage and death certificates, piles of medical reports. And there sat the dreaded packet of letters. Emil reached out and picked up the packet, bound together with a faded blue ribbon. He blew off a layer of dust. They were from Elena, hand-delivered. She'd written to him every day from her hospital bed and continued writing at home until her last morning. Many were signed *Everything*, but Emil wouldn't know that because after the first two he had not read a single one. He threw the letters down, raising another little cloud of dust. He coughed. *Ashes to ashes* ... There were recipes and garden notes on scraps of paper in her curved, watery script, not many of them in English. A few photos of her family were among the papers and one shot of the two of them together. He picked up a picture of Elena as a little girl and saw a serious child's face staring back at him.

She had described herself as rootless; Italian on her father's side, Austrian on her mother's. At her birth the city was under Austrian rule. Tiny Trieste, perched importantly at the top of the Adriatic, was not much more than a harbor running up a hill. Its mixed-up populace, with so many languages, stirred together into a cosmopolitan ragout. The city returned to Italy in 1954, two years before Emil discovered Elena.

Her first words, she'd said, were Italian, her first love the sea. She described her birthplace to him, comparing it to a beautiful woman: "The mountains are her hair, her blouse the soft green of hilly breasts with blue water for skirt, the coastline her crotch, and on top of all this sits her hat of sky."

Charmed to his teeth, Emil asked her if she'd made that up herself and Elena pursed her lips as if a lemon had been shoved between them. He hadn't meant to insult her; it was a lesson in European sophistication. For the first time in his life Emil felt like a rube, which he was, transplanted from a Slovenian village to a Brooklyn ghetto. He caught on fast and quickly learned to hide his ignorance. "Is it like the color of your eyes?"

"Sorry?"

"Those green, hilly breasts?" She turned her face away, but he'd caught her smile. "What else?"

"I do not understand."

"What else is there?"

"At Trieste?" Emil nodded, watching her mouth. She thought a minute, in who knew what language, searching for something to say. Finally: "Trees!" Emil listened to her voice. "At the summer house apricot and peach, pear, and many, many apple. Down the hillside were so many spring blossoms; apples all the winters!" She smiled fully, baring her teeth, looking like a five-year-old, gentle and guileless. Aroused to *his* teeth, Emil wished only to crush her, to take that face and preserve that smile like a stolen flower, that child's smile on her woman's body, crush it between the yellowing pages of some ancient book. She had a single gray tooth in a set that was otherwise flawless and blue-white; he'd crush that gray tooth too, pulverize it to be preserved in a lavender-scented vial, like a saint's relic. It was all he'd been able to do that day to keep from grabbing and forcing himself on her.

Her father's family was originally Venetian, she explained. Glassblowers until the long ago move to Trieste, where they became merchants in fine glass all over the continent. Until the fighting, Elena's world had been gracious and dreamy, indulged. Of having rounded out her youth within a world war, her only comment was, "People disappeared, and then there was no more sugar."

Besides Italian, her German was perfect, and she spoke French and finally English. Of necessity, she knew a smattering of the neighboring, nearly impossible Slovenian dialect. She said, "Essential to have language. In a place like that you cannot go two streets with the same words." Toward Trieste she held a gloomy loyalty but the idea of bowing to a single nation was an absurdity to her. "I see no difference," she said later, in America, "between a gang and an army: one fighting for a street corner, the other for a country; all of it coming to nothing but destruction."

Told of his family's escape from Slovenia, Elena said, "This sounds like a movie to me." One eyebrow lifted, forming a tent of skepticism over her right eye.

"I don't remember too many details, but it was no movie," he answered. Even after he returned to the old country to see for himself, the events of his childhood seemed to him like something that had happened to someone else, more fairy tale than real.

His boyhood village was set deep in an isolated valley of the Julian Alps and *could* have filled the pages of a storybook. Not far from the Italian border, Senice looked sleepy pretty with its chalk-white houses and gray slate roofs gleaming silver in the sunlight, smoke curling lazily above chimneys into a clear blue sky. Wrapped in thick forest, it lay insulated over long, snowbound winters during which gossip was a staple of daily life.

Whispers to heat up a frigid afternoon where winter boredom ruled. Everyone preferred the downfall of a family to rumors of a German invasion as war spread all over Europe. Then it happened: Germany, Italy, and Hungary invaded, marched from Slovenia down to Bosnia. One uneventful afternoon, in a row of uneventful days, five armored vehicles rolled into Senice, the red, black, and white swastika of the Third Reich fluttering. The villagers gathered to watch as soldiers posted a declaration to the effect of the area now belonging to Germany; resettlement would soon begin. The colonel in charge, his snug-fitting smart gray uniform meant to intimidate, wanted to talk to the mayor in the town hall. The villagers laughed. The tavern, they said, was their town hall, and the colonel could talk to the priest if he wanted to judge the people of Senice. The priest could be found in the tavern—holy ground, they added, though the priest stood among them and laughed with the others. The German officer called them ignorant pigs, and they were not troubled further until the war began to turn against the Reich. By then Emil and his family were gone.

At first Emil's father, Ljpoj, hearing the gossip, turned the other cheek. Like Isaac and Ishmael, Ivak and Ljpoj shared a father but had separate mothers. Ivak was so much older, nearly a man when his widowed father took fifteen-year-old Selima to be his second bride. The villagers' tongues wagged. She was too young for the husband who'd imported her, already leaning one elbow in the grave. But she produced another son.

Big brother Ivak was the right man for the job, they joked. They called him Ivak the Seducer. He was flirtatious with the girls (and their mothers). The men drank beer with Ivak, but his half-brother had a face suggesting disdain, and, like his son, who would one day be similarly accused, Ljpoj was too quiet.

Lisle and Emil watched their father that late March morning as he walked alone out of the village, their cold hands held tight in their mother's grip. "Where is my father going?" the young Emil asked. "Can I go too?" For an answer, his mother squeezed his hand harder and dragged him home.

Ljpoj stayed four days among the trees. Each afternoon Emil waited, squatting on the side of the road until finally his father returned. Emil saw him as a dot at the forest edge, growing larger as he approached the village. He ran to him, but his father said nothing. That was the first of several disappearances. The others laughed, called him a fool. Where did he go? Were the White Fairies meeting him in the woods; did he kiss and fondle them?

Ljpoj said nothing.

He was only a half-son of Senice. Perhaps that explained how he could leave. Perhaps it explained the betrayal, if there actually was a betrayal. Perhaps Ivak only boasted, drunk one night in the tavern; maybe he didn't mean to tell a lie but then had to stay with his story to save face once he had begun it. Maybe the desirable Selima had spurned him and a dirty lie was his payback. Who could say for sure? After the old man died, Selima took her jewelry and moved to a shack, alone, on the edge of the village, where anything could happen. Not long after the visit from the Nazi colonel she was found with her throat slit.

The villagers expected revenge. It was assumed Ivak was the murderer and that his brother would kill him. Emil and Lisle were terrified, though Emil didn't quite understand why. But Ljpoj said nothing, only disappeared into the forest again. Even Ivak laughed at him. Not one citizen had a good word to say for the murdered mother. Emil's own mother hissed into her husband's ear, "Listen to me: Don't fight with your brother. Go to the magistrate in Jesenice; tell them what has happened. They will make an inquiry." She pulled at his sleeve. "You don't know who killed that wild woman, out there all alone these past years—anyone, a wolf, might have sliced her for her blood," she said.

Emil was just seven when their father roused the family at three a.m. on a spring morning in 1942. He'd stashed money and provisions all those times he'd left the village. He knew the hunting paths and had gone to the border twice to study unchecked crossings into the Italian Alps. He told his protesting wife to be quiet or he would gag her, and they walked into the darkness, taking two of their goats. They walked five hundred and fourteen kilometers of mountain terrain, crossing Italy and reaching Davos, Switzerland, in sixteen days. Emil trotted proudly alongside his papa on their secret mission. His mama complained unendingly, like yellow jackets at the end of summer.

From Switzerland, where forged travel visas were obtained, the family was handed off from car to car, truck to truck, sometimes on foot, passing, often under cover of darkness, through France and Spain until they made their way into Portugal. In Lisbon Emil, never having imagined the ocean, found his skin itching. With the last of his money Ljpoj thought he bought passage on a freighter bound for South America, but somehow they ended up in Brooklyn.

The familiar mountain skies of Slovenia were swallowed up by the strange and unwelcoming skies of America. Arriving in New York, Ljpoj found himself surrounded by constant pavement, nights that never darkened all the way, and blackening poverty. He purposely avoided a Croatian neighborhood where his Slovenian dialect would be understood, insisting that his family stay apart, learn English, become American. Brooklyn winters full of gray snow, summers of choking heat, and, most alarming, the ceaseless city noise; an immigrant's life in a nervous nation at war.

He found sporadic work as a welder. Everyone said to sign up to go fight the Germans. Emil delivered groceries after school for Big Albert, standing mute on backdoor stoops, waiting for bills to be paid. Late at night his father would read from his son's grammar book, waking Emil if he needed an explanation. He ignored his children unless they spoke "American English." A grinding struggle until Ljpoj finally did sign up.

Emil's mother spat out her fury: "So this is why we came here, for the army, for war? To go back there, where we left, to go and fight for the Jews?" Emil's mother, like the other citizens of Senice, was anti-Semitic as a matter of course, unconsciously afraid of anything foreign or different. Coming to America had not cured her ignorance.

Ljpoj's wartime service meant citizenship and a regular paycheck to the family left behind. He said it was the only way out and promised life would be better after the war; he was a citizen, and all things were possible to a good American! Then he was killed.

Before the end of the war more than half the people of Senice were dead, many from starvation and sickness over long, hard mountain winters with the road to supplies cut off. Ivak, though, survived. Learning that Ivak lived, Emil's mother stopped speaking. She spit on the floor, said, "What kind of a shit of a God allows that for justice?" She spoke in her native tongue because she refused to know English. Emil's sister went to their mother in her chair by the stove that she only ever left to stir the soup. "Mama, here is Emiloshka, alive and strong. Please, Mama, look to your son." Emil, gangly, his face young but his eyes already old, watched, ashamed of his mother's grief. His Uncle Ivak, when they were small, would capture Emil and Lisle and toss them into the air, catching them in his big arms, their bodies like sacks, heads and feet flopping, squeals of fear and delight. He was a big bear of a man, their Uncle Ivak. None of it made sense to the boy. No one told him anything.

Emil was an American when he returned to Slovenia eleven years after the war. He had only shadowy memories of a town where the unexplained took place; blurry recollections of his father's mother, of crunching snow underfoot on the way to Grandmother's shack, of secret places in the woods. Had he only imagined Selima to be a gypsy with bangles on her wrists, skirts that flared, the scent of pine, tobacco, and cloves mingling on her breath? What was real? Had the Nazis murdered her or had her stepson? It was too dark, his sister told him; "Leave it alone."

He returned to the old village anyway, but nothing was revealed.

Emil found no physical trace of his grandmother, not even a mound of dirt in the ramshackle cemetery to lay down a bunch of daisies. He spent a night with a cousin who told him what she knew, and in the morning he went to look for his uncle. He found Ivak in a beer hall on the road to the next village. He was old, and he was already drunk. He stared at Emil, his face dumb, thick and hostile. Emil spoke to him in his old language, but he was clumsy with it. By then he spoke only English; he *thought* in English. To his mother in Brooklyn he still spoke the native tongue, but she hardly talked and there was little to communicate, entombed as she was in Ljpoj's death and her endless resentment. He tried to ask his uncle what had happened to his grandmother, to Selima, Ivak's stepmother. The words came out badly—how else could such a question come out? But he looked into his Uncle Ivak's face and saw that he understood, into his eyes and saw that Ivak was a lost man.

Ivak's eyes shifted like a furtive animal's away from Emil's. In Emil's face was Ljpoj's face, and Ivak pulled away. He rubbed Emil's cheeks with his rough, red hands, and then he shoved him, shouting incomprehensibly, his breath stinking of beer. Emil nodded to his uncle and walked away.

He walked the dusty road back to Senice to catch the first bus back to the capital, Ljubljana. Thoughts of his father tormented: Should Ljpoj have tested his brother, found out if he'd killed Selima and then taken an eye for an eye? Lisle told Emil their father did not want to kill his brother—would killing him bring Selima back? In Ljpoj's heart was truth, she said, and he believed the truth would prevail no matter what. He didn't need his brother's blood on his hands to prove anything.

Emil returned to Ljubljana with six days remaining before his flight back to New York. He spent two hours sitting on a bench outside the bus station then found a crummy, cheap hotel nearby, parked his one bag, and went back outside to wander the city. Emil hadn't come to Slovenia as a tourist; he had no idea how a tourist behaved, so he walked. The city was rebuilding after the war, though the center had been mostly spared. It looked foreign to Emil, nothing like home in Brooklyn. In a pricier neighborhood he stopped in front of a shop that sold glass. He looked into the window to see what made so much light and then opened the door and went inside the crystal shop. He had no money to be in such a place. Inside was magical; glittering, refracted light, rainbows dancing on molded ceilings, on mirrored walls surrounding the room. In the center hung an ornate chandelier with crystal globes clinking gently in the breeze of an electric fan; the music of glass. He felt he had walked into a land of make-believe where spells might be cast on unsuspecting children. And there stood Elena.

A stylishly dressed man faced her from behind the counter, his expression bemused as he chatted with this new woman, oh so casually. Emil had no way of knowing that the shop was owned by Elena's cousin, who had taken up the family business, and that she had come to see him with greetings from her father in Trieste. Between them on the counter was a brochure. She seemed to be admiring what she saw on the pages.

Emil stood entranced as Elena spoke Italian to the stylishly dressed man, her words running together like music. He stared at her. At one point she turned to face him and Emil thought their eyes met, but Elena's eyes passed over him and he couldn't be certain whether she saw him or not. Her expression was distant and—did he only imagine?—sad. She stood with perfect posture. Her simple verdigris shift, draped with a pale green silk scarf, fit over a taut frame. Standing not four feet away, Emil felt he had the right to reach out and put his hand on her. But he had no such right, and when she left the shop the cousin turned his attention to Emil as if Emil had not been thinking what he had been thinking only seconds before, which would have been a violation because it was not just a hand he wished to place on this woman he'd never seen before, nor knew existed until that day.

He studied Elena's walk as her cousin saw her to the door, as he kissed both her cheeks and held her in a brief embrace. Were they lovers; was this man her husband? Closing the door, the cousin turned to Emil, greeting him in Slovenian.

Instead of inquiring about glass, Emil asked the man where one went as a tourist in Slovenia. The cousin asked if he had been to Bled.

"To Bled?" asked Emil. "No, not to Bled." He knew of Bled; it wasn't very far from Senice, but it was a different world altogether.

"But you must go. Bled is a place of enchanting, north of the city in the mountains," the cousin explained in fractured English.

"I've just come from the mountains."

The cousin paused. He looked at Emil, his head cocked to the side. "Forgive me," he said, "but you seem to speak with an accent that is familiar?" Emil shifted his weight, ran his fingers through his hair. "Do you speak Italian?" Emil shook his head. "No? Well, Bled is very pertinent. There is a lake; tourists go for the air, also the famous international casino. To gamble." The cousin made a gesture as if spinning a roulette wheel. "You must go, sir. My cousin, Elena Morandi, who was just in this shop, will go there herself."

"Ah, your *cousin*!" said Emil, way too emphatically, as if it mattered what her relation to this man was. The man mistook his enthusiasm for that of any tourist desperate for the help of one knowledgeable of the terrain. How many times had he seen the reaction? A local will say to the tourist, "The milk is over there, on the table," in such a way, s-l-o-w-l-y, that the far from home traveler can understand, and the grateful traveler will say, hugely, "Ah, over there, the milk is over *there*, yes, I see it now, there, on the table. The milk. Yes! Thank you so very much!" And the grateful traveler will make a small bow from the waist, a thing he would never dream of doing at home. The weary traveler thrilled with every victory in communication. To the manager of the glass shop, Emil was just such a tourist. How could he know that Emil had just severed himself once and for all from his father's Slovenian roots?

Emil repeated, "Bled," as if the word were a prayer or a cure, already feeling in his breast pocket for his map and transportation schedule. He would go back to the mountains. He thanked the cousin for his kind advice and suddenly made a small bow from the waist, a thing he had never done before. And the cousin, in return, made a slight bow to Emil as he smiled knowingly, an expression that struck Emil as irritatingly familiar, if not condescending, and he fought a sudden a desire to smash all the glass in the shop but waved good-bye on his way out instead.

Memories flooded Emil, seated at the dining room table, the girlish photograph of Elena still in his hand, her unread letters on the table. Like a leaf in a river suddenly swollen by spring rains, he floated, pitched along the current of his past.

TWO

And if a man entice a maid that is not betrothed, and lie with her, he shall surely endow her to be his wife. If her father utterly refuse to give her unto him, he shall pay money according to the dowry of virgins.

The Giving of the Law, Exodus

The street outside pulsed with heat. Unwashed city sidewalks sent up a menu of smells for any passing pedestrians to reluctantly breathe. Emil knew too well the sizzle of summer cement, hot vinyl squad car seats, hotter tempers on sweaty citizens; heat waves and guns: an explosive mix. He was cool enough in the dining room with the shades drawn and only muffled street sounds filtering in, the clock behind him ticking off its own idea of time and Elena's letters nagging at him from the table. He sat in a temporary vacuum, his mind weaving past and present.

His mother hadn't liked the clock either. She too had wound it begrudgingly. But Emil thought it wasn't such a bad old clock. Not beautiful or unique with its boxy housing and routine numerals, but it had presence. He'd gone into the clock shop on a whim. His mother had left everything behind, her father's grand clock too. A nice gesture, to give her a clock, but there were those men in the shop. He shook his head. "No," he said, running a finger along the table. He could write his name in the thick dust.

There was a time when delicious meals were served in style at that table.

From time to time Elena arranged dinner parties for friends from the Italian or Austrian Embassy. There was always a stir when a new guest learned he was a cop. A bit of a titter; a cop among Elena's polite dinner guests, well, well. They were never quite sure how far to go. The blunt approach: "Have you seen many dead bodies?" Or the conspiratorial: "How about that police corruption?" And the inevitable, unnerving: "Ever killed anyone?" They meant in the line of duty. They meant for him to put on a show. Holding in their excitement, the women anyway, at the prospect of seeing his piece; might as well be asking to see his member, he'd told Elena. Okay, he exaggerated, but no matter how sophisticated the guest, Emil was regarded as a sideshow, a man with a gun.

Merely crossing the East River into Brooklyn in those days was an adventure; the dicey neighborhood, the untamed culture of an outer borough, and then the shock of seeing how genteelly Elena lived. Their garden set an idyllic tone when all around was the bland repetition of a semi-industrial working class ghetto. "All it takes is cash and a little imagination," he'd say. "And a lot of hard work, I should think," one of the wide-eyed female guests might exclaim. "And Elena," he would add. "She could make Versailles out of a hunk of cheese." For which Elena would treat him to a tiny smile.

"Yes, such a thoroughly charming setting," a smooth Italian guest would coolly add with a European high-horse air, grating on Emil with his gelato voice.

No guests were likely to ever break bread at this table again. Not without Elena, and now body parts turning up outside. Emil chuckled lightly to himself. Better than the sidearm: an actual crime scene with dessert. Ha, ha, coffee anyone, oh, and a ladyfinger with that? A side dish of mystery to stimulate the appetite. Emil found himself laughing soundlessly in the solitude of the dining room, imagining Elena's dinner guests reacting to the news. But in a darker corner of his mind he heard a whispered idea that the severed finger belonged to Elena. It was a sick idea and impossible. He wanted to make amends—if only for her whose finger was missing, for everything, for the Elena he was not finished with, gone—couldn't he at least right *some* wrongs? He was a cop; isn't that what a cop does?

Once elegant dinners were served; now only papers referencing the dead filled the dining room, and the sound of the clock trying, as Elena said, to go backward. He picked up the packet of letters, held them loosely. He didn't want to read them and put the packet back down on the table. Then, angrily, he yanked an envelope out at random, opened the letter and quickly scanned the page.

Emil,

I have been thinking. There is something cruel in a man who does not ask. I will give you an example. Do you remember Lotte from the Austrian Embassy? She came to dinner many times with Ambrose. Once we went to Carnegie Hall with them and you complained the whole way but then enjoyed every single note of the concert. When Lotte gave birth to her only child, Ambrose phoned to tell us the news and you took the call. Do you remember? You told me, but you never asked him the sex of the child.

You questioned your suspects but not those close to you. Do you know this about yourself? You find ordinary life beneath you? Come si puo' domandare niente?

That is how I kept the secret for so long. I tried to tell you about the things that happened in Trieste. But how could I when you did not want to know? At first I thought this was very original on your part; we could skip the ordinary questions in life, we had more important concerns, we were building our world. The past need not exist for us. You had your secrets too. But after enough years went by and you said nothing, I thought that you might not care. That certain questions did not occur to you because you are not capable of caring—not for the answers, no, but for the questions, for knowing others. The word solipsism came to mind, but I am not certain it is the word I mean.

He stopped reading, angrily refolded and shoved the letter back into its envelope and under the ribbon with the others. Was she calling him names from the grave? "Solipsism!" he said, not absolutely certain of its precise meaning—but it couldn't be good. Anyway, he hated letters and she knew it. Maybe her mind was going at the end. No, that wasn't so, and he knew that. "I'll bury the damn letters in the garden!" He pushed the packet away as if merely touching the letters could cause him harm.

Two months after his father died, Emil received a letter from him and became convinced there had been a terrible mistake, that his father was alive and that some other family would have to be notified of the death of their father because his was not dead. He showed his mother the envelope. She shook her head and turned away. Lisle stroked his hair and said no. Furious, Emil slapped the postmark; couldn't she see the letter was sent *after* the War Office named their father dead? It had miscarried, Lisle explained; the war made the mail slow and unreliable; their papa had written before he was sent to Greece; Emil must not think that he was alive. But he'd hidden the letter, unopened, and promised not to read it until his father came home. It had been a bad bargain and the beginning of a lifelong reluctance to open his mail.

At the beginning of their time together Emil sometimes found Elena by herself in tears, and he was helpless before them. Her wounds were deeply subterranean. She had only been in Brooklyn a matter of months before news came of her beloved papa, a telegram announcing that his condition was grave. Elena cried inconsolably and then announced that she would return to Trieste that evening. Emil arranged to drive her to the airport in a police car. Soon after that Emil's mother died. He didn't write or call Elena. He decided she was not coming back. Her father lasted less than two weeks, but Elena stayed on in Trieste.

At first they wrote short letters back and forth across the Atlantic, but they stopped corresponding and there was only silence between separated lovers. She had surprised him by coming to America at all; *that* woman in his house, his miserable mother upstairs, the ugly, defeated neighborhood. It had been too good to be true; she had come to her senses, he thought, and he would have to come to his.

After she left, his mother opened up one morning, asking what had become of the Italian. She spoke to him in Slovenian; he answered her mostly in English.

"The Italian is gone, Mama."

"Did she steal anything?"

"Like what?"

"Whatever they steal. She is a gypsy."

"Like Papa's mother?"

"Like that. Maybe a whore slut into the bargain."

"Grandmama was no gypsy, Mama; why do you say she was?"

"You were too young to know."

"Uh-huh. You don't have to worry about Elena anymore."

"Is that her name?"

"You know her name."

"Her name is nothing to me."

"Nothing is anything to you anymore, Mama. You went away with Papa."

His mother shrugged. It had been a lengthy conversation for them and it bespoke everything there was between them. Lisle told Emil their mother died to make room for Elena. Emil laughed. "Mama died of having no further object for her hatred, and Elena, my dear sister, is gone."

"She will be back," Lisle answered on the cold, damp April morning of their mother's burial.

Elena did come back, and on her finger when she returned was a small opal ring that her father had given her, a ring he had first given to her mother. Emil noticed it right away because Elena wore very little jewelry and had never had a ring on her left hand before that day. She also had bundles of cash with her, her inheritance, she said; twenty-five thousand dollars.

She just showed up. He came in from work and there she was. A cab had dropped her off, she said, the key still in her hand. Emil hid his surprise at seeing her. "What have you done with your mother?" were her first words. "Dead," Emil answered. Elena looked especially beautiful to him, standing in his humble kitchen, more beautiful than ever. She studied his face a moment, hearing of his mother's death, but said nothing. No hypocrisy from her, he could count on that; no false consolation from Elena.

"You are sleeping in the dining room?"

"Yes … I … there was no sense … walking all the way to the other floors." He was ashamed to say he was saving money on heat. At least he'd made the bed that morning.

"I see. No more shiny blue uniform? No longer police?"

"I'm up to detective now." No response. "Here, you must be tired," he said, taking off his coat. "I'll open a bottle of wine."

"Yes," she agreed.

As he opened the wine, Elena, standing at the kitchen table, began to rip out the lining of her coat. She removed her suit jacket to cut out what would have been the shoulder pads but were now wads of bills under a thin cover of cloth. She slit the hem of her skirt and more money fell out, landed all over the table and floor, a tide of American bills from her seams and hems and linings; twenty-five thousand dollars, a lot of money in those days. Emil poured the wine, ignoring the flood of cash. He toasted her health, and they drank.

With some of that money they would close off a room next to the bay window at the rear of the parlor, making a new bedroom for themselves, and they created the apartment on the fourth floor currently occupied by Paulien Vandervell. But before all that Elena began the vast work of digging out the backyard. She seemed to bury herself in the task of making a garden out of nothing. It grew into an enormous project, and as it grew her sorrow seemed to subside. He had joked that the garden was the real reason she returned. In the beginning he held back, did not contribute to her Eden, but was eventually seduced into her plan. Elena and her money changed the tone of Emil's life.

That first day they quarreled bitterly over the inheritance. Emil wanted to know how her father had managed to hang on to this wealth during the war. Elena asked him why he thought her father's property would have been confiscated. "We were without, the same as everyone else. Why would they take our land?"

"I mean not land but glass. Who bought glass during a war?"

"Don't be foolish; not everything stopped still," she said and made a gesture with her hand as if to say, What of it?

"Trieste fell to the Germans in 1943," Emil replied sourly.

"And? Maybe Nazis like crystal?" She twisted her hands as she spoke.

"I'm wondering how your father kept his money, that's all."

"No, you are accusing something, hard and accusing. How do I know what my father did? I was a child. Did he ask me what to do? Did I know what to think? You know nothing!" Emil was quiet; he thought she was overreacting. "Here!" she said. "We will burn it!" She began to scoop up fistfuls of dollars, lifted her skirt to make a kind of basket, throwing bills of all denominations into it. "We will make a great big fire to burn all the evil money." She started into the dining room for the fireplace, her skirt cupped, full to overflowing. "I am happy to—I *should* burn this money!"

He stopped her. "Elena . . ."

Her tormented face shifted into a bitter smile. "It is money after all, no? Dirty money, clean money: still money." She collapsed onto the floor, exhausted, surrounded by the sea of American bills. Emil came over to her with the bottle and wineglasses. He sat down on the floor next to her and stroked her hair. She yielded to his touch like an overwrought, tired child. She was so young.

Emil slumped in his chair, burdened by memories. The ring on the finger outside had to be Elena's, the opal she wore when she returned after her father's death. The thought sent a cold splash of wake up through his gut. He needed to examine that ring! But he didn't move.

The idea of dumping the severed finger kept recurring, of ending the situation where it was, unresolved. Much easier to just bury it; eliminate the whole show, ring and all. That would be the most natural, and not six feet under, the pinkie would be secure in twelve, maybe fifteen inches; to be certain, twenty. To be decent, two feet, and he already had the pepper hole dug. If he were going to lose the evidence, he might as well provide a decent burial. Why not? And throw Elena's letters in while he was at it. Wrap the finger in a little piece of cloth, place it in a small box—like a goldfish or pet bird buried in the backyard. But the finger would be there, and he would know it, inescapably, each time he sat in the garden. He'd never be able to rest of an evening without also sitting in a graveyard, and not only that, but the grave of an unsolved crime.

What if the ring wasn't Elena's? He again picked up her letters, held the loop of ribbon, about to pull it open, but stopped. He pushed his chair back, scraping the bare floor.

What about the dry ice? This indecision—

"Okay!" he said aloud, standing up while dropping the letters onto the table. He was ready to go: get the ice, preserve the finger, get to the bottom of things, put this little incident to bed. His resolve had returned. He grabbed his jacket from the chair, draped it over his right shoulder and walked into the kitchen while shoving his arms through the sleeves. He was about to close the kitchen window in case of rain when he heard a familiar birdsong. He stood still. It sounded like the song of the house finch.

"Are they back?"

He meant Elena's finches. She had given him a garden, and in the garden she loved best the sweet song of the tiny house finch. A modest bird with its dusky brown coat and sudden splash of red. Smaller than a sparrow, the finches had been her little pleasure each spring until one day they vanished. The season came without the song of the finch. Neither mentioned it, each hoping they were wrong. Emil found the answer in the newspaper, in the science section on a Tuesday. The birds had developed a virus to the conjunctiva causing temporary blindness and, once sightless, were unable to hunt and began to starve and die. He told Elena what the article said, and she answered, "I thought they were migrating somewhere else." She blamed herself. They'd been away during a very cold early April. "While we were gone no one put food out each morning."

Emil explained, "Listen to me, Elena. No one is to blame. Did the birds ever die before when we were away? No. They don't depend on us." She was glaring at him. "What?"

"If we fed them, they would have no need to hunt; the location of the feeder is memorized. All they have to do is fly there each day, blind or not. But we were not here; the feeder was empty."

"Elena, be reasonable. The paper said they fall victim to all sorts of dangers once blinded. Do birds fly in the dark? Bats, yes, but bats are not the same. It was inevitable; the finches were disoriented without sight. But they will return; some survived, others will come. It says so right here: *The finch has not been wiped out*." Emil tapped the newspaper to prove his point. Elena looked at him, her small fists tight. "It's right here in print. The scientists know."

"Bats, Emil?" Elena said between gritted teeth. "As for scientists, they *lack* common sense."

But the finches did not return, not while Elena was alive. She had taken their blindness to heart. That it could be arranged to harm such a helpless creature, their fragile bones and wings, all of them at once?

Why? Did the finches bring evil into the world? Did they harm anyone, exploit, cause war? No; in fact, the sparrows bullied *them*—she'd seen this at the feeder. How deserve such a cruel fate? How could this moral lapse on the part of the universe be explained by science?

The day the doctor announced her cancer, Elena's first thought was of the blinded finches. Not that she was as worthy, as innocent as they. She smiled briefly. "Of course," she said, strangely, to her doctor. "Of course, the birds lose their sight and now I am eaten from the inside by worms. And why not?" The doctor didn't know what to say. He folded his hands in front of him on the desk, creating a little barrier. Elena took pity, smiled again; after all, the doctor had nothing to do with her condition; he was only the messenger, and one didn't shoot the messenger; he might have delivered the very same diagnosis to ten patients that week alone.

"Very good, Doctor. How do we proceed? How do we kill this cancer?" There was contempt in her voice; if science could not save the eyes of a bird from a common virus, what could it do with an entity as complex as a cancer? Cut, that's what, slice and dice, as one would sever a cankered branch on a rosebush. But a rosebush might regenerate; the form of a rose is more pliant than that of a human body. She decided then and there that they would never butcher her. She told Emil: no cutting, no slicing, and no pruning—no matter what.

Now, five years later, Emil once again heard the song of the finch. He had forgotten how much he missed hearing them as he worked in the garden or waking early on spring mornings. He looked out of the doorway, leaned forward to see better, but saw no bird. He waited, holding his breath, peering toward the branches of the dogwood and beyond. There was not a single bird in sight, not even a sparrow or starling. Had he only imagined hearing a finch? Where were all the other birds? Hadn't they been there earlier with his breakfast?

There was a songbird in a cage at the fat lady's house where Emil rented a room the evening he arrived in Bled, the day he followed Elena after seeing her in the glass shop. The landlady's face was a layer cake of flesh with two sharp, untrusting eyes piercing out from puffy folds of skin. Her small feet were squashed into a pair of frayed red velvet slippers. On a clothesline in a court below his window hung pairs of voluminous white underpants, and next to them skimpy pairs of men's briefs. Her husband worked, the lady explained, as if letting him know she was not alone in the world, in a mine thirty miles away. In a parlor window beneath Emil's small balcony the caged bird daily sang his plaintive song.

After learning Elena's name and her plans, Emil went back to the bus terminal and made a reservation for the afternoon trip to Bled. He then returned to his hotel to retrieve his unpacked bag. Downstairs, in what passed for a lobby, he rang the bell and politely asked the clerk, who was chewing, having been interrupted while eating his lunch, for a refund. The man behind the desk seemed to forget that earlier he had understood Emil, more or less.

Emil said to him, "I didn't touch a thing, never even used the toilet. I put my bag on the floor, went out, and here I am ready to leave again." From the clerk a blank stare. Emil tried again, slowly: "I cannot stay in Ljubljana. I must go. I assure you, I touched nothing."

The man eyed him dully. In German he said, "You speak German? You want a different room?"

Emil stood a minute, considering. The surly clerk hadn't spoken German to him before; why start speaking German to him now? Emil stood his ground, emboldened by his purpose of following a beautiful woman. The clerk was saying something, suggesting that maybe he'd taken a woman for hire up to the room and was now done and prepared to cheat him. Emil located his native tongue; some of his mother's Slovenian swear words came back to him. He leaned into the clerk's pimply face and said in the man's language, "My money now!" and called him an expletive that implied cows combined with unclean women. Emil's mother's invectives usually involved women she thought of as dirty, and most women, according to her, were filthy as a matter of course.

The clerk shrugged. "How much do you want?"

"All!"

"Not possible. How much?"

Emil named a sum, three-quarters of what he had paid to rent the room for a night. The clerk reached into a drawer and pulled out half the amount Emil had paid. Emil looked at it and nodded, and the clerk handed him the cash. He left the hotel more or less satisfied, found a cheap eatery, ordered a bowl of good Slovenian yogurt, goat meat and dark coffee, and sat there until it was time for his bus.

He had calculated the odds, with only two buses left that day for Bled, and was not surprised to see Elena seated on the bus when he boarded. Emil puffed his chest out as he walked down the aisle past her seat in row eight, next to the window. From his seat, in row twelve on the opposite side, he studied her profile until her head slipped below the seat back.

The bus chugged slowly through city traffic. As it pulled farther out of Ljubljana, Emil began to have doubts. He brooded over his trip to Senice and, despite Elena's presence and his new mission into the mountains, was agitated by the time the bus moved beyond the outskirts, past pretty white houses with red tile roofs and small vegetable gardens, along green and yellow fields, and finally out into open country. He ought to have exchanged his plane ticket, left Slovenia right after the failure with Ivak. He'd thought he would be wiser once his many questions had been answered. As a child he'd been yanked out of one country and thrust into another. It happens all the time, not a big deal—Emil knew that—but he'd never had a chance to ask his father why they had been rushed away in the dark of night. Then the war took Ljpoj, and nothing was revealed and his father remained a mystery, but so what? How many millions went to their graves without finishing what they had to say? How many aborted story lines had death already swallowed? What could he do about it? This whole adventure, digging into the past, was impossible. Now what was he doing? He had no money to be touring mountain resorts.

What if Ljpoj had shouted from the rooftops: *Face me, brother; speak the truth*, would his pride have been any less than the pride that had kept him silent, that had caused him to leave his homeland? If it was pride. Emil the boy had promised to punish his Uncle Ivak; smash his nose, bloody him, scream into his face that he was a rotten murderer. But what if Ivak hadn't slit his stepmother's throat? Maybe the ignorant villagers accused an innocent man. Now Emil would never know, not from the mouth of the accused, not from anyone.

He grew morose; no longer saw the landscape passing by his window. How could he know if his father held truth in his heart, as Lisle said, or was only thickheaded—or, worse, afraid, as the villagers said? Lisle must have known; she believed in her papa. "Leave it alone," he told himself, his brain on fire with impossible questions. The old woman seated next to him, dressed in widow's black, turned to stare. Emil's right leg jiggled nervously up and down. He pressed his knee with his left hand and tried to smile at her. He glanced over toward Elena. He could just see the top of her hair. She was a complete stranger to him but he wanted to tell her everything. He leaned forward on his elbows. The old woman touched his shoulder. On her open, wrinkled palm sat a perfectly formed apricot. She smiled generously, the old babushka, missing half her teeth. Emil shook his head. She said, in her language, "Take it." He took the velvety apricot from her and held it carefully in his hand.

After traveling through high foothills, climbing slowly up and up, the bus came upon the great alpine range, a looming wall of white, a presence all the way up to the sky; majestic, swallowing the road, the trees, the bus, the whole earth into one vast surface of mountain. Emil sat up. The other passengers stirred; his ears popped as they climbed. The temperature dropped. A baby on board began to wail; Emil heard its mother shush it. Elena too seemed to be paying close attention outside her window. Emil felt lighter, not only from the thinning atmosphere but for seeing the mountains again. He had not seen much on his way to Senice. He'd been too tense, looking inward and chewing on himself, carrying his boyhood and Ljpoj and his mother and Lisle on his mind and in his heart, and he hadn't seen a thing. Now he felt almost giddy on the ascending bus. These were the mountains of his birth, and he was of them, and wasn't he as free as a bird in his mountains all alone? He'd once walked these Alps, all the way to Switzerland. Why not free as a bird? He took a bite of the apricot. It was delicious, sweet, ripe, and juicy. He grabbed the old babushka's hand and lifted it to his lips.

They arrived in Bled as the sun was setting in a sky washed in gold. The town was smaller than he'd imagined, knit close around the lake on whose surface rosy gold-tipped glacial peaks were now reflected. He'd had a different picture altogether in his mind, featuring the famous gambling casino and an element of glamour, but there was none of that. It was enchanting, as Elena's cousin had said, with the storybook castle perched on a tiny island in the lake watched over by a fortress on the surrounding mountain. Goats and goatherds could be seen on the outskirts, and sheep grazed in the town square. There were tourists but they were not ostentatious among the townsfolk.

There was only a handful of restaurants and hotels to choose from. Posted outside the tourist board were listings of private rooms to let. He was lucky with the fat lady's vacancy. After paying for his room, he dumped his two shirts and extra pair of pants on the bed and stood on the small balcony, his back stiff from two cramped bus rides. The mountain air was cool and light. Emil breathed deeply, feeling all right, even hopeful. He used the shared bathroom and went out.

He'd followed Elena out of the bus station. She walked as if inhabiting a world of her own, removed from those around her. He was careful to hear the name of the hotel she gave the driver of a horse-drawn jitney, watched as the old man helped her climb in with her bag. He knew it would be an expensive hotel. It seemed logical that she would eat her dinner there unless she wasn't a stranger in Bled and had friends expecting her. Emil decided to find the hotel and eat his supper there. He was very hungry, but he would chance it. If he didn't see Elena in the dining room he would go somewhere else for a more reasonably priced meal. Otherwise, he was willing to spend far more than he should.

If asked what he thought he was doing, Emil Milosec might not have known how to reply. With his father's death he'd become head of the family, whether he cared to play the role or not, and, as the sole male, his word became law. His mother and sister made not a single decision without consulting him first. He was assumed to have answers, was placed in charge of the finances and expected to behave like a man. Lisle in fact performed most of the household tasks, but she deferred politely to her young brother. This was the way a family from the old country did things. It never occurred to Emil to throw off a mantle that was miles too big for him.

His cap pulled low, he walked along the lake. A woman passing by spoke a few words and he understood her greeting. She said in Slovenian that it was a good evening. Emil answered, Yes, a very nice night to walk. His response was automatic, yet, thinking about it a moment later, he was unable to repeat the phrase. He listened to the lake lapping the grassy shore; saw the swans cruising like little white boats. The sky darkened as he walked, and, like an illusionist's trick, the screen of daylight pulled back to reveal a vast length of black cloth sprinkled with stars, cold and shimmering. Those same stars undulated on the lake's mirror surface.

Twenty-five minutes' walk brought him to Elena's hotel. The maître d' glanced at Emil's clothing but seated him at a window with a view of the lake. The room with its Viennese influence had a worn elegance. The silk curtains were faded and frayed, the tablecloths no longer quite white. The effect was of a once grande dame placed on a budget; the war had taken its toll on luxuries. Only four other diners occupied the large dining room. Elena was seated three tables away. Emil, shrinking in his chair, ordered the cheapest item on the menu, beef-broth soup. Elena had before her the remains of a three course meal.

He imagined her arriving, carefully unpacking her sweater sets, folding them into the bureau with her panties, hanging up her blouses and skirts. Her room would be spacious, with fresh-cut flowers. She might have stood on her balcony, facing the lake as the daylight faded, seen the swans glide on the water, long necks arched like royalty.

He watched her drain her wineglass, sign a receipt, smile at the waiter, and leave the dining room, noting her walk, the motion of her hips. But he despised himself for coming to the hotel. He might have waited until morning to find her. Still hungry after two baskets of bread with the soup, Emil paid the waiter and slunk back to his room in the fat lady's house.

The next morning he was back at her hotel bright and early. He waited until she finally came out and followed at a distance as she walked along the lake. Over the next few days he saw her again and again. He visited the Bled fortress the same day she did. He rowed out to the castle on the island, just as she did. The day after that he observed her exiting the Herdsmen's Museum in Bohinj, and at the shops. At nearly every turn Emil was there. He was tracking her, anticipating her movements, spying; the rookie cop testing his talents. He studied her minutely: the clothing and shoes, how her hair was combed, that she was right-handed but carried her bag in her left, chewed her right thumbnail when thinking, and took afternoon tea with milk; no gesture was too small for this detective in the making.

After four days of this Emil was stationed at a coffee kiosk across the street from a restaurant Elena had entered, presumably for lunch. Five minutes later she took him by surprise, walking toward him. She must have come out a back way or through the kitchen. Emil quickly tossed some coins on the counter and walked to the lake, stopping near an old woman with a cart selling souvenirs. He fingered the fabric of a little Slovenian flag. Elena walked toward the north end of the lake but abruptly turned on her heel and strode over to him. She asked him roughly in Slovenian what he thought he was doing.

The souvenir seller put down her knitting and looked up. Emil made no response, having understood the words but feeling unprepared to respond. Elena repeated her demand: "What do you think you are doing, following me? Were you sent? Did someone send you? Who sent?" Again Emil said nothing, an ignoramus in his own country, but more than that he found himself tongue-tied by her presence, addressing him so directly. He busied himself with a souvenir of the lake, a glass globe with snow that fell when the globe was shaken. He shook it hard until the snow, manic at first, settled slowly over a miniature replica of the castle on the mountain lake. He held the globe out to her and tried to smile. What an idiot he must have looked.

Elena changed languages, asked her question in German, demanding again to know why he was following her. Hearing the German, the souvenir lady moved to the side. Emil clumsily pulled bills out of his pocket. At least he knew how to talk money: "Koliko to košta? Ja ću kupiti?" he asked the souvenir seller, but she did not react or even look at him.

Elena stared at Emil. Hadn't he just spoken Slovenian? She said, now in Italian, "Perche' mi segue, eh, perche'?" But this produced no response at all from Emil. He looked helplessly at her, wishing to dissolve into the ground. He turned to the souvenir seller, holding up the globe and his pathetic pile of bills.

Elena shook her hair, tried French. Emil recognized some of her words from his high school lessons. Those agonized classes with the American teacher, Miss Rose Thyme, the white-haired tyrant of French who had cared nothing for the fact that his English had been so recently acquired. It should have been obvious to everyone that he was no good at languages. "No, non," he fumbled out. "Je-ne-parle-pas-Francaise." He thought he'd said it correctly and nearly felt proud.

"Non? Quel langage parlez vous, hah? Quel langage, Monsieur?" And with this she shoved his shoulder. Emil stepped back, surprised by her strength. He remembered how to say he was sorry. "Non. Perdonez moi. I am sorry, English. I speak English."

"You are English?" She spoke English with an Italian accent.

"Non. Je suis Americain." He spoke the French with an undeniable Slovenian accent.

The souvenir seller gathered up her things, hurriedly shutting boxes, removing flags and banners, closing down her cart. She shooed Emil away. He moved out of her path as she muttered while snapping shut the canvas cover and pulling down her shade umbrella. She gathered her strength and with heavy efficiency pushed her cart away as quickly as she could. Whatever this international incident was all about, she wanted no part of it. The war was too fresh in people's minds; fanatics with guns were everywhere; better to go home and hide.

Elena watched Emil, who watched the old woman. He still held the snow globe. "For you," he said in English.

Elena looked at the globe. He shook it, and again the snow inside fluttered and swirled, obscuring the little world of lake and castle within a flurry of white. As the snow began to settle again, Elena spoke. "You do not look American," she said carefully, less sure of her English.

Emil ran a hand through his hair. "Yes. I mean, no."

"What do you want?" she asked him.

"You," he answered simply. "What I want is you."

They looked at each other for perhaps fifty seconds, each taking the other in. Elena broke her eyes from Emil's when a brass band suddenly burst into a perky waltz, oompah-pah-pah, oompah-pah-pa. ... Behind them people had gathered at a white gazebo where the band, bright in red and gold with caps and tassels, began to play in the afternoon sun.

Emil turned toward the unexpected music. As he did Elena reached out and snatched the snow globe from his hand and threw it hard on the ground and then turned and walked away, her low heels clicking severely on the pavement. Emil bent down to retrieve the smashed souvenir. The water ran out; the globe was in pieces. He touched a flake of the snow, briefly wondering what it was made of.

He called after her in English, "I followed you because I didn't know what words to say."

She stopped and turned around, watched as Emil picked up the tiny castle and put it in his pocket. She turned again and continued walking.

The following day it rained. Emil woke up with a fiery headache and feared a cold might be coming on. He hadn't eaten enough in the past few days and felt weak. He went down to his landlady to ask for a pot of tea in his room. The folds of her fleshy face wobbled into a frown. "Tea!" Emil repeated, pointing to the stove. "Tea." How many times had he made tea for his mother; where was the word? Čaj!" he suddenly shouted. At last the landlady understood: His head hurt and he wanted tea. "Yes, thank you. Hvala!" He showed her his bus schedule and pointed to the departure times. "Today," he said. "Later I go." The landlady understood. She nodded vigorously, sending her flesh wobbling up and down, venturing a brief smile.

He sat in his room until afternoon. The rain was steady. Where the mountains had been, low, scowling clouds sat heavily, obscuring the view. The lake was draped in a foggy shawl, the air bitingly damp. In his forever cage the songbird was silent. Finally the rain let up, and Emil crawled out of bed. With his sweater on under his jacket, he went out to buy his mother a gift. He looked into several shop windows but nothing made sense. He stopped at a narrow shop that belonged to a clock repair.

He thought his mother might like a clock. She had complained bitterly of having to leave her beautiful grandfather clock behind. It had been a wedding present, had belonged to her papa and before that to his papa. A ceaseless lament that her china and fine linen—the envy of the other women—had all been abandoned. Which of the women had snagged her forsaken household treasures?

The crowded shop was filled with clocks; on the walls, on a cluttered counter, on chairs. There was a massive ticktock throughout from clocks of all types. A white-haired man bent over a worktable behind the counter did not look up. Emil couldn't imagine spending each day among the clocks; he'd go mad, his mind punctuated by so many minutes asserting themselves. He said hello. The man nodded. "You left a clock?" he asked Emil.

Emil flipped through his language book to find the words. He said, "I wish to buy a clock."

"To buy? I fix clocks." Emil looked up the word, understood. He put the language book back in his pocket. "Some I sell," the clock man added in Slovenian. "Where are you from?"

"United States. From America," Emil answered in his uneven Slovenian. The man leaned in for a better look. They didn't see many Americans in Bled. "A boy," Emil explained. "A boy I am in Senice, from Senice."

"You are from Senice?" Emil nodded. "And you want a clock?"

"Yes. For my mother."

Two men appeared from behind a parted curtain at the back of the shop. Ignoring Emil, one of them asked the old man in Slovenian, "What does he want?"

"A clock. For his mother."

The man said, "Who is he?"

"He's from America."

The other man said, "Him? His clothes are not like an American's. Maybe he is a spy."

The first man said, "Or he was a collaborator."

"No, look at him, too young," answered the old man. Then he asked Emil, "Your mother is in Senice?"

"No, in America," Emil answered in a loud voice.

One of the men said, "He speaks Slovenian?"

The clock-repair made a so-so gesture with his hand to indicate Emil's ability in their language. "I don't know what he speaks."

"So that only proves it," the man continued. "He is a spy." He shrugged, adding, "Maybe a bad one, soft in the head." The three of them laughed.

"At least badly funded," said the other man, gesturing.

"A spy looking for his mother." The three men burst into unkind laughter. But the first man nudged the second man and they stopped laughing. They were looking at something outside the shop. Emil turned but didn't see anything unusual.

He closed his eyes; if he only half listened he could understand. If he stayed in Slovenia long enough he would be back to speaking like the native he was.

"Ask him who he works for," the first man said. His tone was rough.

"No, don't waste time; sell him that clock," the second man said, pointing to a clock on the counter.

"That's Lubec's clock, I'm not finished repairing," the old man said. "He'll be back for it."

"We'll take care of this Lubec. Just say it was broken beyond repair."

The old man looked at the second man. He reached for the clock in question and pushed it toward Emil. "It doesn't work, keeps lousy time," he said. "Like a woman, nice enough to look at but worthless." The old man was talking loudly now, and he laughed at his own joke.

The second man said, "If the hands work, old man, that's all that matters in a woman." All three laughed again.

"Okay," Emil suddenly said, nearly shouting. They looked at him.

The old man asked, "What?"

Emil pointed to Lubec's clock with its simple hands, no filigree or ornate detail, a plain clock but solid. Emil knew less than nothing about clocks and thought this one would be expensive or that they would jack up the price for an American. "How much for the clock?" he asked, trying to sound firm. The first man nodded at the old man, who then named a ridiculously low sum. "*How* much?" Emil asked.

The old man said something to the others in a low voice that Emil could just hear. He said something about it being three o'clock, and he—or someone—would be coming. The second man said to get rid of the fake American.

Emil slapped the cash on the counter. "Okay?"

"*Okay!*" the old man repeated loudly, reaching for the cash. The other two watched as he carefully wrapped the clock in brown paper and tied the finished package tightly with sturdy string, making a little handle loop on top. Emil picked up the package, nodded to the men, and left the shop. The first man followed him to the door; the others were quiet.

Outside, he pulled up his collar and shoved the clock under his jacket. It was raining again, though not hard. He was about to make a dash for a coffeehouse when he saw Elena standing across the narrow street under a wide black umbrella. He called to her in English, "Hey, are you following me?" She almost smiled but said nothing. "I leave today," he said, moving to a shop to the right of the clock repair that had a wider overhang. Elena stayed where she was. "Why don't you talk to me a minute before I go?" he called to her.

"Why do you leave? Afraid of a small rain?" She sounded carefree but her expression was serious, and she bit her thumbnail nervously. Emil noticed.

"You mean 'little,'" he said.

"Cosa?"

"A *little* rain. Not small."

"You correct me?"

Emil shrugged. "Come have coffee with me."

"Why?"

"Why not?"

"Another time," she said.

"There is no other time."

"Peccato," she said in Italian—*too bad*—and she abruptly turned and left, walking briskly, almost at a trot into the lightly falling rain.

THREE

A curse on anyone who strikes another in secret.

Book of Deuteronomy

Emil took his sports coat off a second time and hung it over a kitchen chair. He returned to his flourishing garden, offering innocent pleasures on a day that was anything but. Like a woman spread across a flowered quilt, he thought. "Peccato," he said to the garden. Still no birds twittered. He walked to the honeysuckle draped along the fence, just past the dead pepper patch, blooming early this year. Bees hummed over the flowers, their scent thick in the heat. Smelling the honeysuckle, he remembered a conversation he'd had with Elena one Saturday morning on their way home from the supermarket. He was still with the force at the time, and she'd said something odd like, "Did you ever note that people rarely are tempted by good?"

The car was loaded with groceries, a big haul. The day was bright and promising. Supermarkets had the potential to darken Emil's mood on the best of days, but the chore was done, and he was safe for two weeks or so before they would need to make another haul. At home, while Elena put the groceries away, he headed to the garden. The season was young, plenty of planting left to do before summer's dry breath settled in. The phlox were nearly finished; their tiny iridescent blue flowers lay scattered prettily along the path next to the sharply yellow *Alyssum saxatile*.

The magnolia was close to spent, while the lilac beside the pergola was ripe with clusters of tight buds already hinting at purple; he anticipated its perfume. He'd been thinking of planting a trumpet vine on the fence between his and Franco's yard. Or, even better, a honeysuckle, the heady fragrance to camouflage the city's uglier summer smells, especially in the evening when the scent came on strong. Honeysuckle; how could that name suggest anything other than sex?

After he'd worked a while in the garden, Elena would come out with a light lunch. She'd walk easily, balancing the dishes and the wine and sparkling water on a wooden tray, setting the meal down on the marble table they'd paid too much for at what Emil called a frou-frou antiques joint in Manhattan. The table had reminded her of afternoons in Trieste; hot chocolate in the sun after school with a friend, a sidewalk café before going home to study, and, later, seated at those same tables with a lover—once the war stopped and cafés were safe once again. After lunch they'd lie on the bed across from the bay window that overlooked the garden. Emil would touch Elena as they drowsed, hearing the sounds of the neighborhood drifting in; open her blouse to glance at the soft mounds of her breasts, watch her nipples harden. He might only touch, or penetrate if she were willing, if she'd open up to him; he never assumed. Later she'd join him in the late-afternoon garden, her hands wrapped in tight-fitting goatskin gloves.

An easy emptiness had surrounded his thoughts as they'd driven home from the market. It was the yielding, the letting go to the garden and the fullness of working without a care in the world that made him feel light and good. A garden, he thought, might well be the antidote to murder. He had no wish to contemplate evil or the criminal soul that Saturday; he contemplated the criminal soul all week long. If he was quiet, maybe Elena would not expect an answer to her question; she might talk, and he might only have to listen. He might not have to participate on this nearly perfect day in spring. But she looked at him, her face expectant. He'd have to come up with something. His mind groaned, shifted into gear and words found their way out of his mouth: "That would be backward, wouldn't it?"

"How?"

"People are tempted by bad, not good."

"That is my point. More bad than good attracts."

"Maybe it's only advertising; good behavior doesn't sell news."

"You don't have to turn to the news to see what I mean; there is something wrong with how we decide right from wrong."

Emil twitched. If Elena wanted to talk about crime, she'd come to the right source; he had all the ammunition she could wish for. All the horrors he didn't share with her; murders he'd worked and those that were on the books. The most diabolical acts: A man might bludgeon his grandmother for a ten-dollar bill, while some other character harbored the bones of children under the floorboards or had a secret cell where kidnapped women were chained as sex slaves, then killed. Maybe a diminutive mother starved and tortured her own child to death. The typical response: "That something like this could happen next door …" Or the other classic, of a neighboring killer: "He was always so quiet." On and on until a cop might conclude that all there was in the world was evil. Was that where Elena wanted to go? "But all in all," he said to her, "most people are law-abiding, Elena."

"And who knows what secrets they hide? Corruption is slow. People leak; take a look under the surface to see what swarms inside. We just don't see until it is too late."

"That's kind of dramatic—see what, anyway? I'm not sure I know what you're talking about."

"About what people really are."

"Are we having a philosophical discussion here, Elena?" he said, a spasm of irritation working its way into his voice. "Is that what we're doing on this pretty day?" His voice hardened; he was bullying her, and was sorry for it, but ... "Look, I'm a cop. I can only work a crime that's actually taken place. I don't know what people really are, what lies hidden, and neither do you."

"Yes, and you have not understood a thing, and malevolence continues as a disease. Why do you think that is so? Remember the man in the river." She looked at him out of the corner of her eye.

Oh, no, Emil thought as he drove home that Saturday morning—his day off—the car filled with good ingredients for her to cook, for them to enjoy together, not that. Why would she want to dig up that paranoid political mugging from so long ago, old postwar, communist Slovenia? If she wanted, he'd share the murder he and Mike had handled the day before. Would she like that? He'd admit the inexplicable quagmire of crime in human nature, sure. "Aren't we all mostly trudging along trying to keep our noses clean? Isn't that mostly what most people do?"

"So why become police?"

Emil turned to her in the car. He couldn't tell where she was going, and he certainly did not want to dredge up any murky events from a million years ago. "What gives, Elena? Are you trying to tell me something? A message in a bottle washed ashore? Some pus of confession at the bursting point?" He tried to laugh, to make light of her gravity. He wanted to do something silly, reach over and touch the hem of her dress or put his hand up under it. Touch her cheek because she was so soft and unmanly. But her aloof posture held him in check. He forced another laugh. "Come on now, look at this day. It's splendid. There's a word for you!"

"Splendid," she repeated. "There is a word that seldom fits." She didn't sound like an inquisition now, but resigned.

He opened his window. The air in the car had become swampy with unexpressed emotions. He had no wish to say another word all day if he could help it. A nice, uneventful quiet would suit him just fine. Then Elena surprised him by laughing. He laughed too, though he wasn't sure why. Relief, he guessed, that she had laughed and maybe this awful conversation was over and he could think again about the honeysuckle he would plant, or about touching his wife—massaging her deep wetness—and not about that gory crime scene Friday afternoon. …

It had been raining, a relatively slow day crime-wise. The report came in late: A woman sprawled on her living room floor, beaten to death with a plumber's wrench. Mike and Emil took the call, Mike looking at his watch and swearing. Blood splatters, the television blaring Oprah, loud laughter from the audience. Mike turned the TV off, using a latex-gloved left hand. "Lady must'a been hard of hearing," he said. The wrench was on the floor next to the corpse, her dress front a fouled red mess. "You think the plumber did it?"

Emil went to the kitchen to look at the backyard, to see if there was a garden or not, and a possible escape route. Mike went upstairs and found the husband balled up in a bedroom closet, dying of a prescription overdose; an apparent murder-suicide. The neighbor who'd heard the screams and made the 911 call said of the long-married, supposedly loving couple, "It just doesn't fit the pattern."

"You know about the pattern?" Emil asked.

The neighbor looked to Mike, who said, "Maybe there was a leak, the missus nagging hubby no end to fix? Or maybe you're involved."

The neighbor looked to Emil, who deadpanned, "Don't leave town. We may need to talk to you again."

"What did I do?" the neighbor asked, looking at Mike.

"Thank goodness for finding the husband, huh?" Mike said later in the car. "Or we'd've been at it all night.

He looked up to see if rain clouds were possible, but the smoggy sky was trapped inside itself. "No rain today," he said, moving along the garden path. The phone rang in the kitchen, but as he turned back toward the house the ringing stopped. He wouldn't have picked up anyhow. He fought to resist the lure of the garden, tending to this or that, losing himself in the work. Stopping near the tool bag containing the finger, he listened for Franco or any noises from the Noily side, but he was alone; even the birds had deserted, it seemed. He picked up the tool bag and carried it inside and down to the cool stone cellar where he placed it on a high shelf toward the back.

The rain finally let up for good on that long ago afternoon in Bled. The day Emil told his landlady he would be leaving, then bought the clock for his mother and decided after seeing Elena again that he would stay on another day. He sat in a café eating cold goat meat with hunks of bread until the rain stopped. Entering the house, he tripped over his suitcase standing in the small entryway. It had been neatly packed. His landlady smiled broadly, finished wiping her hands on her apron, and held out a moist palm to collect her key. Emil had paid all he owed; someone else was already occupying his room, she explained. He got the gist. He'd told her he was leaving; it was summer, the time when many visitors came to the lake; a student had arrived who would be upstairs for two weeks. "Good business this year," the lady of the house exclaimed, pleasure creasing her thick face. It was too late for Emil to tell her he'd had a change of heart. Okay, he was ready to go. He stepped into the parlor to remove his sweater, asked if it would be all right to leave his bag for an hour or two? Behind him the songbird trilled his lonely melody. Emil was tempted to think the bird was singing for him.

Seeing Elena outside the clock shop had altered everything; even the rain had seemed less wet. She'd flirted with him, he was sure of it. Maybe not flirted, but she hadn't been hostile. He walked to the tourist board only to find there were no rooms posted. It was the weekend; the town was full; a holiday feel pulsed from the people he passed on the street. The sun had broken out over the mountains and the trees glistened with silvery raindrops; the air was the freshest he had ever breathed. More or less following his feet, Emil walked toward Elena's hotel without allowing himself to think.

He sat on a bench opposite the hotel, alongside the lake, and stretched out his long legs. The sky was iridescent after the rain. Behind him a pair of swans glided effortlessly through the water. He watched them and decided they looked arrogant. The whole town began to seem small and precious to him, nothing like real life at all. He felt disgusted with himself and wanted to go far away from this too tidy, too pretty place. He stood up, shoving his hands into his jacket pockets, and turned to walk back to the center just as Elena emerged from the hotel's darkened entryway across the narrow road. He didn't care; this whole business of following her had been throwing time and money away. He saw that clearly now. But she crossed the road and walked directly toward him.

He took his hands out of his pockets, let them hang idly at his sides. He had no doubt made an ass of himself, and she would be coming over to tell him off. He wanted to leave, but she was definitely coming toward him. She wore a lavender skirt dotted with tiny flowers, a white blouse, and a cropped beige sweater. Emil was struck by how young she looked, almost a schoolgirl. She'd seemed older before, but now he couldn't say; she might be very young, and it occurred to him that she could have been frightened of him. He sat back down on the bench but thought that might be rude and stood up again.

"I saw you," she said. "The window in my room lets onto the lake. You were finding me?"

"I was finding you, yes."

Elena sat and looked him over, still standing. "The rain is stopped," she said. Emil looked up at the sky. She watched him. "You didn't know?"

"If it stopped raining?"

She nearly laughed. "It was me!"

Emil looked down at her; she wore a mocking smile. He studied her face, and she studied his. Her expression changed. "Sit," she said. He obeyed. "Tell me, who are you?"

He sat down, facing her. "My name is Emil Milosec. I came to find out what happened to my family."

Elena listened carefully. "*Your family?* Something happened to your family in the war, do you mean?"

He nodded, but Emil was done talking for now. He'd wanted to tell this woman everything; now he stared mutely at his hands, almost afraid to look at her. Hadn't she seen him in her cousin's shop in the city? Had he really been invisible to her? Was he supposed to admit he'd followed her all the way into the mountains with no other purpose, having dispensed in a flash with a lifetime of questions, dropped everything to follow her?

She studied him again in silence, chewing on her thumb. "Okay, good for now, that is all you can say, I understand. Now tell me what you do now."

Emil shook his head. "I want to get out of here. I want to leave. Will you come with me?"

"Now? To where?"

"Back to the city—to Ljubljana, tonight. Will you come?" Elena made a gesture with her hands, a small sound emitted from her throat, softly, a kitten's mewl of protest. "No," he said. "Of course not. I'm sorry, my request was insane … I'm sorry … I wasn't, I don't know what I was thinking."

"What is 'insane'?"

"What does it mean? It means crazy, loco … um … pazzo!"

"Pazzo?" She stared at him. Then she laughed, covering her mouth, and Emil laughed too.

"*Pazzo!*" he nearly shouted.

She looked at him. "What time are the buses?"

"Tonight?" Emil pulled the schedule out of his pocket. "There's a bus soon, at seven o'clock." He looked at his watch; it was five thirty.

She looked at her watch, sat quietly a few minutes chewing the thumb, and then she asked him, "You are certain of this?" He nodded. "You will wait?"

Emil shrugged. Would he wait? He was prepared to sleep in the woods as his father once had; he was prepared to camp out on this bench outside her hotel forever if she wished; yes, he would wait. "Yes," he told her. "I will wait as long as you need me to wait."

Elena rushed up to her room. She said she'd call the desk to request a light meal to take away, and she'd order a jitney into town. Twenty minutes later she emerged; this time a porter followed with her bag, and she carried a small wicker basket filled with sandwiches. A jitney pulled up to the hotel. She signaled to Emil. He crossed over and helped her into the cart. She ordered the driver to take them to the center. They stopped at the fat lady's house for Emil's suitcase. Elena waited in the jitney. At the station he paid for two bus tickets, but when he turned around Elena wasn't there. He found her hidden in the shadows. He took her bag and led her to the bus.

Traveling back down the mountain in the waning light, he worried a new worry. He'd borrowed money for the trip to Slovenia; he had written to his cousin and told her he would come; it was to be the great homecoming of the lost son, and he wouldn't have to spend money in Senice. Now he had an expensive girl at his side and no means to treat her right. He hated himself for worrying; it made him sullen and silent like his mother, chafing bitterly against the insults of his life. One thing about his father; he had not behaved like a disappointed man. His mother had been proud in Slovenia, and she was pretty, he remembered; proud of Ljpoj, of her place in the village, and her son. She had a vegetable garden that fed the family. In Brooklyn weeds filled her garden. She no longer bothered to make his dinner, just withered in her chair by the stove. Emil loathed what she'd become to the point where he could almost taste his mother's disappointed life. He was a harsh judge, pushing himself hard to make it in America. In contrast to his dour mother, this woman seated next to him was light and color and breath.

In his pocket was enough cash to eat soup for a few days and sleep where he could. He peeked at Elena, seated quietly beside him. Through the opening of her blouse he could just see the curve of her breast. Oh, yes, she would cost plenty; so self-contained and composed, and what else? Sad. Sad like an early death.

She turned to him. Her eyes were direct without revealing very much. He was astonished anew by her presence. "You want to ask me?" she asked him.

Was she mocking him again? Who was this woman he had followed into the mountains and was now luring back to the city? How often had she gone off with strange men like this?

"You want to ask my name, did you? But you know it?"

"I do know it," he said. "Your name is *Everything*."

"That name is senseless. And you propose to take me to bed with that name?"

Emil laughed. Her eyebrow went up. "Oh, I wasn't laughing at you!"

"I think not."

How direct she was. Sure, she talked big now but when they got to the city she'd go straight to her cousin. She must be playing with him, in full control. But she'd come this far, left Bled because he'd said he wanted her to. She said herself he intended to take her to bed. Was that all right? A woman who goes on holiday by herself, an Italian? Maybe she was hunting for a husband. There were women like that, or maybe she was a professional, a high-class tart. Look at her, Emil, you idiot, he thought—this woman could have any man she wanted. Look at her!

"You're Italian, yes?" he asked.

"Italian father, Austrian mother. From Trieste, a place without identity. You understand? You didn't know?"

Emil was quiet for a minute. "Trieste?" He shook his head. "No, I don't know Trieste."

She looked at him. "No?" He shook his head again. That was when she told him of her home, that place of sea and sky and mountain, about the apple orchard. When she stopped talking he had to look away, hide his flammable desire.

Finally he said, "Where will you stay in Ljubljana?"

"Where do you think?"

Emil made no reply. In his mind he called her Everything.

Elena asked if he would like a sandwich, and they each ate one, washed down with a bottle of red wine passed between them; they had no cups. They ate in silence, and Elena soon slept as the bus carried them into the night, toward the city and who knew what, thought Emil as he watched her sleep.

Ten days later they stood on a stone bridge in Ljubljana, arching over the Ljubljanica River, a brackish and lazily flowing river, more a large canal through the center of town. Copper gargoyles stood sentry at either end of the bridge, the copper long since oxidized an acid green. Emil's hand brushed Elena's, resting on the stone parapet. He dared not touch her more. He could count on an erection at the slightest glance; no matter that they were standing on a public bridge in the late afternoon. A small boat slipped below their legs and passed out under the other side of the bridge. He checked his trousers then guided Elena over to the other side of the river. The time was well past for Emil to have left Slovenia. He'd altered his flight once and they would not grant him another extension on his visa. Elena was paying for everything. He was shameless in his desire for her and spent her money. She told him they were not meant to be lovers, but it had happened, and they'd yielded. How did she know they were not meant to be lovers? Emil didn't ask. The following afternoon he would board a plane for the long flight back to New York City; what else mattered but today?

They walked slowly along the river walk until they found themselves in an obscure part of the city where the river had grown wide and become commercial. There were carts and trucks and soldiers near the bank, and larger cargo-carrying hulks on the water, and flat barges. There were signs too of war damage. Some of the barges were being loaded as the soldiers looked on. Wooden barrels lined the wide banks, and warehouses stood along a river road.

Emil and Elena walked blindly, paying little attention to where they went. For days they had walked the city this way. Eating, bathing, walking were only interludes between touching; between late mornings and long nights in their hotel, afternoons spent in bed. They spoke few words to each other. Soon they would part, probably forever, and their caresses were permeated by that inevitable ending. Elena would board a train bound for Trieste. Emil would see her off, and in the afternoon he would go to the airport alone. He avoided thinking of tomorrow, as if that could prevent it from arriving.

They were lost. The area they'd wandered into was worlds apart from the center. A policeman approached. Emil removed Elena's arm from his, where she had looped it tightly so they were connected as they walked. "What are you doing here?" the policeman asked them in Slovenian. Emil answered as smoothly as he could that they were looking for a café, for supper. He said, "My wife is hungry." After two weeks his Slovenian had improved. The policeman looked at Elena the way a man used to unquestioned authority looks, with cutting suspicion and vulgar directness. Elena stood still. The policeman turned back to Emil. "There are no restaurants here; go back the way you came." He pointed, using his automatic rifle, toward the center.

"Of course." Emil said. He took Elena's arm again and they turned around to retrace their steps.

"Emil," she said, her voice hushed, "guns are in some of—how do you call those?"

"Barrels. I saw them; they're rifles. We should not be here."

"For what do you think they have these many guns?"

"Not now, Elena," Emil said. "And not in English."

The policeman followed them. The faces on the people were shut and unfriendly, the air suddenly close and warm. They walked carefully, trying to seem unconcerned. Emil sensed the policeman still behind them. He pinched Elena's arm and whispered to her to drop her purse.

"Why?" she whispered back.

"Just do it."

As he knelt to retrieve the dropped bag, he barely glanced behind him and saw in those few seconds that the policeman was gone, but now someone else was behind them, someone he thought was familiar. But who did Emil know in Ljubljana? No one.

"Is everything as it should be?" Elena asked.

"How many people do you know in the city?"

"My cousin, his family. One or two others. Why?" She sounded frightened.

"I'm not sure. … the policeman is gone, but someone else is—"

"What?"

Emil remembered the man's face. He was one of the men from the clock shop in Bled, the one who'd said to get rid of the fake American. He'd followed him all this way? Had he followed him for days? *Was* he following him? Why? Emil recalled the shop, the two men who had emerged from the back, who'd laughed at him. Were they Communists, or Partisans? Leftover Nazis? Why follow him? Because he was American? Or formerly Slovenian? That made no sense.

As they neared the center of town, enveloped now in peach-colored dusk, the man from the clock shop closed in. "You will stop now," he said, placing a hand on Emil's shoulder from behind. Emil instantly resented being touched. He tensed and then jerked his elbow up, catching the shorter man on the chin. The man fell back a few steps but produced a revolver from his pocket and, quickly regaining his balance, pointed the gun at Emil, keeping the weapon low, not to attract attention.

Emil dropped his hands to his sides. "What do you want with me?"

"I will ask the questions," the man said. Emil got the idea. "I will see your identification papers now, your passports."

"Give him nothing," Elena said in a loud whisper. The man looked at her. "What identification have you?" she asked him. "You are polizia, communista, maybe passport thief?" She spoke to the man in a Serbo-Croatian mix of words. He ignored her.

"This woman," he said to Emil, "who is not your wife, is a kind of thief. Did you know that? We will have no betraying thieves in Slovenia."

Emil lifted his hands cautiously; he thought the man must be an extremist from one side or another. That or simply mad. "I will get my passport, you understand?" he said in English, pointing to his breast pocket, saying again with emphasis, "Pasoš." The man nodded. His back was to the river, and he was standing too close. There were few people out at that twilight hour on that side of the river. The streetlights were not yet lit. They were standing at a narrow place where after the sidewalk ended the grassy bank was less than two yards wide. Emil pulled his passport out quickly, raised his arm and threw it at the man's face. The man blinked, took a step back to dodge the flying booklet. As he threw the passport, Emil simultaneously lowered his shoulder and thrust into the man, shoving and tackling him to the ground. The gun flew. Emil was instantly on top of the man. He felt no surge of rage, no flash of anger. He felt blank and very, very calm. The man was down, and Emil punched him hard in the face. Thick blood spurted out of his nose; he moaned once. Emil punched again, harder, and the man stopped moving. Emil rolled him to the edge of the embankment and pushed. There was a small splash as the man hit the water. Emil watched him sink, then saw his legs kick and thought the man was coming up for air. He unclenched his fists. The night around them was too quiet, too eternal. There was a stillness, an emptiness; what happened to the flow of time? Where were all the people? No witnesses. And where was Elena?

She had the revolver, held it tight in her right hand. She asked in a whisper, "Is he dead?"

"No. I don't think so. He'll be all right. Come on, let's get out of here." He picked up his passport and then reached for the gun, but Elena moved away, her face pale. "Elena? Let's go!" he said.

"More horror," she whispered.

"What did you say?" She stood, stuck to the spot, moving her head slowly, holding the gun. He reached out and grabbed her wrist, pulled the gun from her hand. He held onto her arm and hurried her toward the bridge they had only that afternoon stood so lustfully on. He pulled her to him, checked the revolver, and slipped it into his pocket. "Okay," he said, "not too fast; mingle." The other side of the river was more crowded with people. He held her arm tight. "Listen to me; do you trust your cousin?"

"My cousin?" She seemed dazed. "I trust my cousin. Of course."

"We'll stay someplace else tonight. Would he go pick up our things out of the hotel without asking a lot of questions?"

"Why? Yes, yes, he will do that."

"Good. We have to be careful. We don't want more trouble."

"You know this?"

"I don't know anything."

"But you know that man?"

"I don't know him, but I did see him in Bled. He's maybe secret police. Or Partisan? I don't know."

"You saw him in Bled?" Her expression was agonized; that was the word Emil thought of. "This is already big trouble."

"Not for us," Emil said. He took her small hand and held on to it. "Tomorrow we leave. For tonight, we disappear." He looked at her. "You're not a thief, are you?" he asked with a laugh.

She didn't reply. She looked abjectly terrified.

Emil smiled. "My Everything," he said, lightly touching her hair. He felt exhilarated. Something primal had stirred: He'd defended his lover, they were the beginning of time, he was Adam, she was Elena.

After Elena contacted her cousin, Emil took her to a café and over a stiff drink laughed at his football maneuver. He'd been sent out as a guard in high school, and it had paid off tonight. He was a guy from the United States of America, a man who knew football and how to fight back. He tried to explain to Elena, but she sat closed off and grim, nervously kneading an invisible shape with her fingers.

Later, after Elena slept and the exhilaration he'd felt had passed, he recalled first the policeman following them and then the man from Bled, and he became frightened of something darkly Eastern European. Something he had been free of in Brooklyn but still knew in his bones. It came from inside and it was a fear that could corrode, and he felt the grip of it in his lungs and throat and tried to shake it off. The man came at them waving a gun; it was self-defense—anyone could see that, he argued to himself. He was glad Elena was asleep, that she did not see his fear.

By morning he'd put the man out of his mind; edited, deleted, excised. Elena was quiet and tense. They had breakfast sent up to the room. When the time came—the deathly unavoidable time—he took her to her train. The weapon was in his pocket, wiped clean. At the station he tucked it into the luggage car of a train bound for Belgrade. He stood and watched Elena's train to Trieste pull away and disappear. That she was gone, that he did not expect to see her ever again, canceled everything else in a heaving yawn of emptiness.

He had laughed that Saturday, so many years later, in the car filled with groceries, and Elena had turned to him and smiled, the cloud lifted from her face. He'd flexed the muscle of his cop's manly know-how, had once again put down the serpent of fear. Or so he'd thought. He'd been satisfied; Elena was safe, and he believed she would always be safe with him. And he hadn't given her curious remarks another thought. Until today.

FOUR

This is now bone of my bones, and flesh of my flesh; she shall be called Woman, because she was taken out of Man.

The Fall of Man, Book of Genesis

He stood at the sink washing the dishes dumped there and abandoned since the finger showed up. That night in Ljubljana, the man's legs moved; Emil was sure they had. And that Saturday in the car, was Elena trying to say something specific about the man? The man who'd called her a—what? A betraying thief, was that what he'd said? Was Emil wandering the past senselessly, or were clues coming up that he needed to examine? Clues to what?

A case of mistaken identity is what Emil had assumed all those years ago, without even giving the event that much conscious thought. It was around the time Yugoslavia, and specifically Slovenia, had lost Trieste to Italy. There was plenty of hatred between the Italians and Slovenians, wartime atrocities starting with the Fascists and then the Slovene Partisans retaliating. He'd guessed some political angle related to that. He hadn't thought about it, really. Why would it concern him? And there was Elena in Slovenia, coming from Trieste, some confusion over her identity, perhaps. There was his own mixed-up nationality—it was a volatile time, an era of distrust; who knew who anybody was anymore after a world war?

He'd been almost physically sick, sending her off on the train that day. He wanted to curl into the fetal pose, cry like a boy, spit like his mother, faint like a girl, pull his hair out and wail. She was gone, and there was no way to imagine ever seeing her again. He had to go to work. He owed money, some for school, and then the trip to Europe, and Elena. Elena . . . A man came at them with a gun in war-eaten Europe; real spies were running around all over the place; anybody else would have done the same. "The cold war, for Christ's sake!" he said into the kitchen, as if he'd been accused and that was his defense.

Standing at the sink, his hands soapy, bubbles sliding down the plate he held, Emil searched for a context to events that had taken place nearly forty years ago. Did anything add up? This was what he thought he knew.

One: Elena's cousin owned a glass shop in Ljubljana. Her father owned a glass business in Trieste. What did her father do during the war? Could *he* have been involved?

Two: Elena left Bled with Emil, at his suggestion. *If* she left at his suggestion—a disturbing thought. Did she leave with him spontaneously, or not? Did she go to Bled on holiday, as her cousin suggested, or did something else take her there? But didn't the cousin say she was on holiday?

Three: That rainy afternoon outside the clock shop, Emil thought she came looking for him. But if that was so, why skitter off when he asked her for coffee? Did they meet by chance, or did she have an errand to do with the clock repair? Then the clock guy followed them to Ljubljana. Was that what happened?

His mind now tensely alert, he turned the water on and rinsed the plate. "If I emptied the goddamn dishwasher, I wouldn't have to wash these," he said aloud. He disliked the chore of emptying the dishwasher. He knew it made no difference, hand wash or machine, but the idle activity gave him a chance to breathe as disturbing memories crowded in. He rinsed the rest of the dishes, throwing himself into the task. That was what he was doing in his kitchen in Brooklyn, but in his mind he was in Slovenia, occupying the past, a world that was currently growing more real than the present. He was up to his old trick of sneaking up on the facts.

Okay: How could Elena have been looking for him at the clock shop? He was staying in a private room, not a hotel where she could have easily looked him up—assuming she knew his name, which she did not. He was following Elena, but was she also following him? "Come on, Emil, *think*! You didn't plan to buy a clock." So was the guy from the clock shop—or someone—following *her*? Then him? Then them? Who followed whom first? Knock, knock. Follow. Follow who? Follow me all the way to the end. But if she was on her way to the clock shop that afternoon and was not following him, she would have been very surprised to see him exit the shop with a package under his arm. And then why take up with him later? It was an unsettling thought: that Elena might have become his lover because she believed he was in some way involved in an intrigue that also involved her. Was that possible?

Emil rubbed his head roughly with his knuckles. Thoughts were forming that he would rather shove away. They'd never discussed any of this—he hadn't asked, but it seemed to him now as if two time frames were trying to merge: an insignificant day—returning home from the grocery, during which the troubling incident of the man in the river was brought up—and the present situation of the finger in the garden that had beside it a ring that was probably Elena's. It seemed as if Elena herself were eluding him. What did he know of her past? He'd never met her family. He'd never been to Trieste. Six months after their first encounter she'd called to say she would come to New York. He had just been assigned to a squad and took her call like an eager, drooling puppy. She came for a couple of months and then left again at her father's death, only to reappear with bundles of cash. From his point of view they were lovers who became husband and wife. Was there an alternate truth? The thought felt like the floor falling out underneath him. Maybe he should stop searching for answers altogether.

One of the other cops on his squad liked to call him Tombstone. He'd say, "Do you ever pass the time of day, Tombstone, ask a guy how he's doing?" It hadn't always been that way. His sister used to tease him when he'd ply her with questions, "Ask me no questions, little brother, I will tell you no lies." His mother telling him only God can know.

The conversation with Elena had been left unresolved that Saturday morning, had drifted with her laughter into mutual silence. The silences that intimates often left dangling. He hadn't heard her all the way to her meaning, or he had assumed something about what she'd meant, which amounted to the same thing as not having heard her at all. She'd brought up the forbidden past—a taboo, tacitly agreed upon to avoid. He'd toyed with her, asked her if she had some deep, dark secret to confess.

And now he thought, she maybe did.

How many conversations end satisfactorily anyway? The phone rings, the kids scream, the point is missed or lost or badly expressed, somebody gets angry; it just doesn't turn out as planned, what a person meant to say.

He dried his hands on a dish towel, idly opened a cabinet door and shut it again. *Was* she trying to tell him something that day or not? He was growing frustrated, circling with no end in sight. He wanted to hear

Elena's voice, to replay that conversation, rake the past up out of its oblivion, and make the sound of her come alive again.

No mention is made in the Book of Genesis of the creation of sound. The firmament, the greater light of the day and the moon's lesser light at night; the mists and the four rivers; herbs and animals; and finally Adam and Eve—no word of creating sound. What happened to sound? They forgot? *He* forgot?

Let there be light; let the earth bring forth living creatures, and so on, the Bible says, but of the creation of speech or of sight or of smell or of touch—any of the five senses—not a word; a lapse in the story. Known are the objects of creation, but not *how* they are known. I sense, therefore I am? Then the trouble began: God came looking for Adam and called to him, *Where art thou?* And Adam answered, *I heard thy voice in the garden, and I was afraid*. Why afraid? God wanted to know. *I was afraid because I was naked*. And God was right on it: *Who told thee that thou wast naked*?

Yeah. Or told thee to be afraid? It all came down to old Mr. Snake. How he talked Eve into eating the delectable, forbidden fruit. Blame it all on Eve, weak little Eve, who couldn't resist. That wasn't how Elena saw it. She said Eve was adventurous, took a chance, wasn't stuck in an obedient, ignorant rut like Adam. She ate, and then she handed the apple to Adam, singing the praises of its ambrosial taste: "Try something new, Adam, go on, don't be afraid." So he ate and the fall of man began. Was it bit by bit? Or wham, a head-hitting fall from grace?

Maybe God wasn't around for a few days; maybe they thought they'd get away with it. But then there'd be this new, gnawing guilt on the couple. And once the cat's out, once you know what's what, you can't go back; be like reversing puberty, or virginity. It's a one-way ticket.

Emil had always wondered what was so wrong with sex, why all the biblical no-no? God was up there all on his own; was that it? No lover to soften the night, no sweet place to ease the pressures of a busy mind? No release? No comfort? Why create Eve and Adam with the equipment for it if sex was taboo? Ah, a test: If man behaves, he gets to smell the roses; if not, toil and care, and more fucking. Incarnate: made flesh. *Embodied.* If God is the creator, he created the genitals. "A good trade-off if you ask me," Emil said. He felt anger rising through his own flesh. "I'd have eaten the goddamn apple, you bet I would. Ten times over!"

He threw the dish towel on the kitchen counter and walked into the dining room, stood a minute, fuming. There sat the letters, looking up at him. He turned back to the kitchen. After that first succulent bite, did Adam ever hear Eve again? "Sound, sound, *sound*! Where are the fucking birds?"

He welled with a seamy sense of things left unfinished. Cold again radiated from the pit of his stomach. He massaged his hands, caught another mental glimpse of himself shooting into the pepper patch. How could he explain his behavior? And that was *before* the finger. There had to be a lead somewhere in whatever it was Elena meant by bringing up the man in the river that morning, and that other bit she'd said that day about the nature of evil, and people hiding. People hiding what? What did she care what people held hidden?

He turned to the stove, reached for the espresso maker, methodically filled the ancient carafe with water, unscrewed the lid and slowly measured out just so much coffee, lit a match and set the pot on the stove to cook. He'd have another cup of coffee, that's what he would do, another cup of Joe to clear his head.

He wished he could see her now, could see Elena's face, to ask her what she'd meant that Saturday morning in the car. There were times, like now, when he refused to accept death. She was there somewhere; it couldn't be possible—the total annihilation of a person. If he concentrated with all he had, could he will her back, not her but her essence? That was the sort of childish hope that he believed sent people into religion in the first place. First, wishful thinking: Our dead are safe with God. Second, pure ego: We'll all be dead one day; nobody comes out of it alive. Can't have that, says the ego, can't contemplate total oblivion: not pissing first thing in the morning, no hunger in the evening, no cool, clear water or touching a woman under the covers ... no dreaming, no hoping; no sky, blue and vast ... ergo, the ego will not allow death. Ergo, he could, if he tried hard enough—really tried—conjure up his dead wife. If a garden—life—was God's signature, what was death? His canceled check?

"Oh, shut it, Emil." His voice echoed loud in the silent kitchen.

What *about* the man in the river? He longed to pick out the subtleties in her voice, the innuendo of her body language. How had she moved that morning? How were her hands? Such slender hands, so quick with gesture. Her nervous way of moving her fingers so they gave out to people while at the same time pulling away. A cop, a professional listener, and he had failed to hear the words of the one voice that had mattered most. That was the nature of his regret. If she were here now, in the kitchen, he'd sit Elena down and grill her like the cop he was until he knew exactly every particle there was to know about the man in the river and any other secrets and clues concerning this case that she held deep in her hidden, dead self.

But—wasn't the severed finger the point? And wasn't the ring a master clue?

Emil burst out of the kitchen and ran upstairs. The ring had to be Elena's, and he could prove it. He pushed in the bedroom door, out of breath. At her bureau, to the left of the bathroom door, he tugged and yanked the top drawer off its tracks and dumped the contents. Shimmering panties and satin bras cascaded, waves of fabric landing softly on the floor. Little embroidered jewel boxes tumbled down last on a cushion of camisoles and intimate wear in pastel pinks, yellows, greens, black and navy blue. A string of pearls fell out, and a silver bracelet, some loose earrings. A sheer apricot-colored flowered slip settled last on the heap of finery. He knew that slip; he'd removed it from her body more than once.

Then Emil smelled her. The familiar sachet and perfume mingled with her scent. He didn't know the names of those scents but she was present to him in their lingering fragrance. He caught his face in the mirror above her bureau and quickly looked away. He stood above the pile of her underwear, fingers resting on a corner of the bureau, wanting to sink down, to press his face into her intimacy. Panties lined with a thin tissue of cotton covering a woman's genitals, the smallest swath of cloth. Her vagina, the one that made him dance, the slit that stuck.

His cop's eyes narrowed, and, in spite of how tossed he felt on the sea of her scent, he studied the scene and found what he was looking for, reached down and grabbed the embroidered box that contained her rings. There would be the garnet that had belonged to her great-aunt. The ring his niece had given her from New Mexico, a veined turquoise stone that Elena never wore. The tiny pearl ring he'd bought for her when she'd said she was coming to New York that first time—he'd borrowed money for that too, to present her with a gift. And there should also be the opal that was her keepsake from that final trip to Trieste. Emil turned the contents of the box over onto the palm of his hand. Little rings with gold or silver bands spilled out. All accounted for—all but the opal.

"Bingo," he said.

He knelt down to sift through the lingerie to be certain the opal was not among the garments when an acrid smell of burning assaulted his nostrils; awful, like the smell of burning flesh. Emil rushed back downstairs. The coffee!

There was no flame, only the sharp smell and heavy white smoke. He turned off the gas. The water had boiled out; the coffee was now thick black putty stuck to the top of the pot. He swore loudly in the empty kitchen. Using the dish towel he placed the pot on a wooden cutting board to cool, the empty ring box still clutched in his left hand. He would have to soak the pot in vinegar to loosen the tar. He opened the garden door, adding the burned coffee stink to the thick humid air outside. He sat down hard on a chair by the open door, his shoulders bent forward. "Shit," he said.

He clutched the embroidered ring box as if it were the flotation device from an airplane seat that he hung on to for dear life. Should he have gotten rid of Elena's lingerie? And replaced it with what? Empty drawers? What was wrong with her underclothes staying where they were? He knew she wasn't coming back for them. He wasn't delusional or perverse. But why should he purge his house of his wife's intimacy? What becomes of all the underwear anyway? His sister would have told him it was unhealthy. "Get rid of it, Emil," she'd have said. "It's no good talking to ghosts, certainly no good keeping a ghost's brassieres." If Lisle were alive to speak.

He was surrounded by ghosts.

He squeezed the box Elena had held. She had touched this box, and now it was his to do with as he pleased. And it pleased him to keep it. He opened his hand, squeezed the box again. His thoughts leaped by themselves to a memory of her small hand on his penis. She had touched him, tentatively at first, smiled up at him, then more bold, more sure. Over the years her hands so familiar; soft, private hands, the warm sensing material of her flesh, her hand upon his cock.

At the very beginning, in Ljubljana, early on, in the hotel bed, she had taken him into her mouth, caught him by surprise. She held him, the stalk of him encircled in her insignificant fist; she placed the tip of him into her mouth, moved her tongue leisurely over the surface. Her face down there, below his belly, into the tuft that announced his maleness.

She looked up at Emil and laughed, her eyes merry. "I can sing into it." She was teasing, having fun with him, holding him like a microphone.

"*What?*"

"Name a song. A sexy song. I like big band songs; do you?"

He dropped his head onto the pillow. "Don't, Elena."

"Why not?" She continued, hummed Cole Porter's "Got You Under My Skin," sang a few lines. "I know the words in English, listen: *In spite of a warning voice that comes in the night … don't you know, little fool, you never can win. … I've got you under my skin.* Pretty good, no? Cole Porter, yes? For the big American man." She laughed again, murmured something as she worked him—he could not deny it—expertly. Emil, with his eyes closed, yielded. And what did he do next in that intensely joyous moment—*her* joy—the young and bullish Emil? He pulled her head up and laughed. A laugh that was mean and cold. He told her he did not like her doing that. She was inexperienced, he said, which was a lie. She had done this before. (She admitted years later, after her father was dead, that she'd had lovers in Trieste. "Lovers, *plural?*" he asked, his gut tightening.) He was ashamed of himself only a minute later for laughing at her. And he winced now, all these decades later, to recall his behavior. It stung him, remembering what was hidden in the dusty years. He'd laughed and pulled her away! Had she ever forgotten? Or forgiven?

He stopped her because she was too good at it, and how could he control her if she already knew how to work a man? Maybe it was only her past he'd wanted to control. And maybe a repulsive side of him had reared up, wanting to clip her wings. Not so she couldn't fly, just not too far or high, and maybe that was not possible with the one who ruled the bed.

Today all his memories ended in bitterness, sordid and shaming.

He placed the empty ring box carefully on the table, next to the mustard-colored vase, as if building an altarpiece. A man could drown in regrets.

He stood up, closed and locked the garden door. There was one solid clue he didn't have to argue with: His house had been entered, Elena's lingerie handled, her ring taken and placed on a severed female finger. Again he fought down a sharply rising fury. Calm was required, a cool examination of the facts. The perpetrator had acted with boldness aforethought and flagrant disregard. This was something he could chew on. This was something he could wrestle with. What he needed now was to name a suspect. Could Paulien Vandervell be his primary?

The last two years had played out like a dirge inside his head, a low violin wail of mourning that had never risen all the way to the surface, a silent siren of grief. Emil might end his days as his mother had, buried alive in sorrow. But Detective Milosec was now on the case; he'd been pulled out of his somnolence to pursue a crime whose nature he did not yet know.

PART FOUR

CONVERSATION IN THE GARDEN

ONE

In those days there was no king in Israel; everyone did what was right in his own eyes.

Book of Judges

Emil squinted into the filmy sunlight like a lizard crawling out from under a rock. He blinked. The air was a furnace. He wore a white polo shirt under a lightweight linen sports coat, his appearance coolly relaxed, but inside Emil was coiled tight in the glaring light. Beneath his jacket was the gun he'd fired into the garden the day before, his Smith & Wesson .38 Special. The weapon was slung in its holster under his left arm, invisible to the casual onlooker. He paused on the top step to place a pair of sunglasses over his eyes.

Before exiting, he'd carefully replaced Elena's lingerie. He'd taken the packet of her letters off the dusty dining room table and placed them in the freezer, behind a bottle of Stolichnaya vodka and a frozen T-bone steak.

His car was parked a few blocks away in a private lot owned by Mrs. Santiana. Five other cars were parked in the vacant lot adjacent to her house. Behind the house was a garden. More cement than earth, but the open areas had plantings: cockscomb and four o'clock, other easy to grow annuals, and cherry tomatoes. Mrs. Santiana also had two very healthy peach trees. The fact of the peach trees had convinced Emil to rent parking from her.

Stray cats were a problem. Mrs. Santiana fed them, and they were everywhere all over the car park. Emil sometimes had to wade through waves of swirling felines to reach his car. They pissed and sprayed at will and sat on the car hoods sunning themselves in winter. Mrs. Santiana said she could not turn them away; they were God's creatures that he had sent to her door, so what else could she do? Spay them, Elena tried to suggest. Emil pointed out that Mrs. Santiana would not subscribe to such a procedure; at the very least she would be tempting fate.

"Dios," Mrs. Santiana told Elena, "to cut the little cat down there, no, this I cannot do. If God did, okay, but me, no, I am not God." Mrs. Santiana was cheerful about any burden life imposed on her; feeding too many cats or seeing to her sickly husband, it did not matter. She lifted her cares lightly, hoisted them uncomplaining, bending a little more with each added weight, and still she remained glad. Mrs. Santiana with her luscious peach trees was the gladdest person Emil had ever known, considering, it seemed to him, she had very little tangibly to be glad about. Elena ate the peaches Mrs. Santiana gave her each summer, voraciously sucking their juicy pulp, and let go of the question of spaying the cats.

Mrs. Santiana was after Emil to adopt one of the strays. "You should have a kitten; you are too alone over there since La Señora is gone." She crossed herself and sighed heavily. "La Señora Elena is in the arms of heaven now."

In the arms of heaven's landlord, Emil thought.

"The God above has a plan for each of us, Meester Meelosake."

Emil nodded his head solemnly. "A plan? Even for me, Mrs. Santiana?"

"For you too, don't worry; he has his eye on you, and the little cats too—all of us." She smiled one of her rare smiles, bright enough to lift the whole earth and everything on it if anyone ever saw it shine.

To get to the car park, Emil had to walk past Rudy's Corner Market. There stood Rudy in the doorway of his lousy market with its dim-watt lighting against anyone seeing too well inside, the trademark toothpick balanced on his lower lip. "Morning, Milosec," he called out, though it was nearly noon.

Emil glanced at his watch: eleven ten. "Rudy," Emil replied through a frown.

"Hot enough for you?"

"Hot enough," Emil said without stopping. Albert's head popped out of the sidewalk cellar opening. Albert had antennae. He was supposed to be unloading boxes down in the cellar, but it never failed: His father spoke, and Albert's head popped up out of the hatch as if father and son were attached by a wire, a puppet act.

Emil heard Rudy say, "Have you taken care of that garden?"

He swung around. "What was that?"

Rudy reached for the toothpick with his stubby fingers, swabbed a side tooth for a few seconds before responding. "What's that?" he asked Emil.

"Did you say something about a garden?"

"Me? Nah. I was talking to Albert here. I asked him, 'You taken care with that guard rail?'—you know, to the cellar." Emil looked at him; that was not what he'd heard Rudy say. "You know," Rudy continued, "so passersby don't fall into the pit, break a leg, sue." Rudy pointed to the cellar. Emil looked toward the opening. Albert's head was at sidewalk level, just his big, ugly head grinning at Emil like a Halloween pumpkin. "You can't be too careful nowadays," Rudy added. "People sue as fast as they fart."

"Right," said Emil. Rudy was a lying lout. Or had Emil only imagined him saying something about a garden? Either way it was best to keep moving.

"Everything all right over at your place?" Rudy added. He was smirking, but that was not unusual with him.

What did he mean by *that*? Why wouldn't everything be all right at Emil's? But he'd already said too much to the greasy grocer cheat. Not turning, he waved a hand. "Fine," he said, picking up his pace to get away. "Why not?"

A few minutes later he was closing the padlock over the chain-link gate at Mrs. Santiana's, his car backed out and idling on the street, when he heard Franco call to him from the corner. Emil looked up. His neighbor was walking briskly toward him. Franco's appearance always surprised Emil; for a man whose diet seemed to consist of too many beers, he was still trim. He wasn't tall but not short either—medium—and his crew cut worked with his face, his coffee skin and Mayan nose. "Amigo, I am glad to find you."

"Why?" Emil muttered under his breath. "Why on earth are you glad to find me, Franco?"

They both looked toward Mrs. Santiana who just then came out of her house and stood beneath the red aluminum awning over her doorway. She wore a pink-flowered housedress, her body like a tube of pasta. "Buen día, Meester Meelosake," she called to Emil from her top step. Emil waved and smiled. "Y tu, Franco," she continued. "Como'sta La Señora Marta, eh?"

There followed a spitfire conversation in Spanish between Franco and Mrs. Santiana concerning Franco's old aunt. Emil tried to slip away into his car, but Franco was quickly at his side. "Okay, Okay, sí, Señora," he heard him tell Mrs. Santiana. Then to Emil, "Listen, amigo, I am wondering, could you give me a lift?"

"Something wrong with your car? Or did they finally tow it for those unpaid summonses?"

"You don't have to pay those."

"That's right, I forgot, they write them out for the fun of it."

"Sí. Also, they can never collect."

"You got it all figured out, have you?"

Franco shrugged, lifting his hands, palms outward. "My car needs something in the garage, maybe una carburetor."

"Uh-huh. Well, where you headed, because I'm going over to Queens."

"Amazing, my friend, because I am going there myself."

"To Queens?" Franco nodded. Emil eyed him; Queens was huge. He disliked Queens, which he knew was irrational, based on nothing, maybe the architecture, the blandness of the place, the insane way they named the streets; he just didn't like Queens. Plenty of people from Brooklyn didn't.

As if reading his thought, Franco said, "I don't like Queens, but anywhere you drop me is good."

"Uh-huh, okay, get in. And do me a favor; buckle up your safety belt."

Emil waited until Franco complied, then headed out, going west on Metropolitan Avenue, taking a right onto Kent, heading north to McGuiness Boulevard and across the Pulaski Bridge, which carried him over the Newtown Creek into Queens. They were quiet in the car until Franco broke the silence: "You are well, hombre?"

Emil looked sideways at him. "Couldn't be better. Why?"

"Nothing. You look maybe—what I'm saying—haunted. A little."

"Uh-huh. What's up, Franco?"

"Up? Nothing, the usual. And you?"

"I mean, where are you going?"

"To Queens, like you."

"Queens something liked a hundred square miles, and we're in it now, Franco."

"Sí."

"Where do you want to be let off, 'cause I'm nearly where I need to be."

"Where is that?"

Emil looked at Franco. Franco smiled then looked out his window. Operating on the idea that giving a little something would yield a bigger something, Emil told Franco, "I'm cutting over to a dry-ice place." He turned onto Borden Avenue, crossed over the Dutch Kills, took a sharp right onto 29th Street.

They were in sight of the Long Island Railroad tracks, an industrial zone that could be anywhere on earth with the element common to all such locations: it was bone ugly. Ideal locales to dump illegal waste or dead bodies: along unused train tracks, behind industrial lots, or into the creek. Cops hated calls to places like this. A body could be coming undone for weeks before discovery, a juicy mess, and extra tough to ID. People were never seen; they were there working, but no one walked, no one stuck around, and no one ever saw a thing. This was the bottom end of capitalism, where grunt labor and lowlife corruption toiled side by side, an industrial zone, about as far from Eden as a city can get.

"So you are having a picnic today, mi amigo?"

Emil switched on his right turn signal. He pulled over at a no parking/loading sign next to what looked to be a chemical storage outfit. Multicolored, rusting metal barrels filled a large yard surrounded by a high chain-link fence. Emil wondered how storage containers could be allowed to rust like that; it couldn't be doing the materials inside very much good. "Okay, Franco," he said, looking at him. "What gives? You're up to something, so let's have it."

"Me? No, hombre, I think it is you who is up to something."

The car was running with the air conditioning on. Emil's buttock muscles contracted. He turned off the engine. A few seconds later he and Franco simultaneously rolled down their windows. Heat climbed in like an unwelcome guest with sweaty palms, instantly canceling the cooled air. There was a hum, the at-large, never-ceasing industrial *om* coupled with the muffled sounds of traffic. Otherwise where they sat was oddly quiet.

Hang on just one second; *what secrets?* Emil hit the mental brakes, screeched to a hard stop: In her letter Elena said something about secrets—what was that about? Did she say Trieste? He had the sinking feeling he'd left something undone, like left the gas on; he'd better turn the car around—

Franco was staring at him. Emil adjusted his expression, turned to face his neighbor. "All right, Franco, what've you got?"

"What I have got is some man swinging into your garden like a spider in the night."

"How? Down the *back* wall? How many?"

"Just one."

"Last night? And this is true?"

"Sí, verdad!"

"What happened exactly?"

"I am asleep in my chair—sometimes I fall to sleep in my garden, once in a while." Emil kept himself from snickering at Franco omitting that he'd drunk himself to sleep. "I am awake, and what do I hear? Someone is on the wall. Am I dreaming? But no, I am awake. Quick, I sneak over to the fence."

Emil nodded. "Then what?"

"All in black from head to feet, this hombre; then he is over the wall—at the little pool of fish you have—and, amigo, this guy looks like he knows what he is doing, like in a movie, this Rambo, I can tell you. How does he squeeze his self into the skinny space from that fence to the wall?"

Elena's fear come true: the back wall breached. "Did he have a weapon?"

"Too dark to see."

"All right. Then what?"

"I hear him move. No sound, then small noises, like leaves. Then I hear nothing. Minutes like hours, and I cannot move, and, hombre, I have to use the toilet, because this is why I woke in the first place." He looked at Emil who was staring out through the windshield, listening. "Then I hear a cat, 'Mew,' and then I don't hear any cat, and then the guy is near the tree you have, you know the small one with white flowers?"

"The dogwood?"

"Is that how you call it? Too bad it didn't bark last night. So the guy jumps again—this hombre must be made of rubber bands or else has a spider's web—back up on the wall. Then he is gone."

"Interesting. Why didn't you call the cops?"

Franco shot Emil a look. "First I have to pee," he said, sarcastic. "No offense, my friend, I am not on the same team as those; I don't like police around me. Except you. Besides, what did he do?"

"Trespassing is enough."

Franco made a face. "These cops, they are going to care that a Puerto Rican has been trespassed, and not me but my neighbor? No." Emil smiled halfway. "So all night I am lying inside my house, but I don't sleep. Let's face it, amigo, what does this guy want with me? I am thinking he wants you. I am thinking, did he go inside and kill you? I am thinking all kinds of things. Maybe some guy you put in jail is out and he wants you dead. I think I should call to you to see are you alive or dead? But I'll wait until morning because I think this man did not have time to go inside and kill you. And I was right because here you are. And this morning you were outside. There is a small space in the wall where I can see, so I see you seeing something. I see the bag, and I see the Horse open her window, La Caballería, that woman upstairs, and that you don't want her there. I could be a pretty good detective, no?"

"How long you been spying on me through that small space?"

"See? See how you do that, man? Look how you pick that thing to think about? Is that important?"

"Okay. What else?"

"Did I say else?"

"You didn't have to."

"What did you find in your garden? What is what you maybe need the dried ice for?"

Emil shrugged. "This is all worth noting, Franco; I thank you for sharing the information. But I think it's time you called the police."

Franco shook his head. "I think not, amigo. I think you would call them this morning if you were calling them. No, hombre, this is like the movies too: *no cops*. Am I right?"

Emil's brain raced ahead, but this time the race had someplace to go: The guy who came over the wall must have killed CeeCee Noily's cat, the ginger, who must have come snooping, hearing a noise, thinking maybe a big mouse—more like a rat. He must have tossed the dead cat over into her yard. Why didn't the Noilys' dogs bark? Overfed, useless mutts; lazy beasts. So who was this spider guy Franco saw?

Emil started the engine. "I take it you have no place to be in Queens?"

Franco lifted his hands, shrugged. Obviously he wasn't buying Emil's bluff about bringing in the police. And just how much had he seen through that chink in the fence? Not much, Emil figured, not enough, so he was mostly guessing. He was probably worried about this man scaling the wall, and that might explain why Franco was suddenly so confiding. This is what he concluded as he pulled into the dry-ice place. Then he was thinking that he hadn't watered the garden. By tonight it surely would need water; by tonight all of Brooklyn would be as hot as Mercury. "You want to wait in the car?" he asked Franco.

"And cook like an egg? No, gracias."

Emil nodded. This was plenty awkward, a standoff with Franco, bluffing each other like a pair of school kids, Emil acting like the news of the man entering his garden wasn't huge. He was hoping Franco would drop the matter once they got back to their houses. If Emil was careful to seem indifferent, he might. He didn't figure on Franco having too long an attention span; he could wait him out with dullness till Franco grew bored. If he was along for thrills, he'd soon find out police work was mostly walking and talking and making lists, sifting through clues, slow and patient.

"He was probably a robber with a change of heart," he said to Franco.

"Claro."

"What's that?"

"'Claro?' Sure. And maybe he was practicing to be ninja. Or maybe a biologist seeing how spiders do it, you know, at night, hombre? And maybe whatever we're doing at this dry-ice place is having to do with spider cojones in a jar, huh, amigo?"

Emil was surprised by Franco's tone, as defiant as he'd ever heard him.

After securing the dry ice, the men were quiet again in the car as they drove back into Brooklyn. Emil's idea was to ditch his neighbor.

"Listen, Franco, there's something else I have to take care of, so how about I drop you off?" He pulled over on Franklin Street, took a twenty out of his pocket. "Here's more than enough to get you to your house."

"What's this, amigo? A bribe?"

Emil reached across to open the passenger-side door. "Come on, Franco; we'll talk about the intruder last night later, when I get back."

Franco pulled the door closed. "No, hombre, I don't think so."

Emil resisted a furious desire to smash the steering wheel with his fist. "What do you want from me?"

Franco shrugged. "I can help you."

"How, Franco? How can you possibly help me?"

The oppressively hazy sky felt to Emil as if it were leaning on the windshield, ready to smother him. He couldn't physically pitch his neighbor out of the car.

Franco sat straight, lips shut tight. Emil put the car in gear, stuffed the twenty back into his pocket. "Fine. I'm going to Wittekoff Hospital."

Franco brightened. "You have a hunch?"

After a short drive they arrived and parked in the visitors' lot, and with Franco beside him Emil walked to the hospital's main entrance. Removing his sunglasses, he said, "Last chance to clear off, Franco."

"Let's go, man."

A few people milled about the lobby, and a lone elderly lady was stationed at the reception desk. Emil walked up to her, smiled briefly, and asked for Pathology.

"Are you a doctor?" the gray-haired lady wanted to know. Her cornflower blue eyes were not the loving, grandmotherly type.

"No, ma'am," responded Emil.

"Well, visitors are not permitted in Pathology unless they have an appointment. I don't suppose you have one of those?"

Emil produced and flashed his badge. "I have one of these. I'm Detective Miller, and this is Detective—Vega."The badge was in and out so fast, at most all the gray lady saw was the M from Milosec. Emil kept his thumb over most of the badge.

"I see. Is there some trouble, Detective? I'll ring up security—"

"No, no, Mrs.—" he scanned her name tag—"Ellory; that's not a good idea. We'd like an element of surprise here."

"Oh?"

Emil smiled. "Which way to Pathology?"

"Take the elevator to your left, down the hall behind me. Pathology is on the third floor; take a right off the elevator and go to the rear of the building. But shouldn't I alert administration if something is wrong?"

Emil put his finger to his lips. "Surprise, Mrs. Ellory, can be a policeman's best friend. There may not be a problem after all, and why then upset anyone? We'd want the upper hand just in case. Am I making sense, Mrs. Ellory?" Emil could see she remained skeptical. Mrs. Ellory was the type that did not like secrecy; she was more a spit-it-out-and-speak-clearly type, probably a retired schoolteacher. "You will cooperate, I hope, Mrs. Ellory." He offered her a smile.

She seemed to understand. "Well," she said, "it's back that way."

"Thank you." Emil walked to the elevators with Franco trailing behind. As he walked Franco tucked his striped shirt tighter into his pants. Over the shirt he wore a shiny Mets baseball jacket, bright blue with orange lettering. He ran his fingers along his crew cut, like a patch of new-mown lawn on his head.

Emil held the elevator door open. Franco skipped in. "Did I tell you I could be a detective?" he asked.

"Uh-huh." Emil studied the elevator menu and pushed B.

"Why you do that? That desk mujer say *three*, not *B*."

"We have a little trip to make to the morgue first."

"Okay." He stepped back, deeper into the elevator. "Why?"

"Ask little, observe much, Detective Vega."

The morgue was in the basement. Latrine green walls with pipes and ducts running along them led the way. They passed doors marked "Laundry" and "Boiler Room," walked past a medical waste sorting area and a wide door marked "Garage." The ceilings were low and the air was damp. Way at the back down the long corridor stood a pair of wide, scratched-up brown metal doors. Over the brown paint was stenciled in black "Morgue."

"You get the heebie-jeebies, Franco? Morgues bother you at all?"

"Me … No, ta'ueno. It's nothing to me, the dead."

"Glad to hear it." A saying ran through Emil's head: *From ghouls and ghosties and things that go bump in the night / Protect me, dear Lord, till morning's first light.*

Emil pushed through the doors. Immediately the air was no longer humid, was almost cold. He walked into a cramped, unclean looking, windowless office. An attractive black woman sat behind what resembled a grade school principal's desk, a wool sweater draped over her shoulders. Her face and sympathetic eyes belied a career choice surrounded by doom. She was the last type Emil would have expected to meet in the morgue. He wondered how a job that never took in the light of day, behind a desk that carried documents of the newly dead, had ever attracted such a one as this. But a job was a job, he supposed. On the wall beside the clerk were taped pictures of the living: kids, a baby, a couple on what looked to be a prom date or else a very young wedding. The other desk was empty. Emil glanced at the wall clock: twelve forty-five. Lunchtime; that worked in his favor.

The mistress of the morgue looked up. "Are you gentlemen here to make an ID? No, wait—cops, right? I know it when I see one. What can I help you with?"

Emil smiled. Franco beamed. In his mind Emil had decided to be Mike Dunn, no longer Emil Milosec; it freed him for the deceit that was about to play out—not that Mike had been deceitful. "I'm Detective Miller; this is Detective Vega. Sorry to trouble you, but I'll need to speak to the doc on duty, maybe take a look at a dead girl. You could make my life a whole lot easier if you have a list of recent female deaths, young, say within the last forty-eight hours."

"Sounds all right and no trouble at all if you have any authorization."

Emil saw her name on a desk plaque: LaTeesha Williams. ("Always use a name," Mike Dunn used to say. "A name puts a person at ease.") "Ms. Williams, we are following a tip here, and I have a hunch about it being 'probly nothing, but time is of the essence. Is there any way I could get around waiting for a writ? I need a couple'a facts, maybe a peek and I'll be gone from your life forever." What was he doing, lying into Ms. LaTeesha Williams's very lovely eyes?

"I've heard that line before. But no homicides came through the last few days, I can tell you that for certain."

"Wouldn't necessarily be a homicide."

"And I'm thinking wouldn't be a breast cancer case either."

"Doubtful." Emil's eyes lingered.

LaTeesha Williams shifted her eyes over to Franco. "He the silent type?"

Franco started to say something; Emil cut in: "His first time in the cellar."

LaTeesha Williams nodded. Franco smiled weakly. She stood up and walked the short distance to a row of tall filing cabinets at the rear of the room and picked up four files from a mesh wire basket on top of one of the cabinets, marked "Pending." Franco's eyes were on her behind, but he lowered his gaze as she turned back to them. Neither had Emil been blind to her shape. Her phone rang. She walked quickly back to her desk and reached for the receiver. "Wittekoff Hospital, Morgue ..." She sat down, the files in her left hand. "Yes, okay, *okay*! Slow down; take a breath. Now, tell me, what did he do?"

She glanced up at Emil, handed him the files, and mouthed for him to take a look.

Emil breathed his gratitude. There were four female deaths within the past three days. A heart attack, eighty-three years old; an ovarian cancer victim at forty-five; a brain tumor, closer to the right age at thirty-four; and a hit by car, internal bleeding, age nineteen at time of death—even better. Emil nodded to LaTeesha Williams. She looked up and covered the phone with her hand. "My sons," she said, making a face.

Emil spoke in a low voice: "Can you call the doctor out? I have to get in there."

LaTeesha Williams raised her index finger, indicating for him to wait. "All right, Eric, *Eric*! I'm calling you back in two minutes. Quiet, now! Two minutes." She hung up. To Emil: "With no paperwork? That's pushing it."

"Let me just talk to him. It's important, Ms. Williams."

Shaking her head, she pressed a button on her phone. After a short dialogue about two detectives standing at her desk, she hung up. "Give me those folders, please, Detective. You learned nothing from me."

"Right!" Franco said loudly. Emil shot him a look. Ms. Williams looked at him too. He appeared to have surprised himself.

A doctor in green OR scrubs came out of a room at the end of a short corridor. He looked forever tired. "I'm Dr. Greenfeld; what's this about?"

"Ah, Dr. Greenfeld, I'm sorry to be a bother. Detectives Miller," Emil said, then pointed to Franco, "and Vega. We need a quick look at a Sheila Rapsy and, ah, Mary O'Donnell."

"Why?"

"We have some information—"

"We ship homicides over to County within twenty-four hours, and there haven't been any so far this week, male or female. Nothing irregular about any of my recent deceased."

"We're looking into an odd sort of misbehavior." Emil had put on his officer-of-the-law voice. He wasn't appealing now, as with LaTeesha Williams. This guy, this doctor that he knew had not touched a live patient since medical school, who'd seen it all and then some with extra on top, did not need a song and dance, and he did not need charm, he just needed to know why he was being pestered in his realm of the dead.

The doctor blinked rapidly several times at Emil. "What were those names again?"

LaTeesha Williams handed the doctor the files. He took them and turned back toward the refrigerator room.

Emil followed. Franco drifted in behind Emil. He turned his head this way and that. If a room could be called unhappy, it would surely look like this one, though not so much because of all the dead people passing through as the fact that it was old and stale and sterile. The overriding smell was formaldehyde; the sinks were stainless steel, and stained. Two rows of squat refrigerator doors did not look inviting, instruments and brown glass bottles sat on high shelves, and there was a narrow operating table in the middle of the floor with a rumpled sheet tossed on top. The sheet had drops of blood on it. Franco gave the table a wide berth. Emil glanced back at him. They had left the world of the living.

Dr. Greenfeld pulled the tray containing the brain-tumor victim out of the locker. Emil walked over. Franco froze where he was as the doctor peeled back the sheet. Emil came in closer. "I'm interested in her hands."

"Hands? What for? As I said, nothing's irregular in any of these deaths."

And Emil saw that Ms. Rapsy's hands were indeed intact, all ten digits accounted for. He nodded, and Sheila Rapsy was rolled unceremoniously back into her cold dark box.

"And the car hit?" Emil asked.

The doctor opened the file to the patient's chart. "This one came down on the night shift; let's see ... ah ... Mary O'Donnell ... Sunday—well, Monday, one thirty a.m. The ER had her for an hour ... a student ... ran across, looks like Lafayette Street, driver didn't see her till too late ... fair amount of alcohol in her blood. Uh ... only ID on her was a Pratt student card, had to wait till late Monday to get the records and a positive ID." He looked up. "Her roommate did the honors ...

uh, parents located, Columbus, Ohio; came in this morning, no funeral home in place at this time. You wanna look?"

"Please."

Dr. Greenfeld pulled out poor Mary O'Donnell with her life—as what, an artist, a designer?—spread out before her, only now no more, cut short, no more Mary O'Donnell. Didn't Ohio Mother teach her about running into the road? All blue now, Mary Blue. Why did the chicken cross the road? Emil asked himself.

The doctor lowered the white cloth, uncovering Mary with her pert young dead-too-soon breasts, and Emil saw that the left pinkie of poor Mary O'Donnell was no longer part of her remains. He also noted there was no nail polish on the other fingers. "Bingo," he breathed. To Dr. Greenfeld he said quietly, "You say her parents made the claim already? Good thing they didn't notice, 'cause I'd call that something irregular. Is that missing digit in your report?"

Clearly surprised, the doctor said, "No, it is not."

"Could give you problems."

They both turned as Franco made a small retching sound from the back of his throat. He was hovering by the door. "What's wrong with him?"

"First time on the dance floor. Vega! Go outside, sit with your head between your knees and breathe." Franco ran out of the room. "He had a nice desk job but wanted to see some real action before he retired. I hope this measures up as enough excitement." Dr. Greenfeld made a movement with his mouth that might have passed for a smile. "I guess that's it, then. I'll send in a copy of my report."

"But who cut off the finger? Who're you investigating?"

"No one yet. Maybe one of your guys."

"There's only two of our guys, and I'm one of them."

"And cleanup crews, and who all else could walk in here? Maybe the night-duty doc went on a break to the cafeteria, someone unauthorized walks in, does something weird. Could be a perv before the police arrived on scene did the job, and no one noticed. But I wouldn't worry, probably a freak occurrence. We thought it was a joke ourselves when the call came in, some crank. My professional guess, it's one of a kind." He took a breath. The lies were taking on a life of their own. "Unless we have a serial finger chopper on our hands."

If the doctor enjoyed Emil's little joke, he didn't let on. "Yeah, well, don't send any report if this is the end of the line. That kind of thing goes upstairs, the administration'll make my life hell."

Emil had to wonder that the doctor's life didn't already fit the description. "Sure, Doc, I understand. I'll try not to involve you. And thanks for your help."

Dr. Greenfeld, disgusted, waved Emil away. He lifted Mary O'Donnell's left hand. "This is a very professional amputation," he called out.

"I know," Emil called back.

Out in the office LaTeesha Williams was standing next to Franco with a wet paper towel in her hand. Franco sat drinking water from a paper cup. The color had returned to his cheeks. Ms. Williams looked at Emil and shook her head.

Emil stood over Franco. "Come on, Vega, let's get out of here."

"Sí, Miller, sí." He stood up.

Emil thanked LaTeesha Williams for her trouble.

She replied, "I don't know what for."

Emil smiled. "Me neither," he answered and smiled again, feeling almost sorry to leave her down among the dead. He guided Franco out of the morgue toward the elevator bank. He asked him, "How do you like detective work so far?"

Emil left the hospital by a back exit and found a pay phone on the street. He'd sent Franco around to Mrs. Ellory to let her know all was well; they'd had a false alarm, and no need to mention anything to anyone. Mostly he wanted Franco out of the way for the phone call he was about to make.

He placed a quarter in the slot, called information for the hospital number, dialed it, asked for Pathology, and waited. "Pathology Department?" he said into the phone.

"Yes," a female voice spoke, "you have Pathology."

"Yes," Emil said, "is a Miss Paulien Vandervell under your employ?"

There was a pause. "Yes . . ." The voice on the other end sounded hesitant, if not suspicious. Emil shifted the phone to his other ear as he kicked an unidentifiable black object among the debris at his feet, noting it was soft to the touch. "This is Miss Vandervell's solicitor. We have information she should be made aware of as soon as possible." Another pause on the other end. Emil heard the woman inhaling and exhaling. Finally: "Will you hold, please?"

"Yes, I will, and thank you." He waited in the melting-hot sun for his tenant to pick up.

Emil tightened his grip on the receiver when he heard Paulien say hello with the barest trace of worry in her voice; then he hung up. The idea was to jolt his tenant where she worked. He was arriving at the certainty that it was Paulien who'd removed Mary O'Donnell's left pinkie. He planned to keep eyes fixed on Paulien Vandervell. After replacing the receiver, he moved under the shade of a scraggy maple tree growing unhappily next to the fence enclosing the hospital parking lot.

The city was frozen in the heat, as if a white gel had been poured over every object, creating a still, veiled effect. Buildings appeared mashed together the way they did in a blizzard or fog. Only this haze, this filth was mostly manmade. This air came from bus fumes and trucks and cars exhaling smog, flew over from coal-burning factories in West Virginia and Ohio; far from Brooklyn, pollutants hitching rides on eastbound winds. Too many trees were being cut down. Not only from forests but anyplace anybody felt like cutting them; suburban sprawl, urban development, corporate farms—everybody had reasons. This was civilization's air, and it grew in unhealthy particulates as industry billowed dollars. Emil tried to breathe less deeply, limit the supply of fume-heavy air entering his lungs in the suffocating heat as he worried what the hell was taking Franco so long.

Emil lifted his jacket up off his neck; the collar was ringed with sweat. He looked around. Once upon a time there was a garden where all things freely grew, anything a man could want. All the religions shared the garden idea—or most of them. He understood the need for a garden, the idea of paradise on a long, lonely road. So what happened? God poked around the earthly paradise among his toy creatures made of clay and dust and God-spit, placed among his tame animals and birds, trees, and so on—the whole contented acreage. Then he walked his earth one evening enjoying his handiwork, maybe a little bored, not badly bored, not desperate, just the teensiest bit too contented, and maybe he stuck those two trees down there and cooked up those taboos just to set up a little tension in his perfect world; a minor conflict, a slight irritation for the sake of drama, a twist in the narrative just to see how his people worked it out. A little test, where was the harm?

Along the branch slithers the wily reptile, tongue sensuously flicking, down comes the pretty apple, and—bam! No more garden. No plea bargain, no deal, no second chance: So long, Eve, so long, Adam, put a fig leaf over that and go earn your supper the hard way. Downhill from that day to this polluted one where garbage clings to a hospital fence, one long steady fall from grace. Emil looked at the beer cans, the cigarette butts, a diaper, a single sneaker—minus its lace, dog shit, multiple plastic bags, a broken coat hanger: a random sampling of civilization's detritus stuck like a still life from hell along a fenced-in parking lot. And the thing he had to wonder was this: If God liked that old garden so much and everything in it, why not find a way to save *something*, salvage a couple of acres, an ounce of forgiveness against total banishment for all time. Why dump the whole lot for one slipup? They had to wait until the New Testament for forgiveness, but by then who cared? Who remembered Eden anymore? Man was so burdened with guilt and self-loathing—not to leave out his neighbor—murder and crime that it was too late. Shove your fucking forgiveness, he thought. Look at—

"Hey, Miller!" Franco walked toward Emil, carrying a paper bag with two plastic straws sticking out.

"What took so long?"

Franco held up the paper bag. "Limonada. Good stuff. In this heat, the best. Not too sweet is how the lemon cools."

"What about the old lady up front?"

"Who? That gray-head blanca?" He held a lemonade out to Emil. "And you? Did what you needed on the phone?"

Emil eyed Franco. He reached for the lemonade. "What do I owe you?"

"De nada."

They drank as they walked to the car. Emil wanted to get away from the hospital as quickly as possible. He hoped neither he nor Franco had been spotted by Paulien. "You didn't see anyone in there?" he asked.

"Like who?"

"Anyone familiar."

"I should?"

"No."

"Then no."

"All right, let's go."

"Where to?"

Emil didn't answer.

In the car, Franco asked, "What was wrong with the dead muchacha? This has to do with the man in your garden and the dry ice?"

"Franco, let me ask you. You have any idea how serious the charges are for impersonating an officer of the law?"

"Am I now supposed to be afraid?"

"Look, the less you know, the better. As it stands now, you personally never claimed to be a cop. Say there's a problem down the road, you're better off not knowing, see?"

"What about you?"

"Bad enough. But you're getting yourself dragged into something that doesn't have to concern you."

"That spider swinging down the wall concerned me."

Emil had no answer for that; it was true, like it or not, Franco was already at least tangentially involved.

"Do you know, amigo, that I too like a garden?"

"Uh-huh."

"It's true. There was a great garden, magnifico, where I grew up in Mexico."

"Didn't you say you were from Puerto Rico?"

"Sí, I am. My mother. But my father was Mejicano. He took me to una abuelita, like a nurse, his old cousin. My mother—hijo—was so pretty. They went together to Cuba for nightclubs and dancing, for the good times. He had money out of the ears, muy rico, from Monterrey. He put me in Vera Cruz with the abuelita. He took care of my mother, but then not so much. He didn't bother to tell her he already had a wife and kids. We go to Puerto Rico, then to Brooklyn. And behind my house, hombre, there was a garden. I saw it. My mother's madre lived there, and she made the garden with my old Aunt Marta, who lives upstairs, muy vieja—old, but you know. By the time I lived in the house that garden was turned to nothing."

"Wasn't there a gambling debt?"

"Como?"

"Your mother was good at cards, right?"

"Sí, she was. Why you ask me?"

"Why didn't you fix it?"

"Fix who?"

"The garden?"

"Sí. I would, I mean to, but that whore, culo Kleenex, my wife left."

"That was twenty years ago, Franco."

"Ten, hombre, not twenty." Franco swept his hand along the dashboard. "What was the point without her?"

"What's ever the point?"

"Don't ask me."

Emil turned to face Franco. "You find what you want to do, and if it's hard, you do it harder. That's the point."

Franco was quiet for a moment and then asked, "What do you do hard?"

Emil didn't answer.

They drove in silence for a while. Emil slowed the car on a narrow side street when he saw two men arguing, their voices loud. It looked like the driver of a van had tapped an oversized SUV while backing out. Just the sort of thing two stupid-head guys would make a big deal out of, the men evenly matched for bulk and anger. Emil, the former cop, thought to intervene when one driver shoved the other, but he caught himself and drove on. He was only impersonating a cop.

Franco said, after watching the scene, "You ever see how on TV when they hit the good guy there is never anything on his face? You ever see that? They could punch this hombre with a pipe and he is not scratched once. That's cheap; how dumb do those TV guys think we are?"

Emil said, "Maybe it's only symbolic—the beating."

Franco laughed. "Sí, the pretty hero hurts only on the inside, ha, amigo?"

To get to Mrs. Santiana's car park, Emil had to drive past his house. There was a squad car and an ambulance outside Noily's place, and what Emil knew right off to be an unmarked cop car. A cluster of onlookers from the neighborhood had gathered.

Franco whistled between his teeth. "Hijo. Que pasó?"

Emil barely slowed down. He turned the corner and headed straight for Mrs. Santiana's lot. He parked, locked the car and the gate. To Franco, who had waited, he said, "Will you do this; will you carry the dry ice over to your house for now?"

"Sí, claro." As they walked past Rudy's Corner Market, Franco stopped. "Hombre, let me go into here for one minute."

"No! Why?" Franco ignored him and went inside.

After a few minutes, angry with himself for letting Franco go into Rudy's with the dry ice, he went in after him. His eyes adjusted to Rudy's inadequate illumination after the glaring light outside. Franco had made a beeline for the beer cooler. Emil heard Rudy before he saw him: "Some trouble over at your place, Milosec. My boy Albert's over there now, finding out what."

"Not my house, Rudy; looks like the people next door."

Rudy tilted his head toward the coolers. "You out and about with Montoya these days, my best beer customer?"

Emil snapped his fingers. "You remind me, Rudy, I need toilet paper." He walked a few paces to the paper-goods section and picked up two rolls, placed them on the counter, and pulled out his wallet. "What's that come to?"

Franco sauntered up to the register with three loose bottles of Dos Equis. "Hey, naybor," he drawled out to Emil.

"Drink up, eh, Montoya?" said Rudy with his smirk. He winked at Emil.

Franco made a pronged vee with two fingers and fake-jabbed at Rudy, as if to poke his eyes out.

Emil saw Rudy flinch as Franco broke out into his raucous laugh. He collected his bagged toilet paper and turned to go. But he stopped and waited by the door, held it open for Franco, who had grabbed the package of beer without taking his change.

"Hijo de puta," said Franco under his breath. Behind them Rudy pocketed his change.

Outside, away from the market, Franco said, "I don't like that cabrón Rudy."

"You had to buy the beer right now?"

"Cover, mi amigo," Franco said. "You think I do not know what people say? Franco Montoya, el borracho?"

Emil glanced at Franco, walking beside him. "Just don't say anything to any cops over there, all right?"

"Who talks to cops?"

Franco drifted ahead of Emil as they rounded the corner. Emil held back. Franco reached his house and sat down on the top step. Emil walked up a few minutes later and stopped at the bottom of Franco's steps. A uniform cop came over. "That's close enough, buddy," he said to Emil.

"I live over here, Officer."

"Yeah, okay," the cop said. He had the I-can't-be-bothered-but-I'm-still-in-charge attitude cops get, especially when they have basically nothing to do but stand around. Emil knew the boredom; he'd done his share of hurry up and wait.

"What's the trouble, Officer?" Emil asked.

"Heart attack, guy two doors down."

"Still breathing?"

The officer nodded. "Looks like he picked a fight with his wife and gave himself the attack."

"Otto Noily?"

"You hear it all the time, huh, domestic upsets in the neighborhood?"

"In all the years I've lived here I can count the times I've even heard the man's voice."

"What, the wife?"

"I'd say she's the one in charge."

"She looked pretty shook up."

Emil said, "Sure, life kills, whoever's wearing the pants."

The officer grinned.

Emil was about to ask how the prognosis looked, but the EMS wagon started up, and the uniform went over to make sure no one stepped into its path. Emil watched Mrs. Noily climb into the back of the ambulance. Out of the corner of his eye he saw someone walking toward him.

"That you, Milosec?" the someone called out. The ambulance took off in a hurry.

Emil turned to see Detective Bernie Bracco crossing the street, his approach like he had command of the whole world and was about to let Emil know it. He came out of that unmarked car, Emil let himself know. What was an unmarked doing at the scene of a heart attack? It wasn't Emil's call earlier? He took in that Bernie Bracco had aged some, lost the young man, become the big man with attitude. In a navy blue shirt and smoky gray tie he didn't look Sears-issue; his sports coat wasn't Armani, but it wasn't polyester either. Maybe he had taken something away from Emil, sartorially anyhow.

Emil leaned along the railing to Franco's steps. "Detective Bracco," he said, resisting extending his hand.

"You're looking fit, Detective Milosec," said the other detective, his hand held out, expecting to meet Emil's. Emil relented, and the men shook hands without warmth.

"What brings you over to this neighborhood? Ambulance chasing on a slow day?"

"Nah, nearby when the call came in. You live around here?" Emil nodded. "Know the heart attack guy?"

"Only to nod to."

Emil was thinking as he spoke that Bracco was probably here when the ambulance arrived; he'd bet on it.

"So, ah, you got any more on that, what'd you say was missing, Milosec? Jewelry?"

Emil let out a short, unconvincing laugh. "Just a couple of guys I overheard last evening outside the corner market talking what sounded like a jewelry heist. They looked liked losers, but they might have been talking about a TV show. An ex-cop, I can't stop thinking like you guys." The lies just kept piling up.

"Yeah—"

They both turned toward Franco, who let off a loud belch, seated on his perch at the top of his steps. He'd popped open a beer bottle.

"Who are you?" Bracco asked, his tone mean for its own sake. "And, what, you pull a beer in public?"

Emil said, "He's okay; he owns the building."

"I don't care if he owns the White House; he can't have that beer out."

"Franco," Emil called to him, "why don't you go inside and get yourself a glass?"

"Why don't you?"

"C'mon, don't make trouble over nothing."

Franco stood up, pretending to sway. "I don't care for the company out here today anyway, muchachos." And with that he went inside his house, banging the door closed behind him.

"Nice neighborhood," said Bracco.

"Franco's all right," Emil said. He hoped Bracco was ready to let go of his Joe-public-calls-in-a-crime act, or at least *believe* the act.

"Yeah," Detective Bracco said again. He shot a look over at his partner seated in the burgundy Chevy they shared for eight or nine hours a day.

He mopped a chain of sweat off his hairline. "You did some private work for a while after retiring, that right?"

"Nothing much. Henry Waters used to throw some small jobs my way now and then, odds and ends, a few extra dollars."

"Yeah, Henry's gone now. Went to Hawaii with his wife, some inheritance money she got hold of."

Emil nodded. "That was his dream: get away from the mean streets, find paradise while he still had some finding time left."

"Sure, shave ice on Waikiki. You two still in touch?"

"The odd postcard."

"No more private stuff?"

"Nah."

"Not working a case right now, on your own or anything?"

Emil was glad his eyes were hidden behind sunglasses. "I told you, my nose twitched. I was mistaken."

"What's in the bag?"

Emil laughed. "Who's asking?"

Bernie Bracco laughed.

Emil opened the bag. "Toilet paper. The soft kind. Two-ply."

Detective Bracco looked in the bag. He wasn't satisfied, Emil could see that, but he didn't think whatever was itching Bracco had to do with his phony call. "Yeah, well, I guess that's that. Stay in touch, Milosec."

"Sure, Detective." Emil watched Detective Bracco walk back to his car. He stood where he was until the car started up and waved a manly, noncommittal wave as the detectives drove off. When the car was out of sight he turned and walked up the steps and into his house.

He went straight down to the kitchen. The mere sight of his garden through the glass door offered relief. He switched on the ceiling fan, took off his sports coat and draped it over a chair. The armpits of the jacket were soaked. Emil poured himself a tall glass of water and drank it down. That was bad, Bracco coming around. What was he after? Definitely not that idiot call; not Noily's heart attack either.

He coughed, peeled off his holster; the leather was wet with sweat too. His stomach thumped: Bernie Bracco could've found the gun on him! That would have raised alarms even Houdini couldn't have wiggled out of. He swore under his breath.

He opened a lower cabinet door and placed the revolver and holster inside, up against Elena's blender. He was very hungry. He glanced at the clock: two fifteen. As he closed the cabinet door the song of a house finch rang out from the garden. Emil listened to the lilting sound. His wife used to call songbirds God's disappointed reminder. He was certain now the finches were back, and it seemed arbitrarily unkind not to have Elena there to welcome them.

TWO

If the Lord delight in us, then he will bring us into this land, and give it us; a land which floweth with milk and honey.

WANDERINGS IN THE WILDERNESS, BOOK OF NUMBERS

Elena had a favorite book that caused a vague jealousy in Emil. It was a small book of stories: North African wayfarers and beggars, debauched soldiers, solitary men and woman who'd strayed from their villages. Tales of Algerian girls whose childhoods were full of awed wonder, their dreams without barriers until marriages were arranged and bored confinement crushed them. To Emil the stories Elena had read to him suggested *her* lost childhood, a past he could not replace. Emil suspected that before the war she'd had girlhood dreams that were vivid and a little wild, and that he'd been orderly as child where she was not.

She did everything just so; knew how to converse, the right things to say, how to dress and charm. But *The Oblivion Seekers*, what could Elena want from such a book? One of the stories she'd read stuck with him, the tale of Taalith, who's lost her true love and is expected to marry an old man, but she throws herself into a well, arrayed in her wedding regalia, rather than marry without love. Elena had been torn from what she might have become, and for years he'd quietly feared she would one day leave without explanation—just as she'd arrived.

The book was in the kitchen with him, a gold ribbon marking Taalith's pages. He placed it next to the mustard-colored vase full of pom-pom dahlias and the embroidered ring box. His stomach growled queasily. All he'd eaten all day was the cold toast at breakfast and a couple of quarts of coffee, followed by Franco's lemonade. Acids were gurgling in his gut. He opened the refrigerator door, pulled out a loaf of seeded rye, a round slab of liverwurst, a jar of spicy mustard, and a bit of oak-leaf lettuce. Once in a while Emil liked liverwurst, its tangy bite with the grainy mustard. Poor man's pâté, he called it. He fixed himself a sandwich and poured a glass of chilled pinot grigio and sat down at the table to eat.

The newspaper lay on the table where he'd tossed it in the morning. Another headline in the Science section announced, "Up-Close Look at a Potato-Shaped Space Rock." He smiled.

Thoughtfully chewing his liverwurst, Emil wondered if there were any pickles in the fridge. He didn't think there were, and he wasn't a big fan, but today a pickle seemed in order. Cops ate plenty of salty pickles, or slaw on the side with their diets of takeout lunch. Mike Dunn couldn't do lunch without a pickle. How many meals had they eaten together in the cramped car, the front seat serving as their table? Mike's lunches large, Emil's smaller.

He recalled a gray, blustery day in March. Mike was eating a salami and gorgonzola sandwich. Emil's window was rolled down all the way. The car stank of the cheese. He watched street debris swirl by in a sudden gust. He'd had a bad feeling all day, nothing he could identify or shake, and was quieter than usual. That was when the call came in that a boy's body had been found in a bodega. Mike leaned in to respond. "We got it," he said into the mic, repeating the address. He turned to Emil. "Ready?"

Mike dropped what was left of his sandwich, open in its cellophane wrapper, on the seat between them. "Are you going to leave that there?" Emil wanted to know.

Mike rolled his window down, threw the sandwich to the curb, and turned the ignition key. "And don't give me a hard time about littering; a rat'll eat it. There were two bites left."

The crime was vicious: a young boy brutally murdered, his body partially dismembered. They guessed the victim to be about six years old. The site was the basement of a neighborhood bodega called Cariña's. Uniform cops had already cordoned off the area in front. Two more cops were in the cellar when Emil and Mike went down. A police photographer and forensics showed up shortly after. The cramped cellar began to fill up with personnel. With a dead child the usual crime scene banter gave way to subdued voices, a lumbering, animal closeness among the men.

Emil scanned the scene and stood off to the side, where he noticed a small sneaker sticking out from under some metal shelving. The sneaker looked new and expensive. Emil said, "The boy's not from this neighborhood."

Outside, back on the street, Emil and Mike walked over to a pay phone on the corner. People gathering on the sidewalk were held back by the two uniform cops. Someone had already tossed a bouquet of dyed blue carnations in front of the bodega. Mike called his wife, Danielle. "Where are the kids?" he demanded.

"In school, where they always are in the day. Why?"

"Just make sure they come home—Mikey Junior—you know."

"What's wrong?"

"Nothing," Mike said. "Just make sure," and he hung up. Emil stood rod-straight, arms stiff at his sides, the man on the outside. Would he have come in if he could?

"You okay, Milosec?"

"Sure."

"Pretty grim in there."

Emil nodded. "Goes with the gorgonzola." He glanced at Mike. "I was just thinking, when I was about six, maybe seven, my Uncle Ivak took me hunting."

"With live ammo?"

"Yeah, this is the mountains. Everybody hunted."

"The old country?"

Emil nodded. "I hated it."

"What, blowing the heads off squirrels? You're a kid, that kind of violence …"

Emil shook his head. "No, getting up early, waiting hours in the freezing cold. Up that high, even late spring it could snow hard. I wanted to be home in the warm house. 'With your mama,' Uncle Ivak said. 'I'll make you a man; I'll feed you bread soaked in vinegar, you pussy.'"

"Friendly bunch. They all like that over there?"

"My mother said, 'Go with your Uncle Ivak; that's what a boy does.'"

"Where was your father in all this?"

Emil shrugged. "Off in the woods somewhere. I took one of my mother's porcelain cups, tossed it in the air and shot it. I was mad at her, I guess."

"I bet that put the problem to rest?"

"Trouble is I hit a bird's nest too; blue eggs and white china came falling into the vegetable garden … and feathers."

"A kid of six shouldn't have guns. You felt bad."

"I don't know." He put his hands in his pockets. "Elena says men are afraid of their emotions."

Mike snorted. "They all say that."

Emil turned to look at Mike. "They do?"

"Sure, real men don't cry kind of thing."

"Do you ever cry?"

"Now you're getting personal."

"It was a question."

"Yeah, a womanish question. Don't go fruity on me."

Emil paused, thought about what Mike said. "Could be the women have a point."

The medical examiner's black van came around the corner and stopped in front of the bodega. "Here's the wagon," Mike said. "We gotta go back in."

"Yup," Emil replied. Neither man looked happy.

Emil looked in his refrigerator. There were no pickles; he'd have to chew over the current case without one. The bodega case went cold, Emil remembered. He liked the son of the bodega owner for the perp, but his mama stuck by sonny's shaky alibi. What was a little rich kid from the Upper East Side doing in that part of Brooklyn anyhow; no one saw him? That one irked the precinct for a long time, and Mike in particular. "Sometimes," Emil had said, and none of the other cops wanted to hear it, "people get away with murder."

So the question was: Just how deep was Paulien Vandervell—the Horse, Franco called her—in the plot? Let's say Paulien arranged for Mary O'Donnell's finger to end up in the garden. Was she contacted and offered money? Did she perform the amputation herself? Sneak into the morgue on her Monday coffee break, a clean slice? How could she have known of Mary's accident? Hung around the hospital, gotten lucky with Mary coming in, or else would it have been Sheila Rapsy's finger? Maybe that was why she got the late start today, up all night between the morgue, and his garden. And maybe she cut herself while cutting off the finger. Okay, so what was her motive?

He recalled something Caribbean, obeah women digging up bodies, cutting off the fingers. He'd read that somewhere. Or had Mike Dunn told him? Or maybe Elena? Some magic in fingers cut from the dead. He doubted there was any angle having to do with voodoo and the finger in his garden. Whichever way it worked, why abuse two dead women? Rob the jewelry of one to place on the robbed finger of the other? Don't leave out that the dismembered digit had nail polish applied to it. That was nasty to contemplate: painting a dead, severed fingernail. He had no ideas for a motive on Paulien's part, or anyone else's. But ritualism, black magic—there were Santeria practitioners in the neighborhood, he knew that. Nah, the event in his garden was designed with intentions in the here and now, not the netherworld.

His sandwich eaten, Emil tossed back the wine and rinsed the plate and glass. The dishwasher was still full of washed dishes, but two clean dinner plates still sat on the shelf; no need to empty the dishwasher—

The phone on the wall behind him rang out loudly—once—in the quiet kitchen. He waited. No further rings. He glanced at the clock: two forty p.m. He turned to look at the phone. He looked again at the clock. The answer was: Go see what gives upstairs. Paulien would be at work until five, ample time for a snoop. Opportunity: what cops and crooks shared.

Emil reached inside the cellar door and found the keys to Paulien's apartment. He detoured on his way to brush his teeth and then walked out of his apartment on the parlor level and stepped lightly, taking the stairs two at a time to the fourth floor and quietly let himself into his tenant's apartment.

Paulien Vandervell had lived in Emil's building for a year and a half. The tenant before her was Italian, Ariana somebody, pretty and petite with auburn hair. Elena met her at the Italian Embassy, fresh out of school in Milan. She came to intern, for the opportunity to learn American English. Emil had felt protective, chastised Elena for bringing such a diminutive foreigner into the rough neighborhood, though he didn't mind having her in the house. She'd come down to the garden to help weed and then sit with her face to the sun, her legs in shorts. He liked hearing the women speak their curly Italian in the kitchen. Ariana had paid her respects at the memorial gathering for Elena, her sorrow genuine. He'd heard she returned to Italy soon after.

Elena was cremated and her ashes raked into the garden. The memorial was her friend Lotte's idea; she made the arrangements with her husband, Ambrose. Emil had never understood the attraction between Elena and Lotte, a wide-in-the-hip Austrian with bushy blonde hair, a small nose, and a talkative manner. Ambrose was Austrian vice-consul. He had a head like a wrench, with soft, wheat-colored hair that stuck out in front. He and Lotte were regulars at Elena's dinner parties. Emil arranged for a local undertaker to burn Elena's body and went home to wait for the call that her ashes were ready. Lotte phoned the next day to ask about the funeral arrangements. Emil told her it was all done. Lotte pushed: Surely some gesture was required, and Emil yielded, though the idea irritated him. Probably Elena would have felt the same. About thirty people showed up at Lotte's apartment in Manhattan, mostly to cry in abundance. There were flowers and a table set up with a light supper and ample drink. Emil listened tearless from the back of the room as the mourners had their say. The muffled weeping sounded to him like mice, or like sand being swept along the floor. He drove out to Montauk Point as soon as the memorial service was over.

The day was clear and warm for October. The leaves had shifted into autumn dress ahead of the barren winter to come. He booked a room in a motel overlooking the ocean and spent four mostly cloudy days on the balcony, bundled up, watching the repetitious motion of the colorless surf under an indifferent sky. The steady ebb and flow of the sea soothed, along with a couple of bottles of Jameson's. He slept with the sliding glass door wide open to the sound of the surf and had no desire for words of condolence or comfort. What was done was done (*You are dust, and to dust you shall return* …). No words available in any language could allay that kind of loss.

He returned to an empty bed. A piece of his body felt broken off, an almost physical sensation. He'd read—maybe in the Science section—that an amputee continues to have the sense of a limb long after it has been sawn off, is certain the brain still receives signals from the missing arm or leg, has the impulse to use the limb, and even suffers phantom pain until finally a new reality replaces the old. They used mirrors on stubborn cases, tricking the brain into accepting the loss. The hard fact of Elena being truly severed from him hit home months later with the arrival of spring and the rebirth of the garden. Ignorant garden, not caring who coaxed and cherished it, blindly sending shoots out of the earth, the crocuses pushing hungrily toward the sunlight, utterly unaware of Elena's vanished voice and touch.

He spent that first winter like an open sore, a house with its doors flapping open so anything could wander in. His only cover was a blanket of silence. He was glad for the season; fewer people on the streets, the heavy skies and relentless cold that suited his mood. He'd have been fine if winter had stuck around forever.

Lotte called from time to time to invite him to dinner. He always declined. "You're in mourning," she told him. Was that what it was? He just felt erased. Then the spring, and the garden was his alone and he did the work that had to be done. At first mechanically, but then he was seduced anew and threw himself into the labor. With Elena's income missing, Emil decided to rent the upstairs apartment again. His pension was sufficient but so was his memory of being poor in America. He called Ambrose, who put the word out at the Austrian Embassy. Paulien called within the week. The garden thrived.

Hothouse plants stood crowded together in front of one of the windows at the back of Paulien's apartment: dieffenbachia and dracaena, bromeliads, ponytail plant, and variegated pittosporum, a wall of green that exuded humid breath. Elena kept no such greenery indoors; potted plants annoyed her, false gardens that only collected dust. She said plants like that belonged in hotel lobbies and funeral parlors.

He stood at the middle window, looking down at his garden below and at what he could see of the pepper hole. Not much; a mound of dirt next to some digging.

Paulien was the only renter he'd interviewed. Her passport had been issued in Amsterdam, which made him wonder at her showing up via the Austrian Embassy. But he figured the Euros would be in cahoots on rentals, shared intel on where to live, and that Ambrose knew what he was about. She moved in with furnishings that were unexpected. The apartment came furnished with the basics, chosen by Elena. Paulien didn't have a lot of furniture but what she had was expensive: a red and white striped Victorian couch and a leather club chair and ottoman in the living room. She'd lined the pine sideboard Elena had installed with hand-painted plates from Morocco. She told Emil she'd been to Morocco, but he hadn't seen a Moroccan stamp in her passport. Turkish rugs placed here and there lent an exotic air, along with numerous multicolored throw pillows and the plants. Her belongings bespoke a particular taste; otherwise the apartment felt impersonal. She seldom entertained, was clean, quiet, undemanding, and always on time with the rent. In many ways Paulien was the ideal tenant.

He sorted the mail each day and it was only natural he glance at the return addresses on hers. He was aware that various bank statements arrived regularly, one from an American bank, another from the Netherlands, and recently one from the Royal Bank of Canada. He'd wondered how she managed to have funds for so many banks. He walked to the phone table near the door, expecting to find an address book, but the drawer was empty apart from a pad with the logo of a pharmaceutical company on top and a yellow pencil with a broken nib. She would have taken the pad from work. Where was the address book?

He poked through the apartment, moving a pillow here, a towel there, undergarments; touching things to get a sense of her, the fine line between a cop and a creep, nosing into her stuff. He wanted her documents, bank statements in particular, interested in any sudden pluses or minuses in her accounts, but her papers were either elsewhere—a safe-deposit box?—or gone. He began to have the sense that something was amiss on the fourth floor.

The bedroom closet was half full. A dresser contained feminine items. On the bedside table was a bottle of sleeping pills. In the bathroom cabinet were aspirin, toothpaste, tampons, tweezers—the usual items. No face cream, no deodorant, no birth-control device. And no nail polish. She was carrying that case in the morning; maybe she did have a date tonight. He squeezed his eyes shut to avoid another image of Paulien on her back, legs open. A weekend bag could account for the lipstick and face gels, but the paperwork? Had his tenant decided on an abrupt change of address?

He'd seen a computer on the dining table a few months back when he'd come in to recaulk behind the kitchen sink. It was gone. How much could she have stuffed into that valise? Emil began to consider the possibility that his tenant might have a trail in the criminal justice system. But he'd done a quick background check on the passport. Of course, that could be arranged, false papers. …

He searched but didn't find a duplicate key to his apartment, as he had half hoped he might. But then, Paulien wouldn't be so careless as to leave incriminating evidence lying around, not if she were capable of dismembering a corpse. He looked under the kitchen sink and at the back of the cupboards. He was thinking a hidden something might have been forgotten if she'd left in a hurry, but that was wishful. It looked like he was out of luck upstairs. A European with accounts in foreign banks could easily slip away with her pay from a dirty little job. But she was at work when he called earlier. He could call INS or Interpol. With what? Her passport was clean—even if it was a fake, she checked out when she arrived, so what did he have on her? Nothing more than a cop's suspicion.

He let himself out of Paulien's and locked the door. There was still a chance she'd show up, greedy for her few expensive possessions, but

Emil was coming to the conclusion that he had seen the last of his tenant.

The third floor rooms were not directly accessible from the parlor and garden levels. Emil's mother and sister once kept bedrooms there and a shared bath. At purchase, the building was a warren of partitioned apartments from dozens of illegals having crowded in on the cheap. He and Elena had the staircase built connecting their garden and parlor floors and added their bedroom and bath. They kept separate rooms on the third floor, he an office, Elena a day room where she worked on translations or spent hours reading. The room had an understated luxuriousness, filled with an overstuffed armchair, drapes, and reproduction Empire furniture lending it the air of a French boudoir. The fireplace had a marble mantel with a tiny photo of Elena and her mother as the only decoration. A daybed served for guests, though they'd had almost none. Her large collection of books in several languages dominated the wall of shelves he had installed.

His office was simpler: basic white walls with a few framed awards from the police department. His windows faced the garden and between them hung a small oil painting of a peasant walking through a verdant mountain valley. The painting reminded him of Senice. He'd bought it for a few dollars at a flea market and nailed it up that day, unframed. The television was kept in this room, across from a sagging old sofa. An out-of-date computer sat mostly unused on the corner of a large desk. Elena visited his room for various reasons: tax forms, bills, the television. Emil rarely entered her quarters while she was alive—her folded inner chamber, he jokingly called it. He felt obliged to whisper in there, though it happened sometimes that she'd light a fire and invite him to lie in front of the flames, sex in a plush setting on a cold winter's night.

The garden had mostly spent itself of flowers—the mums and asters still going, the few annuals—when a year came to an end without her. Emil had taken to visiting her boudoir. Who was to stop him? He'd lie on her daybed, the fan going on hot days, staring at her many books. She'd called them journeys and mocked his ignorant suspicion. "You are a hopeless provincial," she'd say and run her fingers through his hair. One day he stood up and ran his fingers along the shelves, and where his hand stopped he pulled a book out and began to read.

Lotte called the day of the one year anniversary. She was lucky he picked up. The answering machine had been thrown out; only Elena had ever used it. "Finally I have you!" Lotte said in her thick Austrian accent. "We want to know how you are. It is one year today … my dear Emil."

Her voice was too sympathetic; Emil was sorry he'd answered the phone. "I'm all right, Lotte."

"Not lonely?"

"No, Lotte, I'm fine."

"Come to dinner, Emil; let us see you. Or we can visit Brooklyn if you prefer." Emil said he would give it some thought. Just now he was very busy clearing the garden for winter. He thanked her for calling and hung up, leaving Lotte stranded on her end of the line.

The third floor was always locked. Emil fit the key into the lock and opened the door onto a long hallway with a bathroom at the other end. He opened the door to Elena's room, resisting for a second time a rising fury tasting of bile at the thought of Paulien entering these rooms. *If* she'd entered. He stood in the center, scanning the scene. Nothing appeared out of place. In his office he did the same. He'd watched that nature program last night and hadn't heard Paulien clumping around on the floor above, but he hadn't paid attention either, so he couldn't say for certain whether she'd been at home or not. From a desk drawer he fished out the tiny castle from Bled, the remains of the snow globe Elena smashed so long ago. He put the castle into his pocket and locked up the third floor.

He'd come up empty at Paulien's and, back in the kitchen, tried to work on Franco's description of this spiderman threading down the back wall in the night. The spider would be mixed up with Mary O'Donnell's finger. But how? Say Paulien severed the finger; which of them placed it in the pepper patch? Or was it somebody else? What about the ring? Did Paulien sneak into his apartment to get at Elena's jewelry? Maybe she entered when he was working in the garden? The parlor door was often unlocked during the day. "So she tiptoes in while I'm outside? And chooses a ring ... why the ring anyway?" No reply from the empty kitchen. "So what's Franco's spider's game? If Paulien passed the pinkie to the Spider, was she working for the Spider or was the Spider working for the Horse?"

Did any of this make sense?

He replaced Paulien's key on its hook and walked to the window. A thin rope with a white plastic bag attached was hanging over the fence from Franco's side, nearly touching the ground. Franco had lowered the dry ice over to Emil's side. Emil went out, detached the bag, and tossed the rope back over the fence. He listened but heard not a peep. "Thanks," he said anyway in the direction of Franco's kitchen.

In the cellar, his jaw set tight, Emil opened the tool bag. This morning the finger had been appropriately pale. It was now afternoon and a purple shade like the end of a bruise had set in on its way to turning black. There was a faint odor of rotten flesh. Emil regretted the deterioration for the sake of Mary O'Donnell. If he'd had a hat on his head he'd have removed it. A minute later, wearing his work gloves, he carefully extracted the finger from the tool bag, pulled a plastic baggie out of his back pocket and deposited the finger and Elena's ring in it. He sealed the bag and placed it in the picnic cooler which now contained the dry ice, though he had the feeling his careful efforts on behalf of poor Mary O'Donnell's missing bit of flesh were pointless.

He went back outside with the tool bag and with a penknife scratched into the dirt for the two bullet casings. He bent low and scraped quietly until he located one. He put it in his pocket and continued to shove deeper into the ground, but he couldn't find the second one. He grabbed a trowel and dug further. Where was it? He'd shot straight into the ground, there'd been no ricochet, both bullets had gone in clean. So where was the second casing? He dug some more, but it was no use.

Emil stood up. A wave of icy panic flushed through his intestines. He looked up at the sky. "Shit," he said out loud. "The Spider took the casings? Who in hell is this guy?"

Emil had not renewed his permit to carry a handgun. In New York City possession of a loaded handgun without a permit outside one's home or business was a class D felony. Further, it was illegal to handle or shoot a handgun unless in possession of said permit. Emil knew the law, and his dread of ending up on the wrong side of it ran deep. From a legal point of view, he was grotesquely averse to taking risks. He'd have dreams if he strayed; car chases, men in hoods, twilit alleys, murder scenarios. He believed his life was governed by reason and law. Not that Emil as an enforcer of the law believed in each and every one; for openers there were too many. As he saw it, laws were supposed to serve a purpose—do this, don't do that—for the good of the whole, so people wouldn't eat each other like fishes.

During his life among criminals he'd heard every excuse imaginable for why X had to kill Y. Religion, as he saw it, didn't do much to prevent homicide. The One True God idea alone, warring over that. On the street there were still Cain and Abel. The very first generation: A brother murders his brother.

"A person makes choices; no myth in the world's ever going to excuse that," he'd said to Mike Dunn.

A Catholic who preferred not to think about sin at all, Mike answered, "I know it doesn't hold up if you stare at it in the daylight, but people need religion."

"Yeah. We've met plenty of very religious murderers, Mike. Not to leave out death house conversions."

"You know, jails aren't really houses of remorse, like we like to think."

"Right. And humanity needs to get over it, religion, find out for ourselves why murder's a bad idea."

"Not gonna happen," Mike said. "Not in our lifetime. Not ever."

"Why not?"

"'Cause where you gonna find the perfect guy to cast the first stone?" Mike said.

Emil asked him, "Why's the guy have to be perfect?"

Sloshing through Emil's bowels and up through the fringes of his mind was the knowledge that his behavior in shooting into the pepper patch reeked of the irrational. And with "Detective Miller's" trip to the hospital he was in it now way over the legal line, up to his eyeballs.

His neck began to throb. Take a look at it, he told himself: An ex-cop fires at random—quick, call the police! But nobody does, and anybody who was going to go to the police would have done so by now out of real fear; hearing shots, bullets flying. Like Mrs. Noily. Bracco might have learned of shots fired—by an ex-cop—even in his precinct. But no one reported anything. Okay, but to take the casing to use as a threat against him? Who would do that? And for what purpose?

He massaged his neck.

Emil feared the consequences of the bullet casing being used against him far less than he feared for his own mental cohesion. He'd stepped dangerously out of character by firing the pistol in the first place. Whatever that meant: character. It was the idea of madness that unnerved him: chiaroscuro of the soul, mental anarchy, pants-wetting, blithering idiocy, spitting and foaming, lunatic utterances, fly perpetually undone, shouting obscenities, leering. The far reaches of personal chaos—this he feared. What if his dreams became his waking reality; what if he utterly lost his reason and began to live a nightmare? He must already look to others like an eccentric: an atheist reading the Bible, scribbling notes, obsessed with the Book of Genesis; the Looney Tune next door with his garden, never talked much; gardeners a solitary lot anyway, mutterers, lost from the time they blew it in paradise, thrown out of Eden, trying to get back ever since; so this cop started firing off his gun one day, no reason, he just started shooting. He'd be like one of his own suspects; the neighbors would cluck … he'd be on display.

Emil turned away from the hopeless pepper patch and reentered the familiar safety of his kitchen, and from there he went upstairs to the bedroom to change clothes. He sat on the edge of the bed to pull off his shoes, feeling himself on some kind of brink and pushing back. He fought the urge to run back down to the pepper patch with a pickax, a backhoe, a pneumatic drill, dynamite—anything—to excavate twenty feet down if necessary until the missing casing somehow materialized in his hand.

"God*dammit*!" he shouted, raising a fist, stopping himself from punching blindly at nothing. "Who the fuck dug the fucking casing out? *Who is doing this?*"

He scrambled to put the pieces together. What time did he shoot his gun? Monday morning, seven thirty … He'd said to Franco seven thirty in the morning was early for a beer, he remembered that. Good. Paulien's shift at the hospital was nine to five. By eight in the morning she was usually long gone. Not this morning. This morning she had the cut, her hand wrapped, blood on the bandage. Okay. How about yesterday morning? How could he be sure what time she'd left for work? It didn't matter; Paulien had to be up to no good, in cahoots with somebody—the Spider, surely, who'd have planted the finger and taken the casing. Why?

"What we have here is a case of cat and mouse, and I'm the mouse," he said quietly, briefly wondering if all widowers talked to themselves.

It was three thirty in the sweltering afternoon. Emil watered his garden. Surrounded by green, concentrating like a child lost in play, he did not hear Franco whistling. He watched as he moved the hose from side to side, creating a gentle shower over the thirsty earth, entranced as rainbow fragments danced in the misty spray above the hose. His feet were bare; he wore lightweight cotton pants held up by a drawstring and a gray, loose-fitting T-shirt. He turned, arrow-fast, ducking on one heel when a sharp stone hit him between the shoulder blades. Dropping to a crouch, he held the nozzle like a gun, pointing where he thought the stone had come from. Seeing Franco's arm waving a white towel from his side of the fence, he eased the water off.

Dragging the hose behind him, he walked over to the fence, the nozzle still clutched in his right hand. "What's the idea?"

"Hijo, finally you pay attention. What are you doing?"

The heat had intensified to ninety-nine degrees. A light, sticky breeze was up, and a thunderstorm seemed possible, but Emil doubted any rain would materialize. The air was a thick, foul mass, like breathing outside the vents of a dry cleaner's; wasted exhalations from polluted city pores. There were still hints of pure oxygen in the garden, though, pockets, like swimming in a lake with warm and cold spots, the garden holding movable promises of sweeter air and calm. But here was Franco. Again.

"What does it look like I'm doing?"

"Not finding out who did it."

"Did what?"

"What I'm saying." Emil listened. "Listen, amigo, I found something out from those two next to you, the two in Mrs. Pest's house?"

"Mrs. Noily, you mean?"

"You know those two who live there? The husband and the wife, la chica linda, who looks at you?"

"What are you talking about?"

"Sí, but that is not important. But what I found out is."

"Can you clarify that?"

"You got the ice?"

"I did. Thank you."

"And the thing in it is safe? Sí?"

"For now. Where we going, Franco?"

"Can you hear me?"

"I can hear you fine."

"Is the Horse home from her job?"

"I don't think so. It's too early."

"Listen to me."

"I *am* listening."

"Okay." Franco lowered his voice to a hissing whisper so Emil had to strain to hear him. "Someone made an offer to buy the Pest's house. Good money. Mrs. Pest was ready to talk, but the mister, Otto, said nothing doing. He said, 'Where will they go?' They have some dogs, no?"

"Yes . . ."

"Okay, Mr. Otto told the buyer to get lost. But Mrs. Pest told the people upstairs she maybe has to raise the rent. She say to the guy with the money, 'How much more will you pay?' And then—*bah*—her cat's neck breaks, she thinks because she ask for more money. You know, greedy. When Mr. Otto finds out she goes behind his back, he is angry, has his heartbreak attack: Bang! And, amigo," here Franco raised his voice, "have I not been saying to you that I will fix my place and sell for—"

"Hold on a minute, Franco, slow down. Who offered to buy Mrs. Noily's house—what guy? And how much money are we talking about?"

"I don't know. But it must be the Spider."

"Which is it? You know or you don't know?"

"Both."

"Uh-huh. I'm going to continue watering my garden now."

"But you cannot do that."

"Why not?"

"Because we have to find out who is climbing over the wall and killing the cat because I think these are the ones who want to buy the whole place, maybe all our houses, get us all rich, but they get richer. See? The something in the dry ice is proof."

Emil picked up the hose. The top third of the garden still needed watering, and that was his sole desire: to water and feed, tend and putter. He wanted no part of Franco's screwy reasoning, or Paulien or detached fingers, or anything else, like developers playing ugly. He was ready to flush poor Mary O'Donnell's digit down the toilet and forget the whole nasty episode. If it came up, he'd say he'd fired his pistol in a fit of pique, Franco could attest to that. He'd pay a fine; they'd take the gun. It wouldn't go further than that. And if questioned, he'd deny the finger ever existed. As for the morgue, impersonating a cop, try pinning that on him. Prove it. That morgue doctor wouldn't be volunteering any complaints. He could still walk away from this. A few fat lies more or less and he could put a stop to the whole sordid business of the last two days. It was a tempting scenario.

He'd intentionally buried himself in his garden, and that was how he wanted it. He was done playing cops catching killers, finished enforcing the law. What had he accomplished anyway? Pulled a few criminals off the street? So what? Take one away and five more spit out to take their place. What had Elena been trying to say: "You haven't gotten to the source"? Society could go ahead and make more rules, a thousand new laws, found a new religion, appeal to human decency—the fact was that no one knew the real root of crime. (*Life for life, eye for eye, tooth for tooth, fracture for fracture, hand for hand, foot for foot.*) Negatives, all built on negatives: Don't, don't, don't. He and Elena had made a garden. The garden was a beginning, their beginning, and if he had any say in the matter, it would be his ending: to be in his garden.

"Amigo? You there?"

In spite of himself, Emil sifted through Franco's words: What did he mean by "the wife who looks at you"? What's her name, the sculptor's wife—Laura, no, Lenore, Lorelei? She'd complimented the garden, "...

what I can see of it." He's saying she's watching me? Could she be the link, not Paulien? No! Crazy idea. And what about Franco and Elena and their pepper patch scheme? For the apple tree. And Franco will paint the wall. Yeah. Elena … apple tree. And maybe Franco made up his spider-man in black, and all this talk is part of some other scheme. Was Franco part of a real estate ploy? Was he paid off to get to me? That's what he's getting at, a real estate scam to explain the finger and the dead cat. If people wouldn't sell nice-like they'd be frightened into selling: harassment. Could there be anything to that?

But what did Emil care if property values flew to the sky and offers were made on rat holes like Franco's and the Noily dump next door? The whole area could turn into a fantasyland of speculation and soaring rents for all he cared. He was settled. Retired from the world and done with it. So far no one had approached him, and his building would be worth more than all the others combined, the garden alone. Franco was hinting at real estate terrorists running around at night trying to get a jump on a market that was about to pop. But if there was any truth to that, all Emil had to do was sit tight. Ignore the market, nurse his tomatoes. . . .

It was Elena's ring that had gotten to him. The dismembered finger was bad enough—that and the personal horror of having fired his weapon for no clear reason. But those two events were not connected; he had to keep that clear in his mind. He was calm now, a man watering his garden on a stifling summer afternoon. He'd get rid of Paulien if she dared show her face again. Call Immigration, start a check on her financial affairs, clear her out for good. He'd change the locks; see if she ever set foot in his house again. Tonight, after the furious sun went down, he would drink his wine outside in the sultry night with the perfume of the honeysuckle, and all would be back to what passed for normal.

Franco called to him, “Hey, Detective Miller?”

“No need to shout, I’m right here. And your theory stinks.”

“Maybe, but where is the hurt in finding out? La chica linda is at the hospital now, to Mrs. Pest with some things for the mister. I ask her from my steps how he is doing and she tells me everything, and asks me is my house for sale?”

“Who?”

“Amigo? I said: la chica linda that lives upstairs in Mrs. Pest’s.”

“Where’s the guy, the husband?”

“Long gone out.”

Emil considered. “How much did you tell them about anything else?”

Franco, indignant, declared, “Me! Detective Vega gave *nothing*.”

“All right, all right.” He was trying to figure what Franco was aiming at, and, more, why he was even paying attention to him. “Why do you call her Mrs. Pest?”

“Have you heard this mujer? She … *disapproves*.”

Emil kept himself from laughing. Franco had landed on the perfect word for CeeCee Noily. Nothing met with her approval; everything caused ceaseless complaint.

“So now would be the time, hombre, to go into her house to find the evidence of maybe bad guys trying to buy us out, you see what I’m saying?” Franco continued.

“You’re saying break and enter?”

“Why break? You know how to do it; you are a cop.”

“Let’s say I do; any ideas what to do with the dogs?”

“Pet them?”

Emil could get into the Noily house easily enough with one of the fire and master keys he’d held on to over the years. But no, uh-uh, he was out of it now. "No hard feelings, amigo," he told Franco, "but this is where I get off. I'm—" Emil looked up when the loud ping of stone hitting glass rang out above him. Franco had pitched a large pebble up to Paulien's window. He pitched a second, a perfect shot up four stories. "Hey! You'll break that window!"

"No one there," Franco said. Next thing his body swung in one quick motion over the fence. Emil stepped back as Franco landed in front of him, to the right of the pepper patch. "Can you get over this way?" Franco asked, waving a hand toward the other fence, between Emil's and the Noilys'.

"I never tried—never mind that, what the hell are you doing flying over my fence like that?" Maybe Franco had been flying over into the garden for years—even when Elena was alive. Maybe *he* was the Spider. Was that how he got the poison into the pepper patch?

Franco moved quickly to the other side of Emil's garden. "Can we use that?" He pointed to a chair.

Emil sighed. Franco was becoming a one man train wreck. "No, here, use this table." There was a square cedar prep table next to the brick cookout Emil had built. Franco moved the table next to the fence, close to the lilac, where no one would see it, namely, Paulien. "Don't crush any plants with that," Emil said, watching him.

Franco paused on the table, turned to Emil, and said, "I was a marine stationed in Nam, you know." In a matter of seconds he was up and over onto the Noilys' side.

Emil went into the house for a stepladder and to put on shoes. He came back out and handed the ladder over the fence to Franco. "You'll need this to get back," he said in a low voice.

"Bueno," Franco said through the fence. Then a minute later, "You coming?" But Emil turned back toward the kitchen again. He came out this time with a ring of keys of all shapes and sizes that he intended to hand over to Franco. He dangled the keys over the fence. "Here," he whispered, but Franco was quiet. "What are you doing?"

"Scraping my shoe."

Emil climbed onto the table to look over the fence. He suppressed another urge to laugh. "Watch out for the feet," Franco said, his expression filled with disdain; his yard might not be much to look at, but at least it wasn't filled with dog shit. There was a hunk of it on the ground with the impression of Franco's shoe in the middle.

Emil pushed hard and, with less ease than Franco, managed to swing himself over the fence into the Noilys' yard. Franco nodded as he threw loose leaves over the dog pile. Emil walked to the back door and listened. No barking. He squatted to study the lock in Mrs. Noily's heavy, theft-proof metal screen door but jumped up, dropping the keys, when Sam darted out of a darkened corner. "Christ!" he said through gritted teeth. Franco covered his mouth. Sam parked himself by the door and stared at Emil. "You again," he told the cat.

Using his T-shirt bottom against fingerprints, Emil held the doorknob while deciding which key might work but then realized the door was unlocked. Mrs. Noily must have forgotten to lock it in the emergency. Now he wasn't breaking, only unlawfully entering. Small comfort. He carefully pulled the screen door open.

He slowly turned the inner doorknob and gently pushed, ready to pull it closed in a hurry if he had to. He waited. No dogs. Were they really that dumb? Did they not know enough to bark at intruders? Emil opened the door all the way and crept inside. Sam tried to squeeze in past him but Emil blocked the way with his leg, shoving him back. He heard the sounds of clicking from upstairs; dog claws on wooden floors. He slipped over to the dining room door and quickly closed it. Franco was now beside him, noticeably uneasy and breathing hard. "The dogs are away?" he asked. Emil nodded.

The Noilys' kitchen was laid out similarly to Emil's, minus the changes and improvements he and Elena had made, like the French door to their garden, the dishwasher, the hand-painted Italian tiles interspersed on the wall behind their stove and sink. The appliances in Mrs. Noily's kitchen were old and colored an on-sale avocado green. The room was filled with stuff: frilly curtains, towels with cute sayings, a lot of loud pinks and yellows. A curio cabinet above the table contained dozens of ceramic poodles in various erotic poses. Emil rolled his eyes. At least the kitchen was clean, easy to figure where things were kept. Emil remembered Mrs. Noily saying to Elena one time that she was a kitchen person. Elena asked him just what that meant. Did she bake a lot, or what? "Talks on the phone, I'd guess," Emil answered.

Where Emil's round oak kitchen table would be were two metal filing cabinets holding up a makeshift desk. A Formica dining table and two chairs covered in flower-patterned vinyl were placed by the dining room door. Franco opened the door a crack but shoved it shut at the sound of a low growl from the other side.

Emil looked up. He was at the file cabinet, a drawer already opened. "What are we looking for, Franco?"

"I don't know. You are the police. Real estate?"

What category? he asked himself. If the supposed offer to buy were very recent, maybe there was no file yet. Out on the desktop were bills: electric, water, telephone, credit cards. Also grocery store coupons, a *TV Guide*, catalogs, a general mess of papers covering the surface. He pushed through the pile with his right hand, fingers splayed. All the usual uninteresting junk of day-to-day life. At a glance, nothing unusual stood out. Franco stood looking over his shoulder.

Phone book, calendar, insurance forms … wait … by the phone a slip of paper with a telephone number and a figure, "$50,000," written on it, followed by a question mark and a printed capital letter: *B*. Emil copied the information down on a scrap of paper.

Franco said, "We finish now? Time to go, huh?"

"This was your idea; what's the hurry? I thought you were a marine."

"I know, but …"

Emil knew Franco was ready to crap his pants; he'd felt that way himself on his first search, and he'd been legal. "Okay," he said under his breath, "this might be something." He'd found a paper with a letterhead Kirk Realty: Commercial and Residential, Serving the Community for Ten Years.

Emil had located his building through an ad in the newspaper. There were only commercial Realtors in the area back then, and those were few and far between. He doubted Mr. Kirk Realty had been in the business ten years. Most people in the neighborhood sold on their own, the few that sold at all.

The letter was dated last Friday: *Dear Mrs. Noily, This letter is to confirm Kirk Realty will make an inspection of your property and commence marketing of your house*—the address, block, and lot numbers followed—*at a price mutually agreed upon. We appreciate your query and would like to arrange a time to see the property as soon as is convenient to ascertain the value and advise …*

"There it is," Emil said, "weary Otto Noily's heart attack in black and white." He copied Kirk's number on the other side of the scrap of paper. He knew the address; it was near the subway. He put the paper scrap into his T-shirt pocket and turned to Franco. "Okay, we can—what are you doing?"

Franco held the refrigerator door open and was reaching inside for a beer. He stopped, put the beer back down and closed the door. "We can go?"

"Did you get your fingerprints on that?"

Franco looked at his hands. "No. The bottle is wet." He wiped his hands on his pants.

"How about the refrigerator door?"

Franco looked guilty like a schoolboy. He found a tea towel at the stove and wiped the refrigerator door and handle. "Okay?"

"And the towel?"

"Sí." He carefully redraped the towel over the oven-door handle. "Okay now?"

"It wasn't folded."

"No?" Franco neatly unfolded the towel. "Bueno?"

"Don't you want to know what I found out?"

"Not here, you loco?"

Outside, Sam the cat waited by the door. His expression was ugly, and it was directed at Emil.

Franco said, "Este gato no te quiere. I never see a cat hate a man like that."

Emil said in a low voice, "Listen, Franco, I'll check on this Realtor, maybe try the other number, but after that," he made a sweeping gesture with his hand, "for me it's over. Do you understand?"

"Wait. You hear that?" Franco hissed.

"Ah, no. Dammit!"

"Someone is here. Madre de Dios, let's away!"

The air filled with the sound of barking. Franco flew like a crazy bird over the fence. Emil followed, his heart thumping in his chest—the indignity of being caught. From his side of the fence he reached over to pull the stepladder up behind him. Franco held on to his ankles as he pulled. He nearly dropped it. They got the ladder over to Emil's side just as one of the dogs burst through the kitchen door, yelping hysterically. They heard a male voice say, "What is it, boy, what's out there, Scotch?" It was Mrs. Noily's tenant. The one Franco had said was gone.

The other two dogs were furiously barking now. Emil and Franco stood pressed together under the pergola, hugging the wall outside Emil's kitchen. Emil held on to the ladder. He'd scraped his shin badly on the pointed pioneer fence; blood seeped through his pant leg. After a few minutes the barking stopped and the dogs were only wildly sniffing the yard and fence.

"Come on, Scotch! Mango! Louie! No one's there. Let's go!" Then, "Oh, fuck!"

Emil and Franco understood simultaneously that he'd stepped into the pile of dog do Franco had camouflaged with leaves. Franco's eyes met Emil's; he bit his lip to keep from laughing.

"Get in here *now*, Scotch! Mango! Louie! Goddammit! C'mon, walk, time for a walk. *Let's go!*" Mrs. Noily's kitchen door banged shut; the lock clicked sharply into place.

Emil exhaled hard. He'd been holding his breath. His shoulders relaxed, and a wave of hilarity swept over him. He fought with himself, but the wave burst out of him, hitting the rocky shore of his massive self-control, sending out a spray of laughter. Seeing the circle of blood coloring his pant leg only made him laugh harder. Then the image of his pistol and the pepper patch came to him. He breathed deeply, his laughter letting go. It was absurd; there was no other word for it, absurd that he had fired into the pepper patch. He said, careful to keep his voice low, "They say if you possess a gun, you will use it."

Franco looked at him, shrugged. "Sí," he whispered. "Gringos are trigger happy hombres."

Emil considered the remark. "They probably are."

He was certain now that he had not intended to shoot Franco, and that realization filled him with huge relief, like a kid who has just passed an exam he was certain he'd flunked. He didn't know what made him fire those two rounds, but at least he hadn't been gunning for his neighbor. He shook his head and started laughing all over again. When was the last time he'd laughed with such abandon?

"Sí, amigo," Franco said. "Sí, to laugh is to live. Now we are getting somewhere." He stood nodding, a look of satisfaction on his face.

Emil wiped a tear from his left eye. His gray T-shirt was bathed in sweat. He lifted his torn, bloody pant leg; he'd have to patch up the scraped shin; the pants were trashed.

Franco said, "We are fallen hombres, but we still bleed . . . and we still can laugh, sí, mi amigo?"

"Speak for yourself, Franco. I'm not fallen."

"No?"

"No."

"Then you are the only one."

THREE

He that smiteth a man, so that he die, shall be surely put to death. And if a man not lie in wait, but God deliver him into his hand; then I will appoint thee a place whither he shall flee. But if a man come presumptuously upon his neighbor, to slay him with guile; thou shalt take him from my altar, that he may die.

The Giving of the Law, Book of Exodus

The sun had finally let go, slid away through the gelatinous ooze of daylight. One minute was dull afternoon, the next dull night; nothing else changed. No relief came with the darkening sky; grimy air stuck to sticky skin, heat fatigue oppressed everyone. Emil looked up. The kitchen ceiling fan whirled above his head with an insistent little click-click at each revolution. It needs oil, he thought without moving.

Earlier, after the episode at Mrs. Noily's, Emil called the numbers he'd written down in her kitchen. He'd told Franco he would and he kept his word. The phone number attached the *B* went nowhere. He tried three times and then called the operator, identifying himself as a police officer, Detective Mueller this time, and requested the address. He was told the number in question belonged to a pay phone in Patchogue, on Long Island. Patchogue, he repeated to himself. What did he know about Patchogue, Long Island?

He next called Kirk Realty's office and identified himself as Mr. Melon, a prospective buyer from Manhattan. He explained that rents had gone sky high where he was living so even the mice were moving out. He was looking to purchase, and was it true he would find improved value in the outer boroughs? The Realtor on the other end was sympathetic, dutifully laughing at the humor regarding mice.

"Yes, indeed, Mr. Melon," Mr. Kirk replied, "the potential here is limitless. Brooklyn is up for grabs; you couldn't've picked a better time to look. When can we schedule an appointment?"

Emil answered, "How about some ballpark figures what to expect? I'm told you need a little more imagination in your part of the borough, that it's rough around the edges. I'm no explorer, Mr. Kirk."

"A little imagination might be in order, but cities are made by men who take chances, Mr. Melon. You and the mice have opportunity here, and that means stepping outside the shoebox." A little humor of his own, but Mr. Melon didn't laugh. "So, any chance of coming out here this afternoon? I could squeeze you in. I'm looking over my listings as we speak."

Emil's voice hardened: "I'm hearing figures like seventy-five to one hundred thousand for a four-story brick, Mr. Kirk. Can that possibly be correct where you're located?"

"That might be a little high, but things *are* inching up. This is the time to plan long range, sir."

"Long range for what? Death?"

There was a pause before Mr. Kirk laughed. "I like your humor. Call me Jim, Mr. Melon—Bill, did you say it was?"

"I didn't, but it's Ed."

"Well, in my view now would be the cusp, the time to make a move, maybe the smartest move of your life. I'm on the side of the homeowner, Ed Melon, a family man myself. It gives me honest to God peace of mind to see a family settle into a home I sold them. When you think about it, it's God's work."

"How do you figure that?"

"Land: real property, Ed. From the Bible on out, mostly all anybody's ever fought over's land; that's been the main angle for two thousand years. Am I right? No need to fight when you've a solid real estate man on your team. See what I mean? And they're not making any more of it."

"Land?"

"Right-o: Mother Earth, terra firma, hills and valleys, fertile deltas, God's little acre …"

"Don't leave out the Garden of Eden."

Jim Kirk belly laughed. "Now, if I could only get my hands on *that* piece'a property! What do you say, Ed?"

"I'll have to give it some thought, Jim."

"Don't think too long. How about a few sites today, make a start, would that work out for you at all today?" The man was as subtle as a plow; he was practically through the phone line breathing his lunch into Emil's face. "I personally wouldn't put it off," he pushed, "real estate being the tricky beast it is. A man has to have insight. The very fact of this call tells me you're the sort."

"What sort is that?"

"I've been in this business long enough to read a man, and I think you've got what it takes."

"To move a market, you mean?"

"Vision, Ed, individual vision into a situation that's ready to explode."

"Would anyone be helping that explosion along?"

"Helping it along? Only sharp men like yourself can do that, Ed. Have you got a car? Or I can meet your subway. We're on the L line. When should I expect you?"

Emil guessed Kirk Realty was bluffing. He'd seen the same signs as Emil, the signs Franco was pushing. He'd probably helped nudge the rents up as the first few pioneers trickled in from Manhattan, with its artificial economy forever jacking prices up. The artists would catch on they couldn't afford Mecca anymore, find cheaper parts of town to tame. The diminishing value of a dollar in Manhattan would cause people to reconsider the inconvenience of a trip under or over the East River. Speculators were always on the prowl, but Kirk hadn't thrown Emil sufficient bait that spoke of a solid market. He concluded the real estate theory Franco was floating wouldn't sail or was premature.

He was about to hang up when Kirk said, "I'm going to level with you, Ed."

"Oh?" Everything else so far was not on the level? Emil didn't ask.

"This part of Brooklyn is going to be a seller's market within a year—six months more like. The artists have come, the investors smell blood, and the developers won't be far behind. This is the last moment for a good buy and then, sayonara, it's over, a whole new ball game. What I'm saying is a housing expansion is already under way."

Kirk had dropped the circus barker's jovial best-buddy-pitchman voice for something more businesslike. Emil asked for his address, just to stall. He said he might come by on the weekend. "Don't wait too long, Mr. Melon. Seize the day; it won't be here tomorrow. I'm saying *I'll* probably be swallowed up once this thing goes viral."

Emil had called Kirk Realty and the *B* number from a pay phone near the subway entrance, along a cluster of shops that sold nothing of much worth. Here too, in what Elena referred to as the hub, the lightbulbs in the shops were low wattage, like Rudy's Corner Market, only here it was more superstition and fear at work. Immigrants, Emil had explained to Elena, afraid the electricity would run out if they used too much of it (somehow he didn't see himself and Elena as immigrants). There were two taverns along the strip. Winter through summer their doors were open to the sidewalk, sending forth whiffs of cigarette smoke and watery beer. A look inside revealed the same worn out customers leaning over their evening mugs. On the jukebox would be Frank Sinatra or Paul Anka, or maybe a polka. These were bars time had forgotten, and according to Mr. Kirk they were situated at the epicenter of the next real estate boom? If that was the case, these working people taking their ease had no clue.

While he was talking to Jim Kirk, Mrs. Noily's tenant—Linda, was it, or Lynne—emerged from the subway, her body revealed in a strappy tank top and short skirt, long legs shooting out. Her light brown hair, pulled into a ponytail, had slipped seductively loose. She looked taller than he remembered from seeing her outside the Noilys'. How could Franco know she was looking at him? But why would he make a thing like that up? Emil quickly turned to face the other way, but she'd seen him and waved. Their block of houses, which was where he assumed she would go, was a fifteen minute walk from the subway.

He hung up the phone and there she was, standing in front of him, long, lithe, and barely dressed. "Hello there, Detective Milosec." Emil nodded, keeping his eyes on the top of her head of shiny, smooth hair. "It's Loretta, in case you forgot."

"Loretta, right."

"Hey, but it's hot, huh?" She sounded flirty, though all she'd said was it was hot. "You heard about Mr. Noily?" She nodded as if confirming something. "I just brought some things over to the hospital for him and CeeCee, including her migraine pills." Loretta licked her lips.

"What hospital would that be?"

"Wittekoff."

"Did you see anyone there?"

"Like who? You mean Mr. Noily? He's in surgery. Hey, you want to get a coffee? It's frying out here."

Emil looked around. "A coffee?"

Loretta laughed. "C'mon." She lightly touched his arm, and he went with her, walked a couple of blocks to a café he'd never seen before. It was a hipster joint with small round tables, some sort of art on the walls. They found a table near the back.

"When did this place appear?"

"I don't know. Maybe like six months ago, seven. Nice, huh? About time too; those dark old-timey bars just about depress the hell out of me."

A waitress drifted over to their table—jeans, vacant expression, a silver nose ring and other piercings that to Emil looked uncomfortable, and not very hygienic. What was he even doing in that café? Nobody in it looked old enough to legally drink. "What can I get you?" the waitress said, as if it were a bother to ask.

"Hi. A mocha latte—decaf," Loretta said.

"You have espresso?" Emil asked. The waitress turned her head to look at him: Was this a test?

Loretta said, "They have espresso." Emil nodded, and Loretta told the waitress, "And one espresso."

"A double?" the waitress asked Loretta.

Loretta looked at Emil. "No, not a double," he said to the waitress. "And bring us some waters. Do you want a cookie or anything?" Loretta shook her head, and the waitress drifted off.

Loretta fiddled with a pink packet of diet sweetener from a container on the table. Emil observed her. "You're always in that garden of yours," she said, looking down. "Like you maybe lost something in there."

"Lost something like what?"

She dropped the sugar packet on the table. "I don't know."

Emil looked hard at Loretta's eyes. Did she know something?

She leaned back and crossed a leg high over her thigh. Emil caught a shot of white panties over crotch. She lifted her arms to recapture the straying ponytail into a red hair band. "So when are you going to show me?"

"What?"

Loretta smiled. "The garden."

Emil pictured LaTeesha Williams, *her* smile and the deep, kind eyes. Other parts of her anatomy volunteered themselves to his mind's eye too: her derrière, full mouth, and breasts. Now here was his neighbor's crotch staring up at him. Up close Loretta didn't seem quite so young; her eyes, anyway, weren't as youthful, their expression watchful.

"Does your husband know you flirt with men?"

Loretta tossed her head back and laughed. She had a feathery laugh that didn't go with her eyes. "Malcolm's not my husband. We live together; we're not *man and wife*. Anyhow, all I asked was to see your garden, not your gun or anything."

"Why do you assume I have a gun?" Had she heard the shots too?

"Once a lawman always a lawman, right? Like in the old Wild West movies: 'The sheriff's in town.' Like *High Noon*. That's one of my favorite movies—Gary Cooper, mmm … you know, you look a little like Gary

Cooper, like mature vulnerable. …" She flicked her silky ponytail with her left hand.

Emil watched.

The waitress interrupted with their coffees, no waters.

Emil swallowed his espresso and stood up. He pulled a twenty out of his pocket. "Will this cover it?"

"Do you have to be somewhere?"

"I do." He coughed once, dropped the bill on the table and turned to go.

Loretta looked up, her lips in a half smile. "Putting someone under arrest, Detective?"

Emil turned to face her; he leaned in and moved the twenty—the same twenty he'd tried to give Franco earlier—closer to Loretta, turned, and walked away.

"'Bye, Detective," Loretta called after him. "Maybe another time …"

He felt her eyes on him as he walked to the exit. What was her game?

Outside felt that much hotter after the icy air conditioning inside the café. There were girls everywhere on the street, younger than ever girls dressed loose in the heat. Emil moved fast, headed north, and turned the corner. He went in the opposite direction of his house in case Loretta would soon be walking that way. Elena said women were beautiful and there was nothing for him to do but suffer. Right.

He walked quickly in the heat two blocks south on Riggs and then doubled back to a side street and passed the Kirk Realty office. A glance inside showed him what he'd expected: dim interior, two desks, one agent, Mr. Kirk himself, a few listings posted in the window on faded index cards, no attempt at decor, and no customers. A sign outside the shop read, "Checks Cashed/Insurance/Notary Public." Sure, a boomtown. What did they call real estate agents? Bloodhounds—and they were right up there with ambulance-chasing lawyers.

He doubled back onto Riggs Street, down one more block south. Ahead was the redbrick steeple of St. Dominic's Church. Past the church, he headed toward a pizza shop, passing a Laundromat and a small zipper manufacturer called Zippit. He eyed a squat, yellow-painted brick building with a sign that announced, "Jesus Is Lord." He had no idea what business was conducted on the premises. He'd seen midsized yellow vans with the Jesus Is Lord logo. Maybe they shipped Bibles, biblical literature. His cop sense made him suspect other goods were being moved alongside whatever religious paraphernalia might be for sale, but that might only reflect his distrust of religious organizations in general, the very idea of peddling faith. Alongside small manufacturing plants that built everything from plumbing parts to plastic dental-floss containers were private homes. On side streets were one- and two-, some four-family dwellings. Their facades were mostly aluminum siding or asphalt tile that looked like linoleum, some in fake brick face or thickly stuccoed like fluffy cake icing. A few were actual old brick. All were tidy with neat rows of garbage cans lined up out front; some contained small gardens inside shallow entry gates or single planters filled with purple petunias or impatiens or marigolds. This was the beginning of the Italian section, and solidly old Brooklyn.

He opened the door to Giorno's Pizza and was hit with a full, rich, tomatoey smell. The owner, Carmine, was perched on a stool on the customer side of the counter, reading the Italian newspaper *Oggi*. He looked up when the door opened. "Hey, Detective Emilio, come va? A very long time, my friend; you've been hiding."

Emil smiled. "Va bene, amico mio, va bene. How's the pizza business?"

Carmine shrugged his shoulders. "The same. You want a caffeè? Sit, I'll make us a cup. Sit." The air conditioner rattled loudly in its sleeve over the door, an old machine that just about broke even between the heat of the oven and the heat off the street. Carmine didn't seem to notice.

Emil and Mike had stopped by Giorno's every couple of weeks when they were on the job together. They both agreed it was the best pizza in the neighborhood. The thin crust was the thing, and the sweet red sauce with a nice amount of cheese on top, not too much cheese like with some pizza joints, Mike pointed out, "where all you end up is chewing on cheese." Mike had a special fondness for the garlic balls, often taking a greasy brown bag full back out to the car. Emil didn't eat the garlic balls; he said it wouldn't do at a crime scene to stink of garlic and herbs. Mike maintained that a corpse couldn't smell anymore, so what was the difference? Giorno's had been around since the early sixties. Emil rarely saw more than four people at a time seated at the few tables in back, and he'd always assumed those few were Carmine's relations. When you entered Giorno's it was as if you had entered a slice of Italy; never a hurry, and Carmine always found time to stop what he was doing to say hello. The takeout business was the mainstay. A city bus stop stood out front, and when the sidewalk window was open and the bus was running slow, as it usually was, Carmine sold plenty of hot slices and cold sodas.

Emil watched as Carmine worked the machinetta. When he was done, he came around again with two miniature cups and four cubes of sugar.

They stirred their sugars in silence. "Good," Emil said of the strong brew. Better than at that frou-frou café with Loretta.

"The heat's on today, and no kidding about it," Carmine said after a few minutes.

"I don't know how you take it with the oven." Carmine lifted his hands; what's to be done, he meant to say, he was used to it. They talked a little of nothing much, then Emil asked, "So, you seeing many new faces in the neighborhood lately?"

"Here by the shop?" Emil nodded. "Well, the bus stop, you see a lot of types." He thought a minute. "Yeah, maybe more kids—young, college students could be. Scruffy-looking kids, some with green or purple hair." He laughed. "Green hair? But what do I care what color if they eat my pies?"

"It's good pie," Emil said. "So I, ah, heard a rumor some rough stuff on the part of certain parties wanting to buy property, *encourage* people to sell. You heard anything of the sort?"

Sometimes Carmine heard things. Mostly in the tightly knit Italian section where there was the inevitable mafioso skim. Carmine was not a snitch; he only ever spoke in very general terms and was what Mike Dunn had called a casually concerned citizen. He had a feel for the rhythms around him and an independent streak; he owned the pizza business and the building it sat in; no one pushed Carmine Giorno around. "Over there, you saying?" Carmine pointed with his thumb toward the Italian side. "Nobody tries any funny stuff over there. Not unless they have something wrong with them that they are cured of very fast."

"I was thinking more down my way."

Carmine reflected. "Could be the Hassid community needs to spread out? They reproduce worse than us Catholics."

Emil smiled. "Not their style, I'd say. They mostly only ever use muscle around the competing Hassidic group. A thing I never fully understood. Anyhow, I think it's just talk, what I heard. Times could be changing, though."

Carmine laughed. Nothing had changed since his father opened the shop, since his family arrived from Bari in 1950. "I'll believe that when I see it. The neighborhood's a little short on charm, in case you didn't notice." Emil smiled. "You own your place, right, Emilio, you're not worried?"

"No, I can't be touched by speculators."

"You're not back on the job?" Emil shook his head. "Private work? Money problems?"

Emil appreciated Carmine's concern. "No and no. Money's fine. I'm curious, that's all. I think maybe people start rumors to try to create a market where there isn't any; then the herd gets going and—you know—New York, the myth, it's ninety percent illusion."

Carmine thought that over. "Nah, I don't know … you hear these things every now and again. This is Brooklyn, Emilio; change comes slow to Brooklyn."

Emil thanked Carmine for the coffee. He said he'd be back for a slice when the hot weather let go of his appetite.

"Anytime, Emilio, anytime. If I hear anything …" Emil nodded. They shook hands, and Emil went back out into the glaring afternoon heat, revived by Carmine's strong espresso and hospitality.

He turned left outside Carmine's shop, deciding to detour north toward the park. A few kids lazed over a ball under some trees near the park's corner entrance. The usual handful of defeated drunks sat huddled on benches, lips blubbery, faces blotched and ruddy. Otherwise the indifferently kept park appeared empty. It seemed to always be empty. Along the west corner stood an Orthodox church, squat but for its onion dome spires. There were four smaller onions and then the great big dome like a full womb in the center, all billowing above a base of pale yellow brick. The domes were the acidic green of long-oxidized copper. Emil was oddly fond of the church, the architecture of it. The structure came up so unexpectedly in the surroundings. Next to the Church of Transfiguration was a square garden, closed in with a chain-link fence. Few plantings of note, mostly shrubs, some that flowered, and solid old trees among a healthy patch of very green grass. No attempt had been made to cloister the grounds, but trees laced the adjacent sidewalk, giving Emil the impression of peeking into a wide-open secret. Inside at the far end were three wooden picnic tables. Emil always expected to see a priest in the garden, walking in flowing black dress or meditating or perhaps just enjoying the day, but he had never seen man or beast, only birds fussing in the trees.

The church marked the temporary end to the light manufacturing that dotted the area. The streets here too were often empty. Barren streets and onion domes; Emil's Brooklyn.

He stood a few minutes in front of the church. There had been no large onion-domed church in Senice, only a small wooden structure, cold as death in winter. Instead of reaching toward the sky, phallic, as the Roman Catholic churches did, like St. Dominic's back around the corner, these domes seemed bound to the earth, breastlike, fertile and mysterious. Studying the structure, he decided that if the idea was to exemplify something spiritual, he'd choose this organic approach over the sky-pricking monuments. Why would the spiritual translate into poking into the sky, away from the ground? Aspiring to the sky—toward heaven—to deny life on earth. Earthly life as in fucking and gardening? He stood in front of the Church of Transfiguration and found nothing forbidding or threatening in its presentation. Then the image of Loretta crossing her leg threw itself in front of him. Fucking and gardening. . . .

As he continued walking in the unrelenting late day heat, two teams of homing pigeons rose into the sky. Released from rooftop pens on rent-stabilized buildings a few blocks from his house, the birds took to the air in tight formation. Twice each day they were let loose. At certain times of year, if he happened to see the early evening flight, their white backs would catch the setting sun, reflecting gold and orange as they flew. A sky performance as the birds suddenly reversed themselves in mid-flight, shifting from flat surfaces that captured the light to a view across their wings, so that for a fraction of a second they'd flicker out of sight altogether. The weaving pattern, up and down, around and around, was hypnotic. Franco had once explained that when the two teams mixed up in flight, sometimes one flock lost a few birds while the other gained. It could go back and forth like that, and sometime birds were lost altogether, fleeing the security of home and flock. Emil watched them swirl, dots dancing through the bright hot sky, lost in a ritual of freedomless flight.

If the real estate people came, buying up housing, what would happen to the pigeons? What happened to the people who couldn't keep up with costs? Where would they go? And the factory jobs? He thought of the closed-up spice factory near his house. Did the new owner know something; was he biding his time sitting on property that could end up as prime real estate, waiting patiently to line his pockets with unchecked wealth?

Carmine was right; theirs was an ugly neighborhood, mostly bare of ornamentation and niceties. Especially ugly after he'd been away, he and Elena, to a pleasing locale so that when they returned home they were appalled by it anew. But it was still a stable area for working families, and there were moments of elegance, like the daily flight of the pigeons, and the big, uncluttered Brooklyn sky that gave it a raw beauty, a kind of grace under pressure. Brooklyn was Emil's home—his family's place of exile from the old country—the good of it and the bad. Was all that set to change? He imagined bull's-eyes on the small family homes he passed as he walked toward his own.

He scratched at his itching brain as he walked, trying to decide if he should dismiss outright Franco's get-rich-quick real estate theory as having any connection to Mary O'Donnell's severed digit. He didn't know what to make of the offer to buy the Noily house, but a little voice that he knew better than to ignore told him not to shut the door on real estate as at least part of the motivation behind recent events. A cop dismissed that little voice at his peril, that mental construct arising from a place that leaped across synapses. Only hints, sure, but the trick was figuring out where the hints went.

A cop keeps hundreds of files open in his head, facts from the morbid to the mundane, information filed away that could lead to a dead end or to a killer. The little detail that doesn't sit right, the notation that seems insignificant and turns out to be the loose screw in the bad guy's story so the whole facade of it falls apart, the minuscule incongruities that expose the lie that spun the web of cover-up. Like any good policeman, Emil was cluttered with mental Post-Its: names, places, alibis, facial expressions, intonations, clothing, license plates and car makers, accents, weather reports, traffic patterns: open files and closed files—all needed on short notice, all taking up space.

He'd never dumped his years of files. How could he? Minds don't delete unless the brain is damaged or the memory erased by disease. Files go dormant or are shoved aside for newer files, but they are there. Memory can be tricked, portions blocked by trauma or grief or fear, but they are still there. Emil's mind was laced with threads, some of which might or might not be tied to current events. Within the jumble of clues he was currently worrying was Elena and that conversation from a few years ago, and those years ago were shifting from hidden recesses to a more present tense, not fully but tantalizingly. Something nagged, and the something was not pleasant. Not the two of them touring, or dining, sipping white wine on a summer afternoon, or sharing warmth on a winter evening. Not fucking and gardening either. No, something was dark in Denmark, he told himself, misquoting.

Back at the house he sorted the mail, placing Paulien's two envelopes faceup on the vestibule console. Her mail was routine. He set his own envelopes—also routine: bills, a credit card offer, a magazine promo—inside the parlor door and then walked down to the kitchen. He filled a glass with water and drank it down. It was a day for water. He hadn't finished watering the garden. The hose was where he'd dropped it when Franco interrupted him. He took his shoes and socks off and walked outside. He pulled the hose to the rear of the garden and finished the job, adding water to the small pool. Goldfish swam near the top, puckering their lips. He remembered he'd meant to feed them. That done, he sat on the pool's edge and from his leafy shelter looked up at the Noily house. It was set back six feet, was not flush with his house, as Franco's was. That little setback was viewed as a plus, keeping the Noilys at a slight remove. He looked up specifically at the third-floor windows.

What was he hoping to see? Loretta at the window, dripping wet, fresh and naked out of the shower? Had the anesthesia of grief worn off? Elena had been a sacrament to him, a communion of sexual desire and ethereal loveliness. Was he waking up to animal desire, the turmoil and bother of lust?

The garden seen to, Emil went upstairs. He was spent by the numbing heat and the unexpected event of so much humanity crowding into one day. He turned the air conditioner on full blast and fell asleep the instant he lay down. He awoke so refreshed he felt almost euphoric, and confused. For a few frightening seconds he did not know who he was. It was all topsy-turvy until the image of the dream he'd just had brought him back to where the day had begun and who he was, or at least where he was.

The dream had him driving through a wide open plain under a milky white sky. A breeze blew into the car window, passing pleasantly along his skin. Mountains appeared; the car slowly climbed up and up. The mountains turned into a flock of swirling birds, black wings beating against his ear. Birds flew into the car, blinding him because there were so many, and he could no longer see the road as the whole sky filled with flapping black specks. He saw the sky had become a glass dome; the birds flew up, smashing into the glass, smearing the surface with blood and feathers, the blood dripping as the car began to fall backward. He tried desperately to steer while moving faster and faster downhill. The brakes failed. He was sliding down, down, down, down—he stood in a playground surrounded by laughing children; they held hands in a circle until one child's hand fell to the ground. He bent to pick it up and when he straightened up he was in the middle of a forest, still holding the diminutive hand. The air was cool and smelled of moist leaves; he heard a stream running; he was thirsty and wanted to go to the stream. He dropped the hand under a pile of leaves. The stream became louder, almost a deafening roar, waking him.

The stream was the sound of the air conditioner humming in the window. He understood the child's hand was Mary O'Donnell's finger, and that she and he were lost.

He lay in bed, staring at the ceiling, shaking off the dream, his breath coming in and out too fast. Knock, knock. Who's there? No one. No one who? No one's there. The unconscious puffing smoke, Elena had said of dreams. He could do without the puffs.

When he had recovered who he was, he got up and stood by the window. The reflected colors of the setting sun rendered the garden in a muted orange wash. He stood at the window a long time, deciding he would stay awake all night to see if anything else might be dropped off in the wee hours. Stake out his own house: Would any other body parts show up or spidermen scale the back wall? For now, below him all was peaceful and quiet.

He took a shower and in comfortable clothes went down to the kitchen to put together his supper. He was looking up, thinking about oiling the bothersome click-click of the ceiling fan, when the doorbell rang upstairs. It was almost nine o'clock. Emil stood without moving a hair. His doorbell never rang at night. Ever. For years. Where he lived people called first. The bell rang again and this time was accompanied by heavy pounding on the front door.

Emil climbed the stairs, his faded espadrilles padding his footsteps. He slipped out of his apartment toward the outer door. Someone was calling his name. Not Franco. The bell rang a fourth and fifth time. "You in there, Milosec? It's Bernie Bracco from the Ten-oh. You wanna open up?" Emil tiptoed over, waited a few seconds, and then opened the door, his surprise unconcealed.

Bracco's arm was still in the air, poised to pound again. "Hey, Milosec, twice in one day, huh? Three if you count that phone call of yours. Sorry to barge in."

Emil looked beyond Detective Bracco to see if he was alone. He was. "This official?" he asked.

"Kind of." Detective Bracco laughed slightly, uneasily. "I think I may have lost a suspect."

If Bernie Bracco was trying to be funny, he'd picked the wrong audience on the wrong night. Emil looked expressionless into the eyes of his former protégé. "Here?"

"Your tenant, Paulien Vandervell."

"Paulien? Is that what you were doing this afternoon?"

"Yeah … mostly." Bracco looked around. "Lookit, can I come in? It's a little, you know, standing out on the stoop …" He waved an arm behind him, toward the street.

The very last thing on earth Emil Milosec wanted on this night, or any other night, but especially this particular night, was a cop nosing into his house. "Will this take long, do you think?"

"Milosec, I could get a warrant." Bracco's face turned mean, but it didn't last. "C'mon."

"A warrant for here?"

"Upstairs, your tenant."

"You want me to let you into her apartment?"

"That's the general idea. Am I not speaking clear enough?"

"Come in," Emil said. His stomach lifted itself back up off the floor, where it had landed when Bracco mentioned getting a warrant. No need to take him beyond the entry, he told himself. But that would look suspicious. He moved away from the door. Detective Bracco walked into the vestibule, closing the outer door behind him.

Emil pushed open the door to his apartment. "You're sure she's not at home?"

"Oh, yeah."

"Okay, why don't you wait here; I'll run down to the kitchen for the keys." Bracco stepped into the living room. Emil took the narrow stairs two at a time. There was nothing irregular about the parlor, he reassured himself. The finger was secure in the picnic chest in the cellar—the gun! It was in the kitchen cabinet. He was sweating. But he'd just taken a shower so the moisture could be explained—*Don't do that!* he shouted inside his head. He found the keys to Paulien's apartment and forced himself to walk slowly back upstairs.

"Nice place, Milosec," the unwelcome visitor said. "Well appointed. Calm, I'd call it. Restrained."

Was Bracco joking around, or was he taking a class in urban decor in his spare time? "The apartment's on the fourth floor," Emil said. He disliked having Bernie Bracco in his building, his house, his life. He walked ahead of the detective and imagined turning and shoving Bracco down the stairs. "So what's this all about? You at liberty to say?"

"Yeah, what the hell, as I said, she's flown."

"Gone?"

"Ah, yeah. We got a tip that your tenant is passing herself off as a pathologist when in fact she has no known MD qualifications to do so. She's Dutch, right?"

"That's right, according to her passport."

Bernie Bracco's breath wheezed as they climbed. "Then you call this morning, funny it was all coming to a head, we put a stake on her today, I was at this address earlier—you know. She's a renter, so I'm only looking at the address. Then, what do you know, you're the landlord. Some coincidence, huh? Almost hard to believe, wouldn't you say?" He paused on a step.

Emil kept climbing. "You could've said what you were after this afternoon, saved some time. I'm not brushed up on my mind reading these days."

Bracco continued up the stairs. "Yeah."

"So you're saying she left from here?"

"Skipped from her job at Wittekoff Hospital. She lived here long?"

"About two years."

"Same employer the whole time?"

"I wouldn't know. Long as the rent comes in on time it's not my concern where she works."

"Which I take it it did?"

"Never late a day."

"Ever notice the pay envelopes, that sort of thing arrive in the mail?"

Emil shrugged. "She worked at the hospital."

"That's all you have?"

Both men stopped.

Emil was five steps ahead of Bracco. He shrugged again. "Any complaints about her job performance?"

"That's the other funny thing; she was good at it. At least here in the U.S."

"Maybe she trained in Europe, just didn't bother to get her license, or whatever they require over here?"

"That's where it really gets fun. Interpol can't get a definite ID on her over there either. She possibly skipped out of Slovenia, her last maybe ID—of all places."

Emil turned to face Detective Bracco. Was that supposed to be a slight, or was he unaware Emil was Slovenian? "I thought you just said she was Dutch. *I* thought she was."

"Yeah, but Amsterdam can't place her, though there was a similar MO there a couple'a years back. Interpol says she sprung out of thin air, no hard file anywhere. What does that sound like to you?"

Both men resumed climbing. "If she's an illegal, why not give it to INS?"

"Well, that's a separate issue from impersonating a pathologist."

"I see your point."

"INS is in now, though. They're sorting out her visa with the Euros. But it takes time."

"You said you had a tip?"

"Some woman, another foreigner. Anonymous. We think Vandervell's been pulling the same impersonating stunt all over Europe. She skips out fast when a problem arises." His breathing chugged like an old engine.

They finally came to Paulien's door; the corridor was hot enough to wilt Sheetrock. Bernie Bracco leaned hard on the stair rail, bent over from three flights up. "I gotta quit smoking," he muttered.

Emil unlocked the apartment door. "If you tell me what you're looking for, maybe I can help."

"I'm not sure myself what I'm looking for."

"I know the feeling."

It didn't take Detective Bracco long to figure out what Emil already knew. "It look to you like the bird has beat it out of the nest, Milosec?"

Emil nodded. "I'd say so."

They stood in the kitchen. Detective Bracco pulled a glass off a shelf. "You mind?"

"No. Go ahead."

Bracco filled a glass of water from the tap and drank, spilling some on his shirt front. Paulien's top-floor apartment had to be ninety degrees. "She must have known we were on to her. The place is cleaned out of papers."

"Some of the furniture is expensive. You think she's really gone?"

"We know she went up to Canada, a flight to Toronto, we think. Our guys were watching and she somehow slipped out of the hospital on us."

"Your guys were at the hospital today?" Detective Bracco nodded, refilling the water glass. Emil's buttocks tightened; sweat popped out on his already damp skin. "What time was that?"

Bracco swallowed. "Around one. Why?"

"Well … Paulien's a big woman, hard to *slip* her anywhere." He forced a laugh.

"Disguised as a male, we believe." Detective Bracco finished his water. "This is all news to you, Milosec?"

"Meaning?"

"Why don't you cut the bullshit: you suddenly call this morning; your tenant's doing impersonations. No connection?"

"None I know of." Bracco laid the glass in the sink. "It doesn't figure. What's her gain; where's the thrill impersonating a pathologist?"

Bernie Bracco smiled, more along the lines of a sneer. "Maybe she had a thing for dead people's tissue. Maybe she ate it, sautéed. So you know nothing more to do with this?"

"The short answer would be, with what?"

"You and she never … you know … in the bedroom, anything like that?" Emil made a face. "So nothing else you can tell me? You're a cop, for Christ's sake."

"She was my tenant, not my suspect. You have the phones checked?"

"Uh-huh, came up empty. You hear any more about that what's it you called me on earlier?"

He kept circling that call. Emil shook his head. "Can't Canada hold her?"

"We're trying; she's off the radar for now." Detective Bracco paused. Long enough to make the innocent squirm, which as the case was, Emil currently was not. "How about a look in your place?"

Was he asking or telling? "You think she's down there hiding? I'm in it with her; we're stealing body parts to sell to the Asians? That what you want to know?"

"I wanna know why I keep getting the bad feeling something stinks around here and you know what it is?"

Emil laughed; he hoped the awkward sound that came out of him registered as a laugh. "You wanna look downstairs, be my guest."

"How come you called the Ten-oh this morning, not your precinct?"

Emil shook his head slowly. "Could be I was homesick for the old squad. But, you know, you're starting to repeat yourself, Detective. Did I teach you that technique?"

"Fuck you, Detective."

"Whatever you say, Detective."

"How come you didn't say your wife is dead?"

Emil felt a flash desire to punch Bernie Bracco in his size-large nose. "Everybody on the squad knew, Bracco. Everybody but you, I guess."

"Yeah, well, look at it from my perspective: You call me, then your tenant *happens* to be wanted internationally and I'm supposed to swing with it? Sounds like lousy cop TV to me."

Emil couldn't argue with that. But even if something was off with him, what would be his motive in calling Bracco? And Bracco would be standing in his tenant's apartment if he'd called him or not. But if Emil said anything more about the two events being unconnected he'd sound like he was defending himself, and cops live to get guys on the defensive. As far as Emil was concerned, Bracco could go ahead and worry the details himself; he was done talking.

The cop and the ex-cop looked each other over, the silence between them thick enough to blanket Brooklyn.

"All right, Milosec," Bracco said. "If she turns up to claim the foliage here, the ottoman—" He kicked the camel-colored leather furnishing. "Or what have you, I count on you to call."

"Without a doubt."

"She have a lot of visitors, male company?"

"Nearly none."

Bracco glanced around. "Don't touch anything till we give you the word."

"Of course. Your search here was off the cuff, I take it."

"Why do you say that?"

"It's after hours; you're alone." Emil could see Bracco was frustrated; no cop ever feels good losing a suspect. "Maybe the Royal Bank of Canada," he said, like it was an afterthought.

"What about it?"

"Maybe she had a letter from that bank."

"See? Now you're making an effort. How'd you find her anyway? Want ad, Realtor in the neighborhood?"

"My wife worked for the Austrian and Italian Embassies. That's how we got the other tenants—through the embassies. I just kept the list going."

Bracco wiped a pond of sweat off his nose. "Fucking heat. All right. Okay for now, Milosec."

"Right."

Emil showed Detective Bracco out. "Even a rumor, let me hear from you."

"I understand."

Emil waited near the window, out of sight, until he heard a car door slam and then the motor kick in and the car drive off. Lovely, he thought. Perfectly lovely. He'd lied some more and evaded, and probably obstructed. He'd be a bona fide crime spree before the night was out. And the cops were at the hospital! How close had he and Franco been to them? He walked back down to the kitchen and poured himself a vodka from the bottle in the freezer and drank it down. "What a day," he said out loud to the glass he held aloft. "And it's not over yet." He poured and downed another shot. Replacing the bottle, his hand brushed Elena's letters.

The quicksand Emil was sliding deeper and deeper into didn't stop his appetite. There was leftover roasted chicken in the refrigerator. Emil pulled it out and cut a few slices off the breast, adding a leg. He'd roasted some red potatoes with the chicken and piled a few of them on the plate. He sliced a tomato and next to that added some sliced cucumber, poured a bit of olive oil and balsamic vinegar over them with salt, pepper, and oregano. With the remains of the bottle of pinot grigio in hand, Emil carried his supper tray outside into the now nearly dark evening. Soft illumination from the kitchen window formed a trapezoid on the ground behind him, a yellow glow. He lit a small copper lantern on the table so he could see his food.

Honeysuckle perfumed the humid air in a thick, enveloping plume. There was something almost lewd about the odor, though to look at the insignificant white honeysuckle flower suggested nothing sultry at all. He breathed deeply; the garden had its own air that hadn't fouled yet in the merciless heat. He chewed his food slowly and savored the wine.

Closing his eyes, he could almost relax; wine, honeysuckle, heat, just his thoughts and his garden. Yet he could not deny a hint of excitement in the air, as if he were on the heels of something big. That would be the second time a giddy feeling had swept over him. But what about this day had been anything close to giddy?

The night encouraged languor. How easy to yield. Forget he was living in a crime scene. Getting the panties off a girl, he thought. At thirteen that was the sole idea in Emil's head. Every other thought or impulse had to pass through that pulsing desire. Elena once said to him, "Boys are made men by their mothers, and they never forgive." *His* mother, that self-pitying victim of circumstance, she'd made him a man? She'd embraced a dead past and clung to it. Though, fair to say, in that past she had been something for a boy to gaze upon and dream. … Panties again … LaTeesha Williams … Loretta, right next door … He should conjugate verbs, that's what he should do. He did that as a teen when the pressure built, lying alone on his bed: I come, I have come, I have been coming, I will come. …

A sudden fluttering in the lilac bush interrupted his musings. A breeze just there, or did something move? The bush seemed to be whispering. He thought he could feel the breath of a woman in his ear, saying words he couldn't make out, only the warm, moist breath of hot night exhaling from her mouth. Is that what Eve did when the serpent came slithering along whispering sweet temptation in her ear? Did she put up a struggle; did she try to hear God's warning before she let go and bit into the fruit? Did she then breathe hot apple breath into Adam's—

These ruminations were cut short by the sounds of rummaging from next door.

"Hey, amigo, you over there?"

"Right here in my garden."

"You find anything?"

Emil couldn't tell whether or not Franco had been drinking. "No, I found nothing. I'm as in the dark as ever."

Franco laughed, though Emil hadn't intended a joke. "That's good, in the dark. The Horse never came home tonight, I think, no?"

"Not so far."

"You suspect her of something?"

"Maybe."

"Who came to your house, if I can ask? Pounding like a crazy guy."

"A policeman."

"Shit, no kidding? For what?"

"Looking for my tenant, as a matter of fact."

"I knew it."

"You knew what?"

"La Caballería is no good. Listen, man, can I come over to your yard, amigo? There is something I want you to see."

Emil sighed heavily; he'd probably never be rid of Franco now, not for the rest of his life. "Yes, okay, sure, come on over." Before the words were entirely out of Emil's mouth, Franco had flipped over the fence and was seated in the chair opposite him. In his hand was a section of newspaper. "What's up tonight, Franco?"

"You are eating your dinner? That is interesting."

"What's interesting about me eating my dinner?"

Franco stared at Emil's plate. "Nothing," he said softly.

"Have you eaten? Do you want some chicken?"

"It looks good."

Emil got up and went to the kitchen. He prepared a plate for Franco, but when he went back outside with it Franco was gone. Emil put the plate on the table and resumed eating. Franco soon tossed himself back over the fence and sat down again. He held a plastic bag in one hand containing a bottle of beer and a small bag of freshly ground espresso beans. "For you," Franco said, pulling the coffee beans out. Emil thanked him and placed the beans between them on the table.

Franco picked up his knife and fork and began to eat. He ate delicately. Emil watched him, surprised. "It is very good, hombre, muy bueno; you are a good cook. The spices are nice."

Emil gestured with his hand that it was nothing. "Rosemary," he said. "From the garden. What've you got for me to look at?"

"Ah, sí." Franco put down his fork, picked the newspaper up from the ground beside his chair, and handed it to Emil. It was the *New York Times* Sunday Real Estate section.

Emil looked at the paper, then at Franco. "You read the *Times*?"

"No, I pick it from your garbage."

Was that a joke? "What am I looking at here?"

"See where I make a circle? Those two houses are two little blocks from where we sit right now, my friend. You see the price?"

Emil looked at the listings. "So what? They can ask for that amount, doesn't mean they'll get it."

"Amigo? I think you are sometimes a burro, a stubborn man. What do you think? You think this is nothing? In the *New York Times*, amigo."

Emil was quiet while Franco finished his dinner. Crickets clicked endlessly in the garden, a sound Emil liked most in summer. He liked that the crickets were out there rubbing their legs together in the dark, that they were at work, eating and mating and whatever else, rendering the night into a living force instead of a dead thing between sunset and sunup.

Franco broke the spell. "I am going to be rich. Do you see, amigo? How much do you think I will make?"

Emil tried not to sound sarcastic. He found Franco's wishful thinking embarrassing. "Like I said, it depends on how much you can actually get. But where will you go, Franco? Once you are rich. And what about the old blind Oscar Park and your Aunt Marta?"

Franco whistled. "Ayee, my old Tía Marta and blind Oscar Park and Oscar Park his dog! In all my happy dreams I forgot those two. I can take Tía to Puerto Rico, to family, but what to do about the other?"

Emil looked at Franco. "What makes you think you can trust these real estate people? They're predators, you know?"

"What do I care; cash money is my trust, ha?"

Depending on the amount, if Franco saw himself stuck in a dead end, this could be his way out. What if he told Franco about the severed finger? Emil guessed Elena's ring meant the message was more determined, that he was being singled out for some special, sinister treatment. But he didn't see how the dismembered digit tied into real estate and decided not to mention it to Franco. He was off on his own journey, and good luck to him.

"What about the spiderman that came down the wall?" he asked. "You lost interest in finding out what the Spider was up to?"

Franco looked ashamed, or was it crestfallen? Emil never believed anything he said; why did he keep trying? "Amigo, what am I doing here? La Señora Elena, she say to me I could do more. She say I was not too late. What am I doing? I am doing nothing. Maybe this is not a bad thing even if it comes in a bad way. Entiendes?"

"What's the hurry? What about painting the wall?"

Franco looked blank. Emil saw he had no idea what he was talking about. Did he even remember promising to paint the wall, or the bullets fired—did he remember that? The light of recognition came into Franco's face. "Ah, sí, the wall next to my garden. I can do that." He brightened. "Makes my house worth more money. And you can do the tree you promised to plant for your wife. Amigo, she told me of her father's orchard. I never see eyes big like when she talked of that. I think she wanted all her life to return to that place."

Emil experienced a spasm of irritation. "I'll plant the tree," he said a little too forcefully.

They both looked up when the lilac bush began to whisper again, then to shake. Franco jumped out of his chair and in an instant pulled a very nasty looking switchblade out of his pocket and snapped it open. He whirled around to face the lilac just as Sam jumped to the ground, landing at his feet. "Madre de Dios! That cat will scare someone to death."

"Or get himself killed," Emil said. He'd watched Franco with amazement, how agile he was and fast with that knife—those were not the reflexes of a drunk. In fact, they could be the reflexes of a spiderman scaling a wall, killing a cat, and depositing an amputated finger in a garden.

Sam meowed loudly and walked his wavy cat walk the few steps to Emil's chair. He sat looking up, his expression not so much begging as insisting on a piece of chicken. Emil tossed him what was left of the leg. Sam seized it in his teeth and ran to a dark corner under the pergola.

Franco closed the knife blade and sat back down. "Is that good, to feed him? He keeps coming back." He put the knife in his pocket.

"I'm guessing no one's fed Sam since morning; the heart attack. Not that I care."

Franco looked at him doubtfully. "No, claro."

Emil stood up. He put his hands in his pockets. "Look, Franco, let's suppose this spiderman who came down the wall—"

"Like the wall I am going to paint? Okay."

Emil smiled ever so slightly. "Right. Now, suppose the spiderman returns—tonight, say?"

Franco broke into his raucous laugh. "I should now pee myself with fear?"

Emil decided to drop it. What would he gain by mentioning a possible nocturnal visit? Franco would want to sink into his beers, dream of selling, getting rich, not take on some maybe bad men showing up in the middle of the night. What could either of them do to prepare anyway? He brushed his hands sideways along his face to the back of his head.

The two men were quiet for a few minutes. Emil stood by the table, leaning in with his hands on the back of his chair, the way he often did when interrogating a suspect, a pose intended to dominate him—or her. Then Franco said, in a voice Emil had not heard him use before, *"Men shall deal unadvisedly sometimes, which after hours give leisure to repent."*

"What's that?"

"Shakespeare, mi amigo."

Emil ran his fingers through his hair. It needed cutting; the back of his neck felt furry. Elena used to cut his hair, and she did a good job. She said Franco sometimes recited poetry; he hadn't believed her, yet the man seated before him had just spoken Shakespeare, and spoken it well.

"Do you know this story of Richard the Third King?" Franco asked without waiting for a response. "He wants everything for himself: the kingdom he murdered for, his brother's right of birth—is that how you say it?"

"Birthright," Emil provided.

"Sí, birthright, his brother's, and also he wants the Lady Anne after he kills her king and the son of her king, her husband! All killed. And he is ugly, esta feo, this Richard with the hump on his back and a dried arm. Finally he has the kingdom and all the blood on his hands. And look what happens to him, amigo? Everything is taken; gone, all of it. But he fights to the death for what he has stolen and wants only a horse to go on fighting. You know this story? He is a bad man, but a brave man. You think a man can be bad and brave?"

Emil sat back down in his chair, opposite Franco. He thought a minute. "Yes, I think it's possible to be two opposing things at once. But I'm not so sure how brave this Richard is."

"No?"

"Just to fight for the sake of fighting?"

Franco laughed. "He has nothing left. He could run away to hide, but he did not. This Richard was more brave than his own conscience!" He reached over to tap Emil's arm. "My father, who did not do for me the way I have seen other fathers do with their sons, this same man sent me to the best schools, first with the abuelita, then in Puerto Rico. The abuelita say to take the gift, and she made me study hard—you can believe. Funny, no? I have all the books—Dante! Milton! Cervantes—most in Spanish, but mine. I can show you if you don't believe me." Here Franco laughed joyfully. "Shakespeare," he said, "he is a man to understand that life is such a funny place to be. Don't you think, amigo?"

Emil nodded. "I don't know much Shakespeare, but I do know how gut-busting hilarious life can be."

They were quiet again for a few minutes, the hot night on top of them like a steaming sheet. By morning the garden too would be fully penetrated with dense, polluted air.

"But amigo," Franco said, and Emil looked at him. "Do you think the police who came tonight knows about the man climbing down the wall, the Spider? Do you think La Caballeria—the Horse—was scared away, big as she is? Or did the policia think she is part of something no good?"

"She may be part of something no good, but the police coming had to do with her immigration status," Emil said. That was at least partly true. Emil had no wish to lie to Franco, but he didn't want him involved any more than he was.

"The Horse is illegal? And she is not even a Mexican? Ha!" Franco laughed. "Who then is the Spider? Do you know?"

Emil shook his head. "I don't know who the Spider is."

"You think I should not sell my building?"

"Go slowly, that's all I say. Go slowly."

Sam emerged from the shadows. He parked himself next to Emil's chair and began furiously licking his orange and white fur. Franco said he hoped the cat wasn't evil, as cats can sometimes be, and that he didn't carry a curse. He crossed himself for good measure. "It is not easy to know, amigo."

"Know what?" Emil asked, resisting an uncharacteristic urge to pet Sam.

"Where evil is; it's not always where you expect, but somewhere you maybe never looked, or where you always do."

Emil expected Franco's gritty laugh, but it didn't come. "Then I won't look under the bed tonight," he said.

Franco laughed at that. "Sí, amigo, if you look for trouble, it shows up."

Around eleven thirty Franco jumped back over the fence. He had thanked Emil for dinner and said good-night. He'd had only the one beer. Emil wondered if he would resume drinking on the other side of the fence. He'd seemed unusually subdued, not the neighbor Emil was accustomed to. He called a second good-night to him over the fence, but Franco didn't respond.

Emil washed the last two plates. He would have to empty the dishwasher in the morning; he no longer had a choice. He made himself a cup of coffee with the beans Franco brought over, using the spare plunger-type cooker because the other one was still stuck with burned coffee and was soaking in vinegar. He poked a spoon into the old carafe. Maybe by tomorrow the coffee tar would come unstuck.

He then walked to the freezer, reached in, and took out the packet of Elena's letters. They were cold to the touch. Emil went upstairs with the cold letters in one hand and the hot cup of fragrant dark coffee in the other. He had no choice now but to read the letters.

FOUR

I shall put enmity between you and the woman, between your brood and hers. They will strike at your head, and you will strike at their feet.

Book of Genesis

Elena's last letter was written in late September. The weather had been clear and cool for several days; the chrysanthemums and asters were in brilliant bloom as if in defiance of drab winter waiting in the wings. Emil went to the bedroom one morning with a freshly cut bouquet and found her on the bed. She looked at first like herself asleep, but he saw her body had become lifeless, was no longer animated; breath had ceased to lift in and out of her. Watching, Emil thought of an empty violin, the instrument where her sound had once been housed silenced. He touched her hair, combed his fingers through, and then let her be. He sat on the edge of the bed and decided the day was as good as any other to die and was not resentful for its being so full of golden autumnal light. Was it the day's fault or the morning's for arriving on time? The last exhalation of a life and time goes on anyway, world without end.

He'd read the first two letters on the days she gave them to him, and he'd meant to read the others but they had infuriated him, written by a person in the next room. Elena told him she would deliver the letters to him each day, but he must go to another room to read them. And he must not comment, although he was free to write back. He didn't tell Elena he wasn't reading her letters but let her believe he was. He disliked mail, and Elena knew that. So the letters sat after her death, collecting dust on the dining room table, until today.

Upstairs with the cold letters and the coffee, Emil turned on all the lamps in the parlor and put Monteverdi's *L'Orfeo* on the CD player at a low volume. Next he shut off the air conditioner and opened the windows in the bedroom that faced the garden but kept the street windows in the parlor closed. He made himself as comfortable as he could before the thick night air filtered in.

He sat with the packet of Elena's letters. There were seventy-three in all, one for each day dating from mid-July to September 28th. The first few had been written in the hospital. Most had been written from their bed, some from the garden or the kitchen. He put his reading glasses on, took a sip of coffee, and made himself ready to read.

He pulled out the letter he'd already read—partly read—the one where she said he didn't care, or something like that. He ran his eyes down the page until he came to the passage:

> *... I thought that you might not care. That certain questions did not occur to you because you are not capable of caring—not for the answers, no, but for the questions, for knowing others. The word solipsism came to mind, but I am not certain it is the word I mean. I thought, okay, he cares in his own way. That is what I decided to conclude about you. But I am not sure.*
>
> *I think you have one final case to solve.*
>
> *Everything*

Irritated anew by the word solipsism, Emil said aloud, "One final case? The letter is two years old!" He reread the part about secrets in Trieste. Something crawled along the hairs of his spine, something old-feeling and inevitable, like an insect of fate.

The letters in the packet were no longer cold, a corpse coming back to life. It might be best to go back downstairs and return the letters to the freezer. And while he was there pour himself another hefty vodka. Or he could go up to Elena's room and light a fire, into her plush room to read the letters among her books. Drink vodka by the fire; plush room, no Elena. If he drank, if he nestled in her room, he would fall asleep, and he must not sleep. It was eighty-eight degrees outside. The parlor was still cool from the air conditioner, and Emil felt chilled. He took another sip of coffee. He'd thought of making a fire on a roasting-hot summer night.

He stood up, restlessness attacking him like rubber bands snapping inside his legs. He sat back down, put his legs out straight and flexed his calf muscles. He was afraid. Afraid of what might happen tonight? No, afraid of the letters. What have the dying to say to the living?

What could the scientists say about death with their endless quest for answers to impossible questions? Following signals from powerful telescopes trained on deepest, darkest outer space, going back a gazillion light-years to the origins of dust and gas and energy and what all else made up the stew that became the cosmos; the stars and planets and solar systems and stuff, and, finally, humanity. The way he saw it there would never be a definitive answer to the formless cosmic muck that became the cosmos of things. He figured the scientists were ultimately out of luck. They were like schoolboys masturbating at the keyhole. They wanted to take it all apart, starting with their mothers, and for what? So not one person on earth ever went to bed hungry again? So the jails could be emptied of criminals, cripples toss their crutches and walk, the sightless see, the deaf know sound, and murders become passé along with Franco's evil—residing who knew where; the world to rejoice in all the secrets opened at last? A map made known, all mysteries exposed? Would a map bring Elena back? Detective Emil Milosec didn't want a map. He didn't want a world without mystery either. The tree of knowledge … what crap! The idea of the rapture, the dead rising into the sky and mixing with the living, repulsed him. He didn't want to meet Elena in the sky. He wanted her to never have left the garden. He'd once been called a dirty atheist. He'd wondered, why dirty?

He pulled loose the faded blue ribbon holding the letter packet together and let it fall to the floor. Emil the cop had no choice. Had the day been a completely different day … but it wasn't a completely different day. He rubbed his eyes, put his glasses back on, and began to read.

My dear Emil,

I am still not used to my role as the dying one. You carried the gun, lived in danger every day. I thought nothing of it in the early days, but, yes, when the phone rang I waited before picking up to put a few seconds before hearing the worst. If I did not pick up I could go on with my day, happy to be ignorant, but if I picked up I had only a few seconds of freedom before everything came crashing down. Can you imagine that? Can you imagine Danielle and her children the day the call came in that Mike was killed? Has she hated the telephone ever since?

In those days I alternately resented you for putting me in that impossible position and feared for you tenderly. Bullets, car explosions, bad luck, I tried to shield myself from your danger. But, really, so many die. Think of the war. In one single day hundreds, thousands, whole villages died. I asked myself: What right do I have to cling to one life?

It became easier that way, to expect nothing. And now so funny because here I sit, sentence passed, time running out until one day— POOF!*—I will be gone. And you? You sound so bold about death: When you go you are gone. Your atheism does that? I never see you worry or hear you complain.*

So I have decided to write to you in my expiration. How do you like that? Now I am tired, tomorrow I will write again.

I am yours,

Elena

Emil,

They have finished sticking the morning pins in me, and pulled the IV out of the vein, given me permission to clean myself in the shower. I repeat my request of our good friend Dr. Drier to let me go home. He tires of my request and weakens. I appeal to his humanity. Mostly I wear him down. My needs are simple; what more can they do for me here?

I didn't ask you if it is good that I return. I want to see the garden. It is July, everything in bloom, the summer heat and all our work yielding its little treasures; the petals peel back, the scent of life and climax of each flower. I have my nose still and my eyes, I can touch, I can press my face to the delicate skin of the flowers and breathe. I can still breathe.

Dr. Drier will speak to you. Please do not force me to stay here. This place is—let me die in my garden.

I despise hospitals. Everyone here is ill! And they smell!

Anxious to leave,

Elena

Emil remembered that awful conversation with Dr. Drier. The good doctor said there was in truth very little that could be done anymore. They would keep Elena as comfortable as possible with morphine. It wouldn't be long, he said, placing a hand on Emil's shoulder. Emil remembered thinking of the candy machine in the hospital waiting area, about putting a coin in and pulling the lever for a Milky Way bar, hearing it slide down the chute and crash-land at the slot below, and thinking that was not the thing to be thinking with the doctor's sympathetic hand heavy on his shoulder. But what was he supposed to think? What words and sentences could he string together to make sense of cancer? Should he say to the doctor, "I understand; now get your hand off me"? But he *didn't* understand, and a candy bar was as good as anything else to think about; it would at least taste good. He nodded to the doctor, thanked him, and went and got the candy and shared it with Elena.

Dear Emil,

This will be short, I am tired. Thank you for talking to the doctors, for learning how to administer the drugs and potions they think will help. You will see how easy I am, I eat like a bird, and my needs are less than a bird's. I will quietly tweet and chirp.

E.

~~Traitor,~~

Why have you turned against me? They said I would go home at the end of the week. Why are you letting a small fever interfere with my freedom? Now I am back on antibiotic drip. Were you looking for a way to refuse? Am I too much trouble? I know where I want to die! Big man without a God, such promise of strength but cannot take a little bit of death at your own door. I knew this about you when we first met, that fundamentally you lack intimacy! All you ever have is theory. No one can live by theory, Emil; you have to touch to live. I knew this so quickly—that facade of yours! It makes me split my sides laughing.

I am laughing at you: afraid of a few doctors. TECHNICIANS! *They know nothing. Sign the forms! For once do not consider every angle, just come take me away from here. You think Dr. Drier is your father, is that it? You're still searching for your poor wronged papa who threw everything up in the air and ran away, torturing everyone with his silence.*

But maybe you have a woman there. Ha! That would suit me—that I could understand. I won't rip her eyes out. Put me in my day room, keep the tart in our bed, I DO NOT CARE, *but get me out, tell these donkeys to let me go home. Otherwise, I will loathe you forever.*

Prisoner

I am still here.

Emil,

They have said Sunday. They want to send a Wagnerian cow home with me. Have you seen her? I won't have anything to do with this nurse, I will play along to get out, then we dismiss her. She can come once or twice to satisfy them.

Soon, yours,

Elena

Dear Emil,

I am nervous as a schoolgirl. Tomorrow I come home. Bring me some shoes to travel in, and that Naples yellow sweater, no, I am too pale for yellow. Bring the light green sweater, or the gray. You decide. Is there wine in the house? Good wine? I want to celebrate!

Everything

Dear Doctor,

I mean you, Dr. Emil. We must play doctor. I will be the submissive patient. You can sponge my body, clean every orifice—and rub me well. What? You think a dying woman has no sensuality? You find I carry the scent of the grave? Some days I lie here and all I think about is sex. My loins still move, my body makes waves of longing. And all you do is feed me soup!

Perhaps it is the morphine talking, not me anymore. You once said I had the soul of a slut. I could not decide to be angry or pleased. Your mother would not like that. Forgive me for mentioning her. This is no time to be mean-spirited. And I wasn't. Though why not? I die; I have no need to be a false witness. For me the score is settled, no deathbed regrets. . . .

I heard Franco ask about me earlier. I heard him call over the fence. Don't be so gruff with him, Emil. Tell Franco I am well, fantasizing sex with ten men at once. I am laughing, in case you want to be pigheaded.

One evening let's have supper outside. The air is so warm and I want to see the nighttime garden. Are there many fireflies? Please do not be afraid, I will not break like a porcelain doll.

Signed,

Slut

My dear Emil,

I wish I could say I found each day precious, but dying is tedious.

I dream of the orchard when I was a child. In spring—how can I make you see? So many flowers! The apple blossoms, the blush of white and palest young green, a whole field all at once. Everywhere I looked under the blue sky, every promise, every dream was possible. We had afternoon tea in the orchard and I thought there could be nothing better on earth than Mama and Papa and Nurse. Yes, one thing, a very large cookie for me. A Linzer tart!

By the time I met you, the orchard was spoiled. The hell had come.

Elena

Dear Emil,

There is something you should know. If I could go to my grave without telling you, I would, but I am afraid for you and I think I have no choice. Where to begin? It has to do with the orchard, and it was a long time ago.

My father did something, a bad thing, during the war. He was not completely to blame, there were circumstances. Sometimes there are tests, terrible tests, in life and the answer is not clear, or maybe it is clear but not easy to see, or to trust. Or to follow . . . But this trouble began after the war, after the years of chaos, not the bombs and guns and noise anymore, but displaced people wandering like ghosts everywhere. Money was only paper, starving people wandered the roads . . . leftovers trying to go home after being torn from their towns and villages. Then the rebuilding began. It looked as if my father's mistake would be forgotten until one day a letter arrived. And then more letters began to arrive and phone calls in the night. They were trying to blackmail my papa. They wanted the orchard, all the property and money. My poor mother was so afraid, she lasted the war, but she became like a child again and had no more strength. In those days I became the mother of my mother.

The man in Ljubljana who followed us—I know you remember—he meant to harm my father, my family. I'm sorry, you do not like to hear of this, but it can no longer be avoided. They came to Trieste. The Italians had just taken over again, so Papa was able to have these men expelled because they were Yugoslav, and Yugoslavia as you know is Communista. And the bad, very bad blood between Italian and Slovene ... My father still retained some authority. They did not question him. Do you see? But those men promised to come to us again, to take forever if they had to, and these are people who know how to keep their hearts black. There was to have been an arrangement, but then we had to send Mama away—to the church because she was nearly insane by then—and you know Papa died soon after. But, Emil, they have not given up in all these many years. I have had letters through the Austrian Embassy. ... For a while nothing, but four years ago it started again. I have hidden this from you. Don't ask me why; you know why.

This must be insane to you, pazzo. Ancient history. When I was no longer able to work, I told the embassy people to destroy any further letters that arrived from Slovenia. I wanted to tell you, but I thought I could take care of it myself, not involve you. My fear now is that this letter writer will persist and go for you, take from you what is yours. Do you see? I beg you, Emil, secure what you have, take unnumbered accounts, hide the money we have collected from stocks—the mutual fund—and the savings, perhaps in a Swiss bank? Please, take precautions today! Also, when you read this do not, I beg you, ask me to explain further; it was all so long ago and all my fault, only do what you must do now to make yourself safe.

You are police; you will know how to protect yourself.

My love, and my sorrow,

Elena

Emil looked up. He removed his glasses, stood up, and walked to the front windows. Carefully, so he wouldn't be seen, he lifted one slat of the blinds. No one was outside his house, only the tree. A few cars drove along the street. A man laughed and then a woman laughed, her footsteps echoing on the pavement, then silence again. He sat back down. He decided to scan through the letters for any further reference to this supposed threat, this "one more case to solve," vainly hoping the morphine was the writer of these letters, not Elena.

He randomly selected pages, eventually finding others involving secrets. And one where she mentioned Franco.

Emil,

I worry about you. You are not suspicious enough. Did you secure the money as I said? Don't be naive. Please, amore, take care. Are you unhappy I never told you before? You never asked! Or if I tried to tell you, you silenced me with your anger.

Take care now—do not delay!

Tutto

You won't be angry that Franco came in while you were out? I tell you only in case he drinks too much and lets it slip. He helped me to the garden. Only for a little while. It was hot outside. I walked on his arm all the way to the goldfish pool. I told him of my father's orchard, and, you know, that lovely man wept. He said he too loves apple trees. Manzana is the Spanish word for apple. I gave him some pepper and nasturtium seeds and told him to plant them. If he starts with peppers and nasturtium maybe he will continue, cultivate the whole garden. Maybe he will plant an apple tree. Or you, will you at last plant me the apple tree I desire?

"Ah, the goddamn pepper patch," Emil said. He picked up the empty coffee cup, Franco's coffee. He placed the cup back in the saucer, adjusted his glasses and skipped to the next letter.

Dear Emil,

I am now alarmed you have asked me nothing about the threatening letters. Perhaps you do not believe me? I cannot face you, but every word I write is true!

Have you guessed I did not tell you everything? It was so long ago. I tried very hard to put it away, to forget how the Nazi officers took my mother and me. I was the logical choice, still halfway a girl, but, no, they took my mother. She was not old yet, still beautiful, and they made me watch, all of them, what they did to her. I saw her eyes with each one. I was sent back to my father to tell him what they did to her. I carried a long strand of her hair that they cut off for him. These were SS, and they said Papa knew where there were Partisans hiding. They believed the men were hiding in the city. You see, the orchard came from my mother's family, was hers, in her name—they didn't know. Papa told them what they wanted. For my mother, for me—because I was next—he told them. Was he a monster? I cannot say. That is what he did. There is no more to say. Others suffered for me. My mama came back with the bald place where they cut her hair. At least they returned her, but she was destroyed. What destroyed her was me seeing, her seeing the last of my childhood ripped away as her body was ripped.

Now you know what no one should have to know.

And I will tell you something about death, Emil. The question is not who deserves to live or who to die; it is a blind desire to live no matter what—

They'd agreed not to talk about the war; she especially, early on, insisted. He felt as if he'd walked into a room in his own house that he knew nothing about, did not know existed. Yet the room had been there all along. It was an upheaval.

He clutched the letter in his hand, crushing it. Then delicately, patiently, smoothed the letter out, as if apologizing to the paper.

There were three more left to read.

Mio caro,

I have difficulty writing today so I will only send my love. And I thank you, and ask that you forgive me for my miserable family. You came to help me once, and I think you did not know the bad people you helped as well. The man in the river … I mourn that man. I don't know how bad he really was. How can we mend the past?

Everything.

Emil sat with Elena's letters on his lap. He didn't read the last two; he'd read enough.

Paulien learned of the apartment through the Austrian Embassy … was she the stalker, the final case to solve? Maybe it was a good thing she'd fled the country. If Paulien Vandervell was up to just half the no good he thought she was up to, what might Emil be capable of if she were upstairs snug in her bed asleep right now? What might he do after waking her up?

The parlor was warm; night had crept in.

Elena expected him to read the letters. She must have known he wasn't. He'd surely have questioned her when he read about her mother and Elena so young, witnessing—how could he tell her he'd meant no harm, not reading her letters?

He'd been a fool.

He threw the letters on the floor. A man could drown in regrets, he thought for the second time, and it was even more true now.

Was the entire narrative of their lives together a lie?

He bent down on all fours to retrieve the pages scattered across the floor but sat up, pulling his knees into his chest, wanting to sob. "It's all broken," he whispered.

He rose and walked slowly to a narrow shelf between the window and the fireplace, stood a minute, then lifted a heavy crystal vase that had belonged to Elena. A cobalt vein ran through the faceted surface, a modern design for the era, she had said. He turned it over in his hands.

Taking two steps back, he raised his arm and pitched the crystal vase with all he had into the marble mantelpiece. The sound of glass crashing into marble shattered the night. The one surviving item of her father's obscene crystal now lay in broken chunks on the floor. He kicked at the pieces. They made a tinkling sound as he shoved them into a pile with his foot. That crystal shop so long ago … the day he found Everything. …

After standing, numb, for several minutes, feeling pulled open, bruised like the flesh of some overripe rotten fruit, he again bent to his knees to gather Elena's letters. Holding them as if they too might break, he rebundled and gently retied the letters with the faded blue ribbon.

FIVE

And the Lord said, "If I can find fifty righteous in the city, I will spare the whole place for their sake."

Book of Genesis

Everyone likes to believe there once was a garden where all things were pure.

Life's a humbling lesson, Emil thought, facing his own gun. The intruder lit a cigarette with one hand, using a beat up old Zippo lighter sporting a Lucky Strike logo, but smoking a Gauloise, inhaled hard, exhaled slowly while demanding the deed to Emil's house. In the other hand was the Smith & Wesson .38 Special. Emil didn't care about losing the house; one was as good as another; a roof, running water, heat. But to take the garden—that was punishing.

He was told to sit. The one with the firepower gives the orders; Emil walked slowly to the other side of the marble table and sat. The garden was quiet all around them, only the crickets with their obsessive rubbing, on and on, and the suffocating heat. It was going to be a long night.

He'd fallen asleep with the letters beside him and been awakened by the smell of cigarette smoke wafting up from the garden, the odor faint but unmistakable. He picked up Elena's letters and in the bedroom, without turning on a light, tucked the packet under the mattress and, still in the dark, went to the bathroom to throw cold water on his face. He used the toilet but did not flush, soundlessly changed into a clean white T-shirt and clean pair of cotton pants, tossing the sweaty garments into a corner on the floor. He then walked deliberately downstairs to see what the night had brought.

He glanced at the kitchen clock: ten minutes to two, the cop in him automatically adding the date, Wednesday, June 21st, 1995, and proceeded out into the humid city night that was hot like a too tight pair of pants; the garden, though, still smelled sweetly of honeysuckle.

The Spiderman was a woman, and she was seated at the garden table with army-straight posture. On the ground beside her was a small pile of cigarette stubs. Was she alone? Emil took her in at a glance: hair brownish blonde, black jeans, and long-sleeved black cotton T-shirt. She looked small for scaling the back wall.

"Have you ever used a gun?" he asked.

The woman's laughter came from a deep place, was sensuous. "Is like asking a man does he beat his wife still." Her voice was cigarette-smoke husky, her accent Slovenian. She sounded enough like Emil's sister to seem familiar.

"You have a key?" Emil asked. She was probably alone.

"I have a key, of course."

"Paulien's?"

"So you understand who I am? No need for games, correct?"

"I'm guessing you are somehow connected to a man who fell into a river a long time ago."

"A man you beat and throw into that river. A man you killed cold, Milosec. This man was my father."

Emil tried out the math; how old could she be? Slovenia, 1956; she would not be forty, would have been a mere child. In the night light of the garden she looked young, her shape firm. “You’re holding a grudge,” he said.

“Tell me,” she asked, “do you speak Slovenian still?”

“Ah … not really.”

“Too bad; it would be easier for me if you did. For example, I do not know this word, ‘grudge.’”

“‘Grudge’? Means to remain angry a very long time.”

“I am not yet two years when you killed my papa; it is good holding grudge in this moment, do you think?”

“I don’t think I killed your father, is what I think.”

Her silence told him his comment was beneath consideration.

“Why don’t you tell me what you want?”

“Already have what I want.” She waved the gun, sweeping the area around them.

“What, my garden?”

“*My* garden now. My house.”

“Why now? Why not take it while she was still alive?”

“It is unfortunate I am not able to leave when I like.”

“I saw his legs move in the water.”

“He is pulled dead from the river.”

“How do you know?”

“They never go alone; friend followed friend.”

“A backup? Why didn’t he kill me?”

“Who?”

“The man following—your father’s friend.”

“She pointed gun to him.”

“*Elena*?”

The woman nodded.

From beneath thick layers of time, unearthed from a life fully lived almost forty years beyond that night, Emil located the buried memory. He saw them standing by the slow-running Ljubljanica, Elena in a light brown linen skirt suit. A fitted cropped jacket and white blouse—a pretty white blouse—opened at the neck. A silver brooch pinned to the jacket lapel, some sort of bird design. He saw her so clearly: hair cut just below her ears and waved; she was slim and beautiful and he was filled with her to the exclusion of nearly everything else on earth.

A man came at them saying things in Slovenian and lousy English—he called her a thieving betrayer—pointing a gun, and Emil, in the briefest of glances, saw his lover's fear. It ran across her face like the shadow of dark birds, a flock of evil black birds. He saw himself too, lean and tall, but could not say what he wore that night. A suit, most likely; men wore suits back then if they weren't laborers on the job. The night was a rich velvet blackness with diamond-hard stars. No, no, that wasn't right; it hadn't yet grown fully dark; a pale twilight lingered before the night closed in. He'd looked up to see a light go on in a window and a shade drawn in an apartment across the river, the fleeting silhouette of a woman.

He saw his chance and took it, punched the man with all he had. There was blood; the man stopped moving, Emil rolled him to the river and pushed. When he turned around Elena was holding the gun. She asked in a whisper, "Is he dead?"

Emil answered, "No. I don't think so. He'll be all right. Come on, let's get out of here." He picked up his passport and then reached for the gun, but Elena backed away, her face pale. "Elena? Let's go!" he said.

"More horror," she whispered.

Emil felt uneasy for the first time since finding the intruder in his garden. Fear crept over him, not of her or his gun in her hands but the same skin-crawling fear as when he couldn't find the other casing in the pepper hole.

What did he see that night?

She didn't back away.

No. She moved to the left, not back: Emil had come between her and the backup, into the line of fire. She was covering him. He had to step to her right to grab her wrist and the gun. He rushed them over the bridge: the lights were brighter; there were people. He pulled her close to check the gun, replaced the safety, and shoved the revolver into his pocket.

That was what happened that night.

He masked his face from the daughter of the man he'd killed, killed with Elena's assist. "Your good papa was blackmailing her father."

She shook her head. "Payment from collaborator is not blackmail."

"I didn't know any of this."

The woman leaned in to look into his eyes. Hers were gray blue and they had seen plenty. No cop could do a better job boring into a suspect's eyes, right through to the back of his skull, than this woman from his home country was doing now. "No matter, simple murder is enough."

Simple murder: One push and an unconscious man is in the river, one subhuman choice. Manslaughter two: reckless homicide. A man whose name he didn't even know. Or was it manslaughter one: With intent to cause serious physical injury to another person, he had caused the death of such person. ...

"Okay. Why not kill her father when the fighting ended?"

"To what gain?" She sounded annoyed. "My father wanted only to compensate these betrayed families. To get property and the money it brings. This land would not stay for long as it was. After the war, changes all over Europe."

"So he turns over his orchard, then, except for losing his property, his problems go away; no war crimes trial?"

"Other moneys too he must pay."

"She was confused," Emil said hopefully. Hoping for what, a different outcome? Forgiveness?

Lighting another cigarette, the woman laughed. "You believe this?"

"Yes, I do."

She threw her cigarette down. "In the end she took choice." The woman shook her head slowly, fingered the gun.

"What did you expect her to do?"

Their voices were growing heated. The woman lowered hers. "She was sent with deed to orchard, and money. Clear instructions." Emil was silent. The woman leaned in. "Ah, but you loved her. You love her still." She smiled. "Sometimes only a trick we play on ourselves is love. Did you never think this? Love is blind, but you know she has experience of many men? We know this to be so—"

Emil put his finger to his lips. The woman looked surprised. Then she laughed, this time with genuine enjoyment.

"You never see estate, I think, this country place of her family? My father told my mother there could never be a more perfect orchard. Like paradise, my father said, hiding that week. The fruit of the peach is finishing, and apples coming, and pears. They ate apricots, like gold coins picked among the ground, so many fat apricots. The hill the trees grow on with mountain behind and small river—how do you call this?"

"Stream."

"Like that. A pretty stream flowing through these trees, silver water under the sky." She lifted her right hand. "But is all gone now to big-price apartments: 'View to the sea.'" She frowned at the thought. "For my father this was a place of innocent, as if no war existed as they rested in this orchard. Until Nazis come shooting and they are ducks in bowls. My papa is one of three to escape. All the others—dead."

"I guess that proves it: Nobody returns to Eden."

"You are making this a joke?"

"Maybe they were looking for a miracle, hoping to be saved, angels descending on fluffy wings." He shrugged, spiteful, but he looked pale and felt as if he had been stuffed into the ground, like the roots of a tree or a coffin. He said, "Would you come inside? Would you take a drink?"

She studied him a moment. "Now you wish to sleep with the enemy?"

Emil stood up. The woman quickly stood too, the revolver ready. Emil looked at his gun held tight in her hand. "I'm offering you a drink on a warm night," he growled. "Take it anyway you like, or don't take it."

The woman nodded. "Okay, not a problem."

She stuffed the nearly empty pack of Gauloise into her shirt pocket, the lighter into her jeans. Emil wondered if she'd ever worn a dress, and about her legs. She was a lefty, he noted, like her father, and shorter than Elena. Her father hadn't been tall; Emil had had the advantage that night in overpowering him.

"We will go to kitchen now. Careful, slow." She indicated with the gun that Emil enter first. They both stopped and turned, hearing a noise from Franco's side of the fence, like leaves or paper. In one smooth motion the woman stepped behind Emil and trained the gun on the fence while keeping him within easy range. They waited in silence until there was no further sound. The woman waved Emil inside.

He turned the ceiling fan on along with the light above the round oak table. The mustard colored vase of pom-pom dahlias glowed under the lamp; otherwise the kitchen was dark. A few petals had fallen onto the table, like fragments from a still life. The embroidered jewel box was there, next to the vase and Elena's copy of *The Oblivion Seekers*.

"Water, vodka … milk?" he asked his uninvited guest.

The woman sat down on the chair facing the door to the garden. The screen door let in no air. "Ah, vodka, why not." She looked up as the ceiling fan began its irritating little click-click. "Needs oil," she said.

Emil picked out four glasses, two for water and two for vodka. The woman followed his every move. Her face was positioned just beyond the reach of the lamp's circular beam, but her hands and the gun were well lit. He noted the surprising smallness of her hands and the smoothness of her skin.

"I have all your moneys now," she said as if continuing a thought. "But not to worry; pension I could not go to, a little other. And I have the insurance your pretty wife gave over before she becomes very ill. She is smart, your wife. She finds a way to do this with insurance men. This was secret from you, yes?"

Holding on to the glasses, he said, "Did you break into my mutual fund account?"

She smiled. "Of course; it cost money to be in America."

"Those accounts are protected."

"Very little in this world is protected, Milosec." She smiled again, almost sweetly.

He'd been naive; Elena in her letters had said as much. "You're having fun with me," he said.

"Fun? No, not yet."

Emil stood at the refrigerator. He opened the freezer door, felt the cold breath of it on his face. His jaw clenched; his hand gripped the door. He knew of no such insurance. Elena must have tried to shield him with this policy. Freezer, he thought, taking the bottle of vodka out. *Freeze her*. How to get the gun out of her hands? He could throw the bottle at her?

He turned to face her. "I don't have to give you a thing, you know?"

"No? You wish to continue living, give me deed to the house. Otherwise …" She lifted her shoulders. "This house will bring a good price. Watch and see."

"You're betraying your promise that with the insurance money she'd be rid of you," he said, pouring vodka into two tall shot glasses. He was guessing Elena would have made such a deal.

"Too bad for me to be such a liar." Her tone was ugly. "But your Elena Morandi was neither a person of her word, so …" She shrugged. "I am sorry a little for you. I think you are like the big Hollywood man: Always protect woman—"

"Don't make me laugh," Emil cut in. "I'm the one who murdered your papa, remember? I made sure he never tucked you into your little bed, taught you your prayers. …" He might as well put the fact of having killed her father to some use, pin some pain on her.

"Okay, I take what was hers."

Emil carried the glasses to the table and sat down. "The Nazis threatened them. Why else would her father give up those he was protecting?"

"It is possible there are threats, and worse. But the life of wife and daughter for the lives of how many others, with freedom they fight for? To work with Nazis?" She leaned forward and spit on the floor, as his mother once had. "All of humanity for one little girl? No. Never!"

"You're a fanatic," he said. "Plenty of people walk around—armless, torture victims—without spending their lifetime looking to even the score. What's so special about what happened to you? It was a war—it's what happens in war."

The woman said nothing.

"They could have taken the deed in Bled, killed her then?"

"You want always to kill, this is American way? They did not know he sends his one daughter child. Only someone will come to give over deed et cetera at three o'clock on a certain day."

"The clock shop," he said quietly. "I stumbled in and stepped on the plan."

"What stumbled?"

Emil shook his head. "Nothing."

Neither of them had touched the water or the vodka. Emil reached out and picked up his glass. "To truth," he said, watching her.

"You have Lubec's clock?" she asked, ignoring his toast. Her face slanted into a grin, watching him.

"Yes. . . ." He pointed to the dining room.

"This was good joke at that time. Old Lubec has his clock disappear. I know the whole story."

The stupid old clock no one liked.

He fell for a woman, chased a skirt. Everyone was suspect; everyone suspected everyone else—except for Detective Emil Milosec, who suspected nothing. "The whole episode is a house of cards. What if I hadn't gone into the clock shop?"

"How is this house?"

"A case of mistaken identity," he said, saying each word precisely.

"Ah, Milosec." She leaned in. "She double-crossed. If you truly did not know, then even you she double-crossed."

She was right: Elena knew what she was doing, even if she decided only in the last minute, seeing him come out of the clock shop.

"She went to Vatican with her mama, with money from selling that orchard. Our money goes to fucking church."

Elena had come to him that first time from Rome. "Then why not prosecute? You'd look like you cared more about the money than justice?"

"What is justice, Milosec? A dream. That money was needed."

"It always is."

The fan swirled the sultry kitchen air around on itself. The woman spoke in a low, droning voice barely above a whisper in the mostly dark kitchen with only the pom-pom dahlias in bright contrast to the general mood of distrust attached to an unwelcome intimacy. He wasn't listening, and he was no closer to grabbing the gun. How could he, how could anyone say how they would react in a war? At what point did the Jews of the Warsaw Ghetto understand with the certainty of breath that they were being hunted down like trapped animals? How would a mind comprehend such a reality? Go on living each day until one day it was their turn?

Was it her papa's idea to send Elena to New York that first time? Send her far away for safekeeping with the big American?

The woman had stopped talking.

"Did her father know he was dying? Do you know that?"

"Not dying, killed himself. But he makes a mess with rifle, lived for ten days." She looked briefly past Emil. "We took long time finding her again."

Twenty-five thousand dollars: her inheritance money that rebuilt Emil's house; the money that made the garden. "So it all comes down to real estate."

"We did not invent the world, Milosec, not you, not me."

"What happens next, according to your plan?"

"You have Slovenian passport still. There is pension money you have, go to Senice." Emil laughed quietly. "What is joke now?"

"Senice. You can't know how funny that is." What would have happened if his family hadn't left Slovenia? Would his mother and sister, would *he* have survived?

"Okay, ha ha. You give this property to me, your cousin from old country, and return to home because you are lonely." She shrugged. "Easy."

Emil stopped smiling. "I could call the police."

"To tell them what?"

"There's the finger for starters."

"What do you say?"

"Why did you bother with it?"

"I do not know this finger."

"You didn't plant a severed finger in my garden—and the ring—and kill the cat?"

"Severed?"

"Cut, dammit! *Cut* finger." He made a slicing gesture over his left pinkie. The woman shook her head. "The shell casing—"

"Milosec. . . ." she cut in, twisting the palm of her right hand upward.

"You have no idea what I'm talking about?" He thought a minute. "*Paulien*," he said quietly. "The Horse is the Spider," he added, more to himself.

"Ah. Not horses and spiders—people, this Paulien likes to play with dead things—things once living human."

Bracco's phony pathologist.

They were quiet a few minutes on their separate sides of the table, the ceiling fan clicking overhead.

"One question, Milosec, I am thinking while you are sleeping, why is there no apple tree among your garden?"

"No Tree of Life either," he said.

The beginning of crime: a couple of trees, a taboo. *A tree to be desired to make one wise, she took of the fruit thereof, and. . . .*

Emil had had one final conversation with Mike Dunn about the forbidden trees of Eden. "Putting them in there and then saying don't touch," Emil had said to him, "what does that tell you?"

"About what?"

"About crime."

It was early one winter day; the car was on with the heater running. Mike held on to a Styrofoam cup of steaming coffee. On the seat next to him were the remains of a ham sandwich. He looked out of the window. "What does it tell *you*?"

"Maybe that crime is hardwired, factored in as part of the plan—preordained."

Mike looked at Emil in disbelief, eyes wide. "'Preordained'? And what plan is that? I thought you didn't believe in a plan."

"I don't."

"So? Look, you're giving me a headache."

Emil nodded.

"Why do you bother with all this Bible stuff anyhow? You don't even go to church."

"Elena says I go to church in my head every day."

Mike laughed. "Well, you ought'a try going to a regular church in the real world for a change, let someone else do the heavy thinking."

"I just . . . I don't think any of it works—religions makes it worse."

"So you've said. . . ."

Mike inhaled deep, glanced in the side-view mirror as a guy on a bicycle rode past. He faced his partner. "Lookit, Milosec, certain matters—religion, sex, money with some—people get hinky about, you know what I mean? Like, it's private. Know what I'm saying? And it's not going to go anywhere. See?"

"You sound like my mother, Mike."

Mike said, "Yeah. Listen, what I'm saying is: You don't know the answers, and I don't; nobody knows. Some people think they know, but they don't."

"Right."

"So just leave it alone." Mike finished off his coffee and placed the cup on the floor. He put the car in gear. "Okay?" He looked at Emil, nodded. "Okay. We got somebody killed over in South Slope, call came while you were getting the coffees."

"So, ah . . . don't say religions breed ignorance?"

"No, see, don't because what it sounds like—what it comes across like is—"

"Contempt?"

"Yeah, that's it," Mike said, pulling the car out into traffic. "But in a nice way."

Emil said, "You didn't tell me your name."

"For why do you want to know my name?"

"To know who my cousin is to whom I'm about to be so generous, just in case anyone asks."

"I am Zoran."

"Zoran," he repeated. He finished his drink. "To the garden," he said.

Zoran lifted her glass and, without taking her eyes off Emil, finished her vodka in one toss.

"This plan of yours," he said, "this will bring you pleasure?"

"I am not caring about pleasure. I am tired, Milosec. Tired of … I do not know this word. …"

"It's 'revenge.'"

"Maybe that."

"And how long does the glow last?"

"What glow?"

"Getting even after all this time?"

"Took too long, okay, my people are patient; we do not forget. You are Slovenian; you know."

No, Emil did not know. And he wasn't convinced there were others. There may have been a retribution cabal once, but Zoran might well be operating on her own now, maybe as a black marketeer tired of looking over her shoulder.

"How much time have I got?"

"Five days, one week, enough to gather your moneys. Tomorrow you turn deed of property to me. You get airplane ticket … go somewhere, disappear."

"Not a lot of advance notice, Zoran. What about Paulien?"

"What about?"

"She might come back."

"That low Hungarian?" Zoran sneered.

"But she's Dutch, Vandervell."

Zoran shook her head. "Not Dutch. She makes her own identity. She is up to some problem in Slovenian hospital. She is real doctor but have some problem. My people find she needs to—how to say—got lost? We see she can work for us. We obtain her papers for here."

"Some *problem*?"

"She is not taking live patients; living people are not her thing, so …" She lifted her shoulders. "Okay, not nice work. When I find apartment you name at embassy to rent, I tell her to go to that apartment. Easy."

"And she returned the favor with the keys and spying on me. But I'm guessing she didn't know the whole story?"

"Knows what she needs only."

"Why did you tell the police about her?"

Zoran lit another cigarette. "I cannot have this woman here longer. She makes mistakes, is not—what word?"

"'Reliable.'"

"That."

Emil shifted in his chair. "Is it a good idea to team up with criminals, Zoran? Puts a stink on the best of intentions. Not to leave out she might want her own revenge."

"You advise me now?" Zoran looked briefly worried but then

shrugged. "Paulien is maybe … maybe… not-social, is sick?" She touched her head. "Whatever—she cannot go to police." She made a gesture of dismissal. "Did work we need, now is gone. Good-bye."

"Assuming she stays gone …"

They were silent again, effectively out of things to say. His weapon was now out of reach on Zoran's lap. His only chance was to knock the water over on her—or, better, the vase, hope she'd hesitate before firing. What were his odds? Stunningly not in his favor. He reached out anyway, carefully moved his arm toward the vase, the side of his hand, palm facing in—

"*Stop! Do not move!*" Zoran stood up fast and, snakelike, slid behind the table to the back of the kitchen, near the dining room door. She signaled Emil to shut off the light. The closest switch was next to the garden door. He pointed, Zoran nodded, and he walked to the door. Thirty seconds elapsed; that was all. Emil had not heard a noise and for a split second wondered about his hearing. That thought was immediately replaced with the hope that the noise had come from Sam the cat or some other innocent source and not—

Within that thought Franco entered the kitchen doorway, and Emil heard the switchblade snap open.

He yelled, "Franco, *no*!" He shut the light while moving to the right. Simultaneously, a burst of yellow flame shot out.

Uselessly, Emil ducked as the sound of his gun rang out deafeningly through the kitchen, the house, the world, the universe, and Franco was thrust backward, folding at the knees, ejecting through the kitchen doorway before crumpling to the ground.

The silence that followed echoed in Emil's head. He stepped out of the kitchen. The ground seemed to envelop Franco. Emil knelt down beside his neighbor. The entry wound was surprisingly small but a pool of blood streamed from the point of exit in Franco's back, spilling onto the brick patio, running the way the ground happened to slope, toward the vacant pepper patch. Emil placed a hand gently on his neighbor's chest, just above the wound, and let it rest on Franco's lifeless form.

"Get up," Zoran said, turning the light back on.

"Be quiet," Emil said without moving.

SIX

What kind of God is this? First, he envied Adam that he should eat from the tree of knowledge. … And secondly he said, "Adam where are you?" … [And] "Let us cast him [out] of this place lest he eat of the tree of life and live forever." Surely he has shown himself to be a malicious envier. And what kind of God is this?

Elaine Pagels, The Gnostic Gospels

When Elena died, he had dreams. In one they sat together on the edge of the bed, looking at a photo album until it began to glow. In another he called out to her on the street, but she didn't turn around. He ran up to her, calling her name, reaching out to touch her shoulder, but as she turned to face him he lowered his eyes, telling himself the living were not meant to look into the eyes of the dead.

He would imagine seeing her at a red light on a crowded corner, and he would stand still as the sign said, "Walk," and after it blinked, "Don't Walk." He'd stand there until everyone else had crossed and he was alone, until the street sign again said, "Walk," and he understood he had not seen her at all.

As a cop Emil had witnessed so much death, but rarely as freshly raw as that of his neighbor lying on the ground before him. Kneeling beside him, Emil wished the still- warm Franco a safe passage. A passage to where and how he didn't know because where were all the dead anyway? Did they dissolve as if they never were? Or, as Elena wrote, "POOF"? How could it be that what was alive with a beating heart one moment, fully expecting to see another day, suddenly was no more? Where was the logic of life and then no life? He felt a furious objection rising up inside and at the same time a wave of long-held grief that threatened to gush.

His voice grim, he said over his shoulder, "What now?" Zoran was quiet behind him. Emil repeated the question: "What's the plan now, Zoran?"

She coughed. "You will telephone the police; you will say how this man came in like an animal and you have to shoot."

Facing Franco, Emil said, "No, you have that wrong. I will not say I shot this man. Shoot me now if that doesn't work for you."

"Stand." This time Emil did as he was told. "Telephone police." Emil nodded, walked slowly into the kitchen, and at the wall phone dialed 911. He told the operator there had been an accident, that a man had been shot.

When he hung up he saw Zoran at the freezer, the bottle of Stoli in one hand, the gun in the other. She grabbed a glass, poured, and swallowed down a double.

"It's not so easy, is it?" he said, watching her.

"What now, Milosec? What is not easy?"

"Killing a man."

The police lowered their guard some when they learned Emil was one of their own. They would go a little easy on his "cousin," newly arrived from a Communist country. She'd be understandably jumpy, those lousy Reds over there, and that low dog Slobodan Miloševic with his ethnic cleansing, dragging America into it. Zoran managed to work in enough information to gain some sympathy. The patrol officer who'd been first to arrive let it be known that Franco Montoya was known to the police. He told the assigned detectives, "The deceased has a few D-and-D run-ins to his name. A known borracho."

"That right?" Detective Colm O'Branahan asked Emil. "The man a drunk?"

Emil said, "I suppose so, but I didn't know him to be violent." Zoran's eyes were on him from where she stood just inside the dining room, like two steely cubes of ice.

The police had Emil's gun. He didn't know if Zoran had another one stashed someplace or if she was now unarmed.

Detective O'Branahan's partner, Detective Ernesto Guzman, volunteered, "A hot-tempered Latino with a few beers too many turns into a firecracker on a short fuse." He looked at Emil as if seeking confirmation of this homegrown theory from a veteran of the force, but Emil remained expressionless.

Emil heard Zoran light a cigarette behind him—heard the Zippo snap shut—when he asked if an autopsy would reveal anything. "I mean, assuming there'll be one," he added.

"There will be," Detective O'Branahan answered, adding, "You thinking he was high on something else besides beer?"

Emil only wanted to plant the idea of an autopsy; he already knew, with the knife, the killing looked pretty much like self-defense, open and shut. He knew too they'd be sending Franco to Kings County Morgue. If for some reason they took him over to Wittekoff Hospital, Dr. Greenfeld might recognize Franco as Detective Vega. "I just wondered," he said.

Detective Guzman didn't seem to be buying any line but the drunken one, as if he wanted to clear out of Emil's house fast and not look too deeply into the matter. "Could be lucky the gun was in the kitchen," he said, sounding like a poor imitation of officious. "A drunken personality's erratic, you know, hard to predict. We see it all the time."

Detective O'Branahan stared at his partner. Emil wondered how much they hated each other's guts, an Irishman paired with a Puerto Rican. "He never made a threat to you in the past? No words exchanged—I don't know, noise complaints, loud parties at night? Nothing seething between the two of you? Maybe a bad mix, you and him?"

"I wasn't born here myself, if that's what you're getting at," Emil said. Detective Guzman looked at him and the faintest of smiles passed over his face before quickly fading out.

Zoran had turned lights on in the dining room prior to the patrol cops' showing up. She'd taken off the black long-sleeved T-shirt, beneath which she wore a sleeveless white top with a boat neck, revealing a good deal more flesh. She'd moved their glasses to the dining room table, refilled them with vodka, and taken off her shoes too, made it seem as if they'd been relaxing, catching up on old times when Franco came at them.

"So you fired?" O'Branahan asked her. He'd moved his bulk into the dining room.

She said, "My cousin does not hear the sound outside. He is too trusting, I think. I move quicker than he. We know even in my country how crazy is Brooklyn."

Atta girl, Emil told himself; it figured she could lie like a small time whore. Spread the charm on thick; bring Brooklyn in—perfect.

"You know about us over there, huh?" Detective O'Branahan said. He didn't wait for an answer. "Okay, wait in here, Miss," he told her, indicating that she take a seat.

It was clear who wore the pants in the Guzman-O'Branahan partnership. Back in the kitchen, Detective O'Branahan said to Emil, "How'd the cousin know where the gun was kept?"

He pointed to the cabinet. "First thing she did was poke around the kitchen. She'll be staying here. … I guess she plans to do some cooking." Emil thought, Now ask me if I renewed, if I had a valid permit for the gun. "I'm not sure the permit's up to date either," he offered.

O'Branahan sniffed, arched his eyebrows. "That'll be a slap on the wrist. So why do you suppose your neighbor went nuts?"

Emil shook his head. Eye contact was becoming a problem because he could see O'Branahan wanted to believe in an ex-cop. "Most nights he'd just sit in his yard singing to himself, downing enough beers to quiet the demons. I wish to hell he'd have done that tonight."

O'Branahan said, "You sure about your cousin in there? There's no jealousy angle going on?"

"Montoya never met her," Emil answered blandly.

The Irish detective squinted. "Out of the blue he barges in baring a blade. Doesn't figure."

"I'm surprised myself. But he did serve as a marine in Korea—or was it Vietnam? Maybe he thought he was back in battle, nightmares, post-stress … who knows?" Now *he* was fabricating like a small time whore.

Emil turned to see Zoran watching him from the dining room. It occurred to him that if Detectives O'Branahan and Bracco ever compared notes, this little sham would come apart all over the carpet. But competing precincts, what were the chances? And Paulien? Would she know the game was up and not look back? What about her pretty Moroccan plates and furnishings upstairs? And whatever collection of other body parts she might have played around with? He hadn't looked in her freezer. Neither had Detective Bracco.

The uniform patrolman came back into the kitchen and whispered something to Detective O'Branahan. The Irish cop scowled, scratched his nose. "The lady next door says she thought she heard gunshots from Montoya's place the other day. You know anything about that?"

Here was Emil's chance to come clean, confess: Sure, he knew all about those shots; he fired them. He also obstructed justice and impersonated an officer of the law, and there was a bit of evidence tampering while he was at it, not to leave out failing to report a crime—c'mon down to the cellar, boys, have a look—and should he mention his "cousin's" father, that Emil had killed him?

He said, "Yeah, Mrs. Noily called me about that. I told her it was probably a car backfiring. If he had a gun, wouldn't he have used that tonight instead of a switchblade? The situation could have turned out very different with a better weapon in his hands."

There was a tense silence while O'Branahan sized things up. The dining room clock sounded to Emil like eternity ticking off the minutes. He wondered if Zoran realized it was Lubec's clock.

"Maybe it was you firing your weapon?" O'Branahan suggested.

Emil laughed as casually as he could manage. "Sure, target practice in the backyard."

O'Branahan coughed twice into his hand, scratched his nose again, and looked around the room. He glanced over at Guzman leaning on the kitchen counter. The situation didn't sit right and O'Branahan knew it; he just didn't know how much it didn't or exactly where the bad fit came from. "You have anything to add?" he asked his partner.

Detective Guzman shook his head. "Look at the angle of the body. Forensics said he was blown out the door. It fits; I don't see there are any surprises here."

Emil figured Guzman for a tired cop on the night shift who would rather be at home in front of the TV, not sweating a case that might be a little fishy but not worth the trouble. Then he surprised Emil by adding, "We could give the ex-Commie cousin a lie-detector test if her prints are not on the weapon, no powder residue. But what's the point? Like you said, the guy must have went nuts. Where are the complications?"

O'Branahan chewed the inside of his lip. "Well," he said, displaying infinite patience, "motive is missing if you don't buy the went-nuts theory." But the veteran policeman had already drawn his conclusion, though he wasn't happy with it. "All right, I'll need the two of you to come down to the station for a statement. Sorry, Milosec. Procedure—you know." Emil nodded.

O'Branahan signaled to the techs from the coroner's office. Emil watched them tag and bag Franco's body. He thought of Mary O'Donnell's finger in a plastic baggie down in the basement. It looked like he'd be throwing the pinkie out after all. He fingered the tiny plastic castle from Bled that he'd put in his pants pocket before coming down to the garden. A man's castle is his home.

The detectives and Emil and Zoran filed out after Franco's body. A small crowd had gathered outside his house, the second crowd on the street in a day. CeeCee Noily stood with her arms folded across her chest. Her tenants, Malcolm and Loretta, stood beside her, Loretta in some sort of scanty night outfit. Albert stood there too, in red-striped pajamas, his pumpkin head gaping. A few other neighbors watched the spectacle from across the street. No one was in cuffs, but somebody must be in trouble. CeeCee Noily nodded her head with an I-told-you-so look on her face. Mrs. Santiana stood by in her housecoat. She crossed herself when Franco's body was wheeled out.

Ten minutes later Emil was seated in the back of a cop car on his way to the precinct, with Guzman behind the wheel. Zoran sat next to him, and he sneaked a quick look at her profile in the orange glow of the passing streetlights. He had not come clean and now they were in it tight as fleas. He wondered briefly how airtight was the lack of a trail between her and Paulien, also how real her visa was, should anybody care to check. And if they fingerprinted her, what might that reveal? There was still a chance the game could blow up in his face.

What he sensed in himself was relief, though he could not easily say why. Relieved of the long haul of being Detective Emil Milosec, the ruse of a personality held in place for so long? Maybe that was why people went senile; they got worn out by the constant burden of who they were supposed to be. He didn't see any point in confessing to the legal system. No gulag, like with Raskolnikov. Emil wouldn't cower before any God, but he'd been expelled from Eden all right.

Stripped bare, the garden first, his identity next. He'd always wanted to go to Scotland, to the Hebrides, a place severe and wind-scoured where a thought had no place to hide; some called the Hebrides the edge of the world. Once upon a time Emil had walked an alpine wilderness with his family. He should have been afraid, but he wasn't; it was the greatest adventure of his life. He experienced an inappropriate urge to laugh, picturing himself in a hair shirt, maybe with a few goats, on a rocky highland slope. What did Franco say? "To laugh is to live."

Amigo.

And Zoran? It starts all over again with a new killing. Franco with his poems and his Shakespeare, snuffed. Zoran would continue to believe her cause was just, fool herself for as many years as she could. She'd have Emil's garden, could immerse herself in its indifferent beauty, but that wouldn't change the fundamental fact of her having taken a life for no good reason. Emil had his part in that death too: Had he not gone to Slovenia to find his Uncle Ivak, not followed Elena and bought the goddamn clock, Franco would still be alive. Cause and effect? Free choice? Who knew?

Knock yourself all the way back to Cain and Abel. His father had resisted killing, but his policeman son had not. What could he do with that?

They moved through a night that was oppressive like someone had cranked up the oven to broil. Guzman drove slowly. People without air conditioning sat out on their stoops, though it was nearly four and they should be in bed if they had jobs to go to once the sun came up. What would happen to all these stoop dwellers when the real estate boom everyone said was coming popped? When the developers turned this sleepy town of brick and mortar into glass and steel? Good-bye, Rudy's Corner Market—and good riddance. But there was Mrs. Santiana and her peach trees and thousand cats. And there was Tía Marta and Oscar Park, and the artists settling in, Giorno's Pizza, and the flight of the pigeons. ... It was early yet, but the waters were shifting. Emil believed that now.

He sneaked another look at Zoran. She looked small in the big American car. He'd never sat in the back before, marked or unmarked. He thought that over, but, no, he'd never sat in the suspect's seat.

Elena said to him once, "You and I are on the outside, Emil. Do you know what I mean?" He thought he did know, now. He really never had any business being a cop. She'd known that all along. Did she ever fully figure out that he had nothing to do with the events in Bled, that he was just some joe who happened upon the scene and happened to fall for her all the way to the ground?

Detective O'Branahan yawned. He tapped the dashboard. "Guzman, you think you could drive a little faster? I'm falling asleep here."

Detective Guzman turned to his partner. "What's the hurry, Colm? Sleep. It's a heat wave; the night is quiet. Even the bad guys perspire." He pronounced it "per-spy-yer," the way Franco would have.

O'Branahan said, "Yeah, well, we're not on a goddamn date, so c'mon, how about it?"

Cop banter, Emil thought; the way to get through a long, hot night. He knew it; Mike Dunn had known it.

Detective Guzman said, "Okay, big guy, we'll go fast." He turned to his passengers in the back. "I'm gonna speed up," he said. He attached the red beam to the roof, hit the siren, and leaned on the gas. They were all pressed backward as the car picked up speed. Emil watched the Brooklyn night whiz by in a blur. Time seemed to go out of focus, or at least soften around the edges.

One of Elena's big band songs came to him as he leaned back in the police car cruising through the steaming summer night: *Say I care forever, and I mean forever / if I have to hold up the sky* ... He figured, for what it was worth, he was still holding up the sky. It looked like he'd be holding it up someplace else from now on, and maybe that would be all right, starting out empty.

It was Elena's garden. As much as for any other reason, he'd kept the garden up for her. Now that too had ended; beginnings into endings, on and on.

Acknowledgments

I thank early readers: Mark Saxe, Alison Slon, Barbara Collier, Scott Neary, Marcy Rosewater, Thaddeus Rutkowski, Peter Brown. Also thanks to Traci Parks and Genia Gould, and Tess Congo. Thanks to Peter G, Jr. for technical advice on guns and police procedure. For the patience of family and friends while I disappeared for long stretches into Emil's garden, thank you. To the Col., you gave me the title, Dad. Thanks to the Virginia Center for the Creative Arts.

I especially thank my editor Fred Ramey, and all at Unbridled Books. Thank you Malaga Baldi.